W9-CRP-869

Praise for

*Delicious and Suspicious*

"Sassy." —*Publishers Weekly*

"An entertaining read . . . Just like the pork barbeque and spicy corn muffins that fill the bellies of the fictitious patrons of Aunt Pat's, the Southern flavor is what makes this novel unique. The characters live and breathe on the page, not as stereotypes of Southerners but as colorful personalities that complement the Memphis setting." —*Romance Novel News*

"This entertaining regional amateur sleuth gives the audience a taste of living in [Memphis], especially owning a restaurant in a tourist-attraction city . . . With a strong, fully seasoned support cast who enhance the whodunit, *Delicious and Suspicious* is truly scrumptious." —*Genre Go Round Reviews*

"A saucy Southern mystery!"
—Krista Davis, national bestselling author of
*The Diva Haunts the House*

"Don't let that folksy facade fool you. Lulu Taylor is one intrepid amateur sleuth."
—Laura Childs, *New York Times* bestselling author of
*Skeleton Letters*

"Lulu Taylor serves up the best barbeque in Memphis. Never been to her restaurant, Aunt Pat's? Well then, pick up a copy of Riley Adams's enjoyable *Delicious and Suspicious*, slide into a booth, and follow Lulu as she tracks down a killer with the help of her wacky friends and family. You'll feel transported to Beale Street. Oh, and did I mention the mouthwatering recipes at the end?" —Julie Hyzy, author of *Grace Interrupted*

"Riley Adams's first book, *Delicious and Suspicious*, adds a dash of Southern humor to a sauté of murder and mayhem that is as good as cold banana pudding on a hot summer day. Lulu Taylor is a hoot! I look forward to reading the next book in the Memphis BBQ series!" —Joyce Lavene, coauthor of *Harrowing Hats*

*Berkley Prime Crime titles by Riley Adams*

DELICIOUS AND SUSPICIOUS
FINGER LICKIN' DEAD
HICKORY SMOKED HOMICIDE

# HICKORY SMOKED
## HOMICIDE

## Riley Adams

**BERKLEY PRIME CRIME, NEW YORK**

**THE BERKLEY PUBLISHING GROUP**
**Published by the Penguin Group**
**Penguin Group (USA) Inc.**
**375 Hudson Street, New York, New York 10014, USA**

Penguin Group (Canada), 90 Eglinton Avenue East, Suite 700, Toronto, Ontario M4P 2Y3, Canada
(a division of Pearson Penguin Canada Inc.)
Penguin Books Ltd., 80 Strand, London WC2R 0RL, England
Penguin Group Ireland, 25 St. Stephen's Green, Dublin 2, Ireland (a division of Penguin Books Ltd.)
Penguin Group (Australia), 250 Camberwell Road, Camberwell, Victoria 3124, Australia
(a division of Pearson Australia Group Pty. Ltd.)
Penguin Books India Pvt. Ltd., 11 Community Centre, Panchsheel Park, New Delhi—110 017, India
Penguin Group (NZ), 67 Apollo Drive, Rosedale, Auckland 0632, New Zealand
(a division of Pearson New Zealand Ltd.)
Penguin Books (South Africa) (Pty.) Ltd., 24 Sturdee Avenue, Rosebank, Johannesburg 2196,
South Africa

Penguin Books Ltd., Registered Offices: 80 Strand, London WC2R 0RL, England

This is a work of fiction. Names, characters, places, and incidents either are the product of the author's imagination or are used fictitiously, and any resemblance to actual persons, living or dead, business establishments, events, or locales is entirely coincidental. The publisher does not have any control over and does not assume any responsibility for author or third-party websites or their content.

PUBLISHER'S NOTE: The recipes contained in this book are to be followed exactly as written. The publisher is not responsible for your specific health or allergy needs that may require medical supervision. The publisher is not responsible for any adverse reactions to the recipes contained in this book.

HICKORY SMOKED HOMICIDE

A Berkley Prime Crime Book / published by arrangement with the author

PRINTING HISTORY
Berkley Prime Crime mass-market edition / November 2011

Copyright © 2011 by Penguin Group (USA) Inc.
Cover illustration by Hugh Syme.
Cover design by Annette Fiore Defex.
Interior text design by Laura K. Corless.

All rights reserved.
No part of this book may be reproduced, scanned, or distributed in any printed or electronic form without permission. Please do not participate in or encourage piracy of copyrighted materials in violation of the author's rights. Purchase only authorized editions.
For information, address: The Berkley Publishing Group,
a division of Penguin Group (USA) Inc.,
375 Hudson Street, New York, New York 10014.

ISBN: 978-0-425-24460-9

BERKLEY® PRIME CRIME
Berkley Prime Crime Books are published by The Berkley Publishing Group,
a division of Penguin Group (USA) Inc.,
375 Hudson Street, New York, New York 10014.
BERKLEY® PRIME CRIME and the PRIME CRIME logo are trademarks of Penguin Group (USA) Inc.

PRINTED IN THE UNITED STATES OF AMERICA

10  9  8  7  6  5  4  3  2  1

If you purchased this book without a cover, you should be aware that this book is stolen property. It was reported as "unsold and destroyed" to the publisher, and neither the author nor the publisher has received any payment for this "stripped book."

In memory of
Elizabeth Riley Adams,
Elizabeth Adams Stringfellow,
and Mary Ligon Spann

# Acknowledgments

Many thanks to my editor, Emily Beth Rapoport, for her editing expertise and support. To my agent, Ellen Pepus, for her help and advice. To Hugh Syme for the cover illustration, Annette Fiore Defex for the cover design, and Laura K. Corless for the interior text design. Thanks to authors Jim and Joyce Lavene, who are great friends and mentors. To my fellow mystery-loving cooks at Mystery Lovers' Kitchen (www.mysterylovers kitchen.com) for their generous support and friendship. To my family—especially my husband, Coleman, and children, Riley and Elizabeth Ruth . . . who make life and writing fun.

Chapter 1

Lulu Taylor just happened to be trying on a vibrantly colored floral-print dress in Dee Dee's Darling
Dress Shoppe when she heard the shop bell and then a familiar voice.

Lulu would be able to pick out Tristan Pembroke's voice
even if she were in a crowd of hundreds at the state fair. It
was lined with snobbery and condescension, which Tristan
seemed to think sounded well-bred. Well, Lulu had *known*
Tristan's mama, and wouldn't she be horrified to see her
little girl today?

Lulu wasn't actually too thrilled with Dee Dee, either,
but she had the only dress shop that stocked the Sassy Se-
niors line of dresses. Although Lulu had a closet full of
floral dresses, her motto was that you could never have too
many flowers. That's the very reason magnolia blossoms
swam in glass bowls at her barbeque restaurant whenever
they were in bloom.

She liked Dee Dee even less when she heard her say in a cigarette-hoarsened stage whisper, "We can go ahead and talk now. It's just ol' Lulu in the dressing room, and she couldn't hear a drunk elephant if he crashed into the room."

Obviously, Dee Dee hadn't learned the difference between being ignored and not being heard. They were totally two entirely different things. Lulu felt in danger of losing her religion but prudently bit her tongue—since there was clearly going to be some sort of transmittal of interesting information. With those two it wouldn't be a pearl of wisdom, or the secret of life. . . . But it was likely going to be *interesting*. She strained to hear—and her ears were *not* defective.

"Okay, here's the scoop," said Dee Dee. "Tamara Lynn is going to wear the teal-colored plunge-neckline gown with the drop waist. And . . . so is Pansy."

"Mmm-hmm," said Tristan, making sounds like she was taking notes. "Well now, that's going to be real interesting. Pansy's mama will blow a gasket when she finds out."

"And you wanted to hear about Clarice's talent. She's singing."

"Well of *course* she's singing," snapped Tristan. "The girl can barely even tie her own shoelaces at age sixteen! Singing is her only talent."

"But I know *what* she's singing and what she's doing *while* she's singing," said Dee Dee in a smug voice.

Lulu couldn't resist peering out the side of the dressing-room curtain to see Tristan's face. And didn't she look put out! A red stain splotched across her high cheekbones on her pretty face, and she was running a bony hand through her straight, black hair. "Never mind being all secretive,

Dee Dee! Spill it!" Lulu noticed that Dee Dee was reading out of a big notebook on the sales counter. Dee Dee always looked like a caricature of herself, with hair dyed an unlikely shade of blond, huge glasses that took over most of her face, and eyebrows drawn on in a very dramatic fashion.

"I guess her tacky mama finally messed with her brain because she's doing a *baton* routine to 'Dixie'! While singing!"

There was a stunned silence, and Dee Dee started cackling. "Your eyes will pop out of your head if you don't watch it, Tristan!"

"Whatever possessed her?" said Tristan in a musing voice.

"I think," said Dee Dee with satisfaction, "that you can take the woman out of the country, but you can't take the country out of the woman." She suddenly squawked loudly. "Lulu? You okay in there, darlin'?"

Lulu played up her deaf role. "What, hon?"

There was a *tip, tap, tip* of Dee Dee's heels on the hardwood floor of the dress shop. "I said, are you *okay*? Need me to find you another size? I noticed that you've been shrinking a little—you're not quite as tall as you were. Need a smaller size?"

Lulu gritted her teeth in irritation and rattled the hangers together a little to show she was working hard at trying on dresses. "I'm doing fine, Dee Dee. Just trying to decide between a couple of dresses." As if, thought Lulu, there was a huge difference between the dresses she was trying on.

The heels tapped back away. "Okay. Let me know if you need any help."

Tristan's and Dee Dee's voices murmured together for a

minute, and Lulu couldn't make out a single word. Then she heard the cash-register drawer open and heard Dee Dee say, "Thanks for your business," in a caustic voice, "although I'm thinking that soon we'll need to renegotiate fees. I'll talk to you about it later." The door chimed as Tristan left.

Lulu walked out to the register with one of the dresses.

"I thought you might like that blue-and-white floral," said Dee Dee, wagging her finger. "'Looks like Lulu,' I thought when I saw it. That's why I put it aside for you."

"It reminds me of my Aunt Pat's china pattern," said Lulu. "Cheers me up just looking at it."

She was about to vaguely mention that she thought she'd heard Dee Dee talking with a customer a few minutes before (and see how much nosiness she could get away with) when a flash of red caught her eye. It was her redheaded friend and Aunt Pat's Barbeque restaurant regular Cherry Hayes, with her face stuck against the glass window.

Cherry pushed the door open energetically, and the bell tinkled with alarm.

"I thought I saw your Buick out there, Lulu, as I was driving by on my motorcycle. Find anything fun to buy?" Cherry brought her eyebrows together in a ferocious frown as she looked doubtfully at the merchandise on the racks. She was holding her motorcycle helmet, which had a picture of her first love, Elvis, on it. The helmet was usually either sitting on Cherry's head or very close by. Cherry swore it kept her safe throughout the day and that Elvis acted as her guardian angel.

Lulu chuckled. Unless Dee Dee had radically changed her buying practices, she doubted she was going to stock any wildly patterned, vibrantly colored minidresses. And that was the kind of look that Cherry went for.

But to her surprise, Cherry absently put her helmet back on her head and started pushing through clothes on the racks. She gave a gusty sigh. "I think I'll shop. Shopping always cheers me up a little." Cherry looked sideways through her fake lashes at Lulu, prompting her to inquire further.

"Something happen, Cherry?"

Cherry looked stormy. "That troll Tristan happened. I saw her leaving the shop as I was about to come in. Remember how I'm trying to join the Memphis Women's League?"

Lulu nodded slowly. "I think so. Although I don't remember *why* you are." She simply couldn't picture Cherry Hayes eating crustless cucumber sandwiches with a bunch of ladies who formed the elite in Memphis society.

"At first it was because Evelyn has always talked about how great the club was," said Cherry, mentioning their mutual friend. "So my neighbor Pepper and I decided we wanted to be part of the fun, too. But *now* I want to do it because they're so determined to keep me out." Cherry absently took a blouse off the rack, pulled a horrified face, and put it back up. "Actually, the only one who's blackballing Pepper and me is Tristan."

Lulu leaned in a little, since Dee Dee looked like her ears had pricked up. "How'd you learn that?" she asked in a low voice, thinking Cherry might take the hint and speak a little quieter.

Cherry wasn't one to take hints, though. "I'll tell you how I heard," she said. "Evelyn told me all about it. Said that Tristan suddenly acted like she was a blue blood and was all hoity-toity about membership. 'Cherry and Pepper aren't the kind of candidates we're looking for. *Indeed*, I cannot envision the future of the Memphis Women's

League with Cherry and Pepper as part of it.'" Cherry pretended to sip from an imaginary teacup, with her pinky stuck way out like she was having high tea.

Lulu heard Dee Dee snicker, and Cherry spun around and stared her down, eyes narrowed. Dee Dee suddenly got real busy with her paperwork.

"And then, you know, I saw her when I was parking my bike. So I said to Tristan, 'Hey, *thanks* for inviting Pepper and me into your club.' You know, really sarcastic. But I think Tristan's dumb as a post. So she says, '*I* didn't invite you, Cherry. Or Pepper, either.' Just real hostile." Cherry looked glum that her efforts at sarcasm had been wasted. "All those years in beauty pageants must've fried her brain."

Lulu nodded. "That's right—I'd forgotten she'd been involved in pageants. Magnolia Queen?"

Dee Dee bellowed from across the room, "Magnolia Queen, Azalea Queen, Barbeque Queen. That was all back in the day. Now she coaches contestants and judges pageants."

Ah, thought Lulu. She'd forgotten Tristan's connection to the pageant world. Some of her conversation with Dee Dee was starting to make sense.

Cherry quickly blushed a shade of red that matched her hair. "Oops. Sorry, Lulu. I've got foot-in-mouth disease. I forgot that your granddaughter is in pageants."

Lulu chuckled. "I'd forgotten Coco is, too! Don't worry about it. I know you weren't talking about Coco."

Dee Dee perked up over at the register. "Lulu," she called loudly, "be sure to send Coco over my way if she needs a special dress for a competition. I've got a few little-girl dresses that would be the perfect thing."

There was nothing wrong with *Dee Dee's* hearing,

thought Lulu sourly. She'd been honing in on their conversation the whole time.

Cherry sighed again. "Okay, I think I'm done here. Shopping's not helping me forget my troubles this time. Or maybe," and this time her voice did drop a little, "I need to go to the Hipster Honey store and find some cute clothes."

Lulu said, "Cherry? Just forget all about this Memphis Women's League bull. It's not worth the aggravation."

"Darn straight it's not!" said Cherry, hotly. "Just the same, though, Tristan Pembroke better watch her back. This brouhaha ain't over yet."

*Chapter*

2

Lulu relaxed as she walked in the door of Aunt Pat's. Just walking in from Beale Street and seeing the familiar wooden booths, red-checkered tablecloths, and paper-towel rolls on the tables made her blood pressure go down. The walls were covered with photographs and framed family memorabilia—which made Lulu feel like she was surrounded by family at all times. She loved, in particular, being greeted by a black-and-white photo of her dear aunt Pat. With her eyes twinkling and mouth pulled into a gentle smile, she looked like she could pop right out of the photograph and visit with her.

Colleen Bannister walked into Aunt Pat's to give Coco a ride to a pageant, since Lulu's daughter-in-law, Sara, had to stay at the restaurant to work, and Colleen had to go with her daughter, Pansy, anyway. It was a wonder, thought Lulu, that Colleen's hair could actually fit under the door frame. It was truly a work of fine art and sprayed within an inch of its life. And the amount of makeup that Colleen slathered on her face was probably enough to beautify three different women. You could see, though, where Pansy got her beauty-pageant looks from. Colleen was divorced, and Lulu was always surprised she wasn't dating anyone.

Sara stuck her head out of the back office and peeped about; seeing Colleen, she hurried over. "She's almost ready, Colleen. I'm sorry it's taking Coco so long today. She was showing off her new pageant shoes to some customers, and I think she somehow *lost* one of them."

"Oh, it's fine—I'm not in any hurry. I'll just have a little something to eat while we wait. I was feeling a little hungry, anyway."

Colleen sat down at a table and ordered a couple of side orders and a drink. Sara and Lulu sat down to join her and watched in alarm as Colleen abruptly burst into loud sobbing.

"She hates her," said Colleen as she carefully dabbed a tissue under her eyes to keep her copious mascara from streaming down her cheeks. "Tristan Pembroke *hates* Pansy!"

Lulu Taylor gave Colleen a big hug. "Now, honey, you know that your Pansy is the prettiest thing in Memphis! And the sweetest. I'm sure nobody could hate her."

"Then why does Pansy never win any pageant that Tristan judges?"

Lulu's attempt at comfort went wildly askew, as her efforts only seemed to make the tide of mascara rivulets come faster.

Sara said glumly, "If Tristan hates Pansy, she must hate Coco, too. I've noticed a similar pattern when Tristan is one of the judges at Coco's pageants."

"Besides, just because Tristan is always at these beauty pageants doesn't mean that she's causing our girls to lose," said Lulu.

Colleen held out a perfectly manicured, moisturized hand to Lulu. "Wanna bet? I'll even shake on it, Lulu. I'm good friends with another one of the judges. And she has *had* it with Tristan. Says that she throws her weight around with the other judges and threatens to get them kicked off the circuit if they don't go along with her voting."

Lulu shook her head in confusion until the little bun of white hair at the top of her head wobbled back and forth. "But *why*? What could Tristan possibly have against Pansy or Coco?"

Sara said, "She's just bitter because her own daughter wasn't pageant material. Like it even *matters*," said Sara, tapping her glass of sweet tea on the table. "We don't even take it seriously."

But Lulu noticed that Sara sounded more like she was trying to persuade *Colleen* that they didn't take it personally.

Colleen pursed her ruby-lipsticked lips. "Sara Taylor, you know that Pansy and I are not competing for *fun*. We're competing to *win*. Nothing makes that girl happier than having one of those ten-story crowns on her head, all glitzy and shiny, and everyone standing up and cheering themselves hoarse. And she's worked on her talent until she's one of the best fiddle players in Memphis—and I'm including the adults. And she has lots of other talents, too. You should hear her do impersonations of people. And her dance routine is absolutely amazing—everyone says so."

Sara looked doubtful. "You're not turning into one of those stage mamas, are you? The kind we're always laughing at for putting fake teeth in when their little precious has lost a front tooth?"

"They're called flippers, not fake teeth," said Colleen in a put-out voice. "And if they'd been around eight years ago when Pansy first started out, you better believe I'd have stuck them in her mouth fast as lightning."

Sara looked thoughtful as she wound a long strand of curly red hair around her finger. "I never went the pageant route myself, of course," said Sara, making a face. "But Coco just seemed so interested and kept asking to do it. So I finally gave in and said yes."

Colleen said sweetly, "Well, you *could* have done pageants when you were little—you're definitely pageant material, hon."

Sara made a face. "Well, it's nice of you to say so. But with my big bones, I was definitely not designed with pageants in mind. But Coco is."

"I'll say she is," said Colleen enthusiastically. "She has the most darling little face, with dimples and that thousand-watt smile. She's that natural blond that the judges just love. And you can tell by watching her sing that she's loving every minute of it—and she has the sweetest little voice I think I've ever heard come from a nine-year-old."

Sara said, "I'm glad you can tell she's having fun. Because if she wasn't having fun, there wouldn't be any point at all."

"But there *is* a point to it, Sara. College scholarships. We simply don't have the money to put Pansy in school. Even a state school! That's the kind of thing you need to be thinking about, Sara. Think about the scholarships that Coco could be getting, and get a little more competitive."

Sara ran a hand through her riotous red spiraled curls. "She's only nine years old, Colleen!"

"Financial planners say that it's never too early to plan for your child's education."

Although, thought Lulu, she doubted that beauty-pageant earnings were the planners' recommended savings route.

"Besides," said Colleen, "you get just as anxious during the pageants as I do, Sara. I've seen you strung tight like a bow. The only reason you're not kicking up a fuss about Tristan ruining Coco's chances at pageant wins is because she's showing your art at her benefit-auction party this weekend."

Sara said, "That's not true. I've never gotten into the pageant world like you have. It's one of those things that I sort of tolerate."

"Well, mark my words, y'all. If Tristan Pembroke gets any whiff of your passion for art—if you let on that it's more than a way to kill time—then you're in trouble. She's the kind of person who loves to crush your dreams. And she'll just stomp right on your art if you let her."

Lulu said quickly, "Sara knows not to listen to criticism. She's run into that kind of thing before and knows how to ignore it. Besides, y'all, maybe we should change the subject before Steffi comes out here."

Colleen froze, a forkful of coleslaw halfway to her mouth. "Steffi? Not Steffi Pembroke?"

Lulu straightened the checkered tablecloth. "The very one."

"You mean to tell me that Tristan's daughter is working here? As a waitress?" Colleen's stage whisper projected across the Aunt Pat's dining hall.

Lulu nodded.

Sara's jaw had dropped a little. "When did this happen, Lulu? I worked the lunch shift, and she wasn't here then."

"I got her set up with her apron a few minutes ago. You see," said Lulu in a low voice, "we could definitely use another waitress. You know how crazy Aunt Pat's gets in the evenings when the bands start playing. Having another waitress will really help us out. And—well, she asked me for some help. She had a fight with her mama, and she's kicked her out of the house. Tristan even threatened to write the poor girl out of her will. I know she graduated from college a few months ago, and waitressing wasn't exactly at the top of her job-hunting list."

Sara shrugged. "It's a job, though. And it brings money in on a pretty regular basis. Sounds to me like that's what she needed if she didn't have a place to stay. Hush. . . . She's coming up."

Steffi, thought Lulu, looked absolutely nothing like her immaculately groomed, still gorgeous mother. But, thankfully, she had none of her mama's hateful ways, either. Lulu always had the feeling that Tristan Pembroke had taken it as a personal affront that her daughter hadn't inherited her beauty. Steffi was nobody's pretty child, with her double chins, pasty complexion, and lifeless hair. But her personality drew you right in . . . especially the way she stood up to her ruthless mother time after time.

Steffi said, "Lulu, I wonder if I'll ever get the hang of this. I didn't realize how clumsy I was until I tried balancing a tray of food. Everything keeps sloshing into everything else!"

"You'll get used to it," said Lulu with a laugh. "Just give yourself some time."

Steffi turned to Sara. "Sorry I didn't mention to you when I saw you at Mother's that I was going to start waitressing here. But I didn't actually know, myself, at the time." She made a face.

Sara shook her head, a smile spreading over her good-natured freckled face. "Don't worry about it, Steffi. Lulu was telling us it was an all-of-a-sudden kind of thing."

Steffi rubbed her face, tiredly. "It sure was. I'm lucky I have a place to go in case of an emergency."

"That's something I forgot to mention," said Lulu mildly. "Steffi is in my guest room until she saves up enough to put down a deposit for an apartment. And maybe a little savings buffer for emergencies."

Big tears welled up in Steffi's eyes. "Thanks so much again, Lulu. I don't know what I'd have done without you. I'd have asked my aunt Marlowe, but she's been out of town on a business trip." She looked up and saw some orders ready for tables. "I'd better run." And she darted off to deliver the orders to the tables.

Colleen said slowly, "That was very sweet of you, Lulu, to keep Steffi at your house until she gets back on her feet." She paused, took a sip of her sweet tea, and said, "But what the Sam Hill are you *thinking*?"

Lulu blinked. "What do you mean?"

"I mean that as soon as Tristan Pembroke finds out that you're aiding and abetting her daughter in standing up to her, then you're going to have a huge mess on your hands. Huge! She might come over and roll your front lawn with toilet paper. Or maybe call a friend on the Board of Health and have Aunt Pat's shut down for violating some crazy rule no one's ever heard of. She'll arrange to have a personal beverage planted right in the middle of the food-prep area. You never know what that twisted woman is going to do!"

"Pooh," said Lulu with a wave of her hand. "I can handle Tristan Pembroke. Besides, our arrangement is just a temporary thing. Steffi needed a place to go, and her aunt, her favorite relative, is out of town on business. She doesn't have the cash right now for an apartment, and I had the space for a guest. It worked out real well."

"I'm just saying to be careful," said Colleen, irritably. "Tristan's tougher than she looks. I wouldn't mess with her."

"Well, *I'm* about to have to mess with her," said Sara grimly. "Y'all won't believe it when you hear what she's done to me."

Lulu sat back in the booth. "What? I thought she was helping you out with your art, Sara. You're one of the big, featured artists in her benefit auction. It's only you and a couple other artists, right? I thought it was going to be your big springboard for your art career!"

"It is; it is," said Sara in a hurry. "But then Tristan messed me up on something else. It's like it isn't in her to actually do something nice and then leave it alone. She commissioned me to paint a portrait of her. I was sort of rolling my eyes at the time, you know—who does something like that? Usually people want a portrait of their child or their beloved dog or something like that. A portrait of *herself*?" Sara shook her head.

Lulu said, "I'll admit that it's real tacky, honey. But it sounds to me like she gave you more work to do, and that's got to be a *good* thing."

"It was a good thing until Tristan decided she hated her portrait and won't pay me for it. After all that work I put into it, too." Sara looked steamed.

A deep voice behind Sara said, "Hold on a minute. Are y'all talking about Tristan Pembroke? And pay?"

Lulu smiled up at Morty, one-third of the Back Porch Blues Band, a regular customer of Aunt Pat's for the past sixty years, and a good friend. He was in his eighties, resembled a black version of Mr. Clean, and kept calling himself retired, although you couldn't tell it. He was still playing gigs as if he were a fully employed, much-younger man. "Yes, Sara was commissioned for a portrait, and Tristan has only paid her half of what she's owed."

"Shoot. I hate to hear that," said Morty, shaking his head. "She hired the band to play her benefit gig. And she's not paying us in advance, either." He looked glum.

Sara said, "It'll probably work out all right for you, Morty. Unless, that is, she doesn't like your music." Morty frowned in confusion, and Sara said, "That's what happened to me—she didn't like the way the portrait turned out."

Colleen said, "Isn't that just like Tristan? Why? Didn't you draw her pretty enough to suit her?"

Sara pointed her finger at Colleen. "Bingo! Hit the nail on the head. No, apparently I didn't depict Tristan quite as gorgeous as she thinks herself to be. I'll admit that the more time I spent with her, trying to help her organize the art side of the auction, the more I disliked her. My dislike *might* have spilled over into the portrait. Just the same, she commissioned the painting, and she was responsible for paying for it. Nobody's going to buy a portrait of someone else. I've half a mind to try to put it up for auction at the benefit." She snapped her fingers. "Know what? That's what I'm going to do."

Colleen looked nervous at the very thought of it. "It doesn't sound like a good idea to me. Tristan will be furious! And if she thinks the portrait isn't a good likeness, then she's sure going to be upset at a whole party viewing it."

"What else can I do?" asked Sara with a shrug. "The benefit will be the best time for me to get rid of the portrait. I'll be sure to give it to the auctioneer after all my other paintings have been sold. At least I'll get something out of the work I put in—and there'll be a donation to charity, too."

There was a booming laugh, and Lulu looked up to see her favorite policeman, Pink Rogers, smiling down at them. He wore, as usual when he was off-duty, one of the pastel button-down shirts that had earned him his nickname. But then, at a very fit and trim six feet seven inches and two hundred and fifty pounds, who was going to give him grief over his choice of clothing?

"I was just wondering what was going on at this table, that's all," said Pink, grinning. "I don't know when I've seen such stormy faces. Even Morty looks upset, and he's usually such a laid-back guy."

Colleen scooted over and patted the space next to her on the booth. "Well, have a seat and I'll be happy to fill you in, hon." Lulu could tell that that wasn't exactly what Pink had in mind—he was a sitting-at-the-lunch-counter kind of guy. But he took a seat, and Colleen said, "We're all furious with Tristan Pembroke. Mad enough to spit!" Lulu flagged down a waitress and asked her to bring Pink's usual order, since she knew her regular always ordered the same thing.

The indignant Colleen filled in Pink with her story. "Pansy won Miss Peach, Miss Magnolia, and Miss Barbeque," said Colleen. "But she'd get a whole lot further if certain people weren't cheaters. And so would Coco," she added. "There's no reason why Coco shouldn't have won a Little Miss pageant by now. It's all Tristan Pembroke's sabotage."

Pink was looking like he wished he'd sat over at the lunch counter and hadn't come over to their table at all, thought Lulu. "I remember hearing some sabotage story some time back. But you're saying she's doing other things to make Pansy lose?"

"Oh, she does little petty things from time to time that don't help—like stealing Pansy's duct tape."

"Duct tape?" asked Pink in a weak voice.

"It helps keep dresses and swimsuits in place," said Colleen. "It's *very* important to keep stuff from falling out of their swimsuits. But Tristan does other things, too—she votes against her and makes the other judges vote against her, too. And y'all know what she did to Pansy a few months ago—it made *big* news." Lulu didn't actually know about it, but Colleen wasn't giving her a chance to ask her. "And Tristan is clearly using some insider information to get ahead when she's coaching girls. All I have to say is that she better look out. One of these days, I'm coming after her."

Pink raised his eyebrows at Colleen.

"Oh, shoot. I keep forgetting you're a cop, Pink. Don't worry. . . . I'm not planning on putting a hit on Tristan."

Pink looked relieved and picked up a spicy corn muffin for a big bite.

"Not yet, anyway."

Chapter

3

Later that afternoon, Lulu's son, Ben, said to his wife, Sara, "Mother is going to be so excited. For a while I've been following this guy online who has a food blog that's gotten really big. He does interviews with chefs, posts recipes, interviews cookbook authors . . . the works. He has a following in the thousands on his blog and is huge on Facebook and Twitter, too."

Sara said, "Why would your mama be interested in that, Ben? She's not a blog reader and sure isn't on Facebook and Twitter."

"He's packed up shop and moved to Memphis, that's why. Think about it, Sara—it's a fantastic opportunity to introduce him to Aunt Pat's. Besides, barbeque just isn't *food* in Memphis—it's a *culture*. He's going to be dying to find out more about how barbeque meshes with life here in Memphis."

"If you say so," said Sara doubtfully.

"I was talking to Derrick the other day, and your nephew knows more about social-media branding than you can shake a stick at! I'm thinking that's the way to move Aunt Pat's into the twenty-first century, Sara. We'll embrace the food bloggers—especially this guy, who is such a huge influence. They have a much bigger audience than the newspaper food critics. We don't have to rely on only local traffic—we could make Aunt Pat's a real destination!" His eyes shone.

"So you're thinking about getting your mama to call him up and invite him over to the restaurant? Maybe make sure he has a first-class meal with us? Then he'll blog about it to all his followers?"

Ben hesitated. "Well, yes. That's what would make sense, of course. But the reality is that Mother shuts down whenever I mention the Internet to her. She'd reject this idea right out of the box. So I went ahead and e-mailed him. . . . See, Sara, you e-mail people like him. He's an *online* guy. He's planning on coming by tomorrow and checking out Aunt Pat's."

Sara had a feeling that she still wasn't getting the full story out of Ben. "And that's it? I guess he'll probably want a couple of pictures of your mom. She's kind of the face behind the restaurant now, even if she isn't spending as much time in the kitchen as she used to."

"Yesss, that's pretty much it. Pretty much."

"What else is there, then?" asked Sara.

"As a reader of Gordon's blog—that's his name, Gordon—I've found that he's a really nice-looking guy. Nice looking for a man, I mean. And he's older—not too old. Actually, he's in his sixties, just like Mother, and seems really active. He's obviously real sharp, too, to be doing all this stuff online at his age. So I thought maybe he and Mother would hit it off a little bit. I told him that Mother would be pleased as punch to show him around Memphis, seeing as how he's new in town,"

Sara shook her head. "Ohhhh, no you didn't! You know your mama is perfectly happy by herself! If she was interested in going out with people, Ben, I think she'd be able to handle setting herself up on her own dates."

"She needs some prodding," said Ben firmly. "Mother needs to try to relax and have a little fun. She's so serious all the time. And she doesn't seem to do anything with her appearance; she looks like a little old lady with her hair in a bun and her flowered dresses. I think she needs a little shaking up." He thought about this for a moment. "Maybe Mother needs a makeover. She'd look cute as a button if she updated her look a little bit."

"Humph," said Sara.

"I had my own makeover a few years ago, remember? The before-and-after was real dramatic. I think it made a real difference in the way I looked and felt, too. I felt younger and more energetic, so I *was* more energetic."

Sara sighed. She wasn't sure that Ben's comb-over, which made his hair resemble a helmet, and his mustache, which conspired to make him bear a startling resemblance to Captain Kangaroo, qualified as a makeover. But she loved him too much to point that fact out. "Ben, I think you better let your mother do her own thing. If she *wants* to update her look, she'll do it. Besides, I'm sure that Gordon is going to like your mama anyway."

Ben brightened. "I'm sure he will. Think of all they have in common—food! The way to a man's heart is through his stomach, and I'm going to make sure it's an expressway right through it. I'm cooking up a plan to give him some real, mouthwatering southern cuisine—and tell him Mother made it."

"So you're thinking that this guy isn't just going to move Aunt Pat's into the twenty-first century—you're thinking he's going to move your *mother* into the twenty-first century."

"I can dream," said Ben with dignity.

"I've got a funny feeling about this," said Sara as she, Steffi, and Lulu walked up to Tristan Pembroke's front door for the art benefit. "You know that feeling you get when you *know* you're going to get some bad news?"

"Now, Sara, it's not like you to be silly," chided Lulu, smoothing down the new floral dress she'd gotten from Dee Dee's shop. "You're going to have a wonderful time and sell a ton of paintings," she said with determination as she plastered a smile on her face and walked in with what felt like throngs of people.

Steffi said, "Thanks for the ride over, Sara. I know I wasn't on Mother's guest list, but I wanted to see the auction. What time were you saying for us to leave, Sara?"

By the look on Sara's face, Lulu could tell she was ready to leave right then. "Maybe thirty minutes after the auction, if we could. That'll give me enough time to talk to the guests who bought my paintings. I'm thinking that should be around eight o'clock. I'm already worn out and want to get back home and hit the sack."

"No problem," said Steffi. "I have a feeling I'll be ready to escape Mother by then. She's sure to be shooting me looks for being here." And Steffi disappeared into the crowd of guests.

"I don't understand why that child wanted to come," clucked Lulu. "It's not like her mama didn't give her a clear enough message that she wasn't welcome. Poor baby."

Sara shrugged. "Teenagers. She's being passive-aggressive and proving to her mom that she can do whatever she likes. Besides, there's safety in numbers. No wonder she wanted to go with us. What I don't understand is what *I'm* doing here. I'm already ready to head back to the car."

"This will probably be a great night for you, Sara. These folks *look* like they buy art. You'll probably even unload that portrait of Tristan. And I know you'll be glad to get it out of your house."

"Isn't that the truth?" said Sara, looking balefully at the covered painting she was lugging in. "I didn't even know all these people were going to *be* here." She set the portrait down to rest a moment before picking it up again. "Tristan has this many friends?"

"She probably doesn't—people are just looking for a fun evening out, and the tickets weren't even all that expensive at fifty dollars a person. And you don't have anything to worry about, Sara—folks are probably going to come up to you to chat about your art. It's not like you have to go up and make a speech or anything."

"Except," said Sara in a low voice despite the loud party going on around her, "that I'm planning to unveil this portrait of Tristan that she hates."

"I wouldn't worry my head over it, Sara. Maybe it'll sell at the auction. If not, you've not lost anything—and you'll have filled your tummy with some scrumptious food."

Unfortunately, thought Lulu as she took a big sip from her punch glass, the food wasn't so scrumptious after all.

Cherry took a big bite of the chicken, then proceeded to chew, and chew, and chew, making a face at Lulu.

"Cardboard. That's what this stuff tastes like. She should have gotten Aunt Pat's to cook for the party," said Cherry, finally giving up on the chicken and discreetly depositing it into a napkin. "This is the worst food I've ever put in my mouth! Tristan must have gotten the hospital to cater this benefit."

"What a shame," said Lulu, sadly surveying her plate. "The food *looks* good. It smells good, too. Nice presentation—they just overcooked it. And undercooked it. And overseasoned it *and* underseasoned it. I missed lunch today, so I'm starving. I might slip into Tristan's kitchen and find something to spice it up a little bit."

Cherry's face brightened. "Maybe you can sneak in the kitchen and snag some salt and pepper. I was going to toss my food in the trash, but I think Mama would haunt me. She was always worried about those starving children in . . . well, wherever it was that they were starving back when I was little."

So Lulu walked right into the kitchen on a rescue mission, and no one paid attention to her being there at all. The catering staff was too focused on producing more of their culinary disaster.

Lulu finally tracked down some salt and pepper. What catering company would underseason food and then not even have salt and pepper out to resuscitate it all?

Lulu was heading out of the kitchen when she heard Tristan's voice, high-pitched and annoyed, coming alarmingly close to her. She glanced around the kitchen and didn't see a good place to hide—until she noticed that the door to the large pantry was open wide enough to stand behind and be shielded from the rest of the room.

"Get more plates cleared out there! Everywhere I look there are plates and glasses and forks—stacked up on all my tables. It's *not* just about putting the food out there, people! It's about getting the dirty plates *out* of there, too!" She gave a gusty and exasperated sigh, and the catering staff that Lulu could see were nodding their heads and rushing back out to the other part of the house. In seconds, it was quiet enough in the kitchen for Lulu to hear Tristan's tapping heels. Lulu clutched the salt and pepper shakers until her fingers turned white and prayed that Tristan Pembroke didn't find her cowering in her pantry gripping seasoning for the tasteless food.

Although Lulu couldn't imagine how things could possibly get worse, they did when Lulu heard Tristan make a startled, un-Tristan-like yelp and then heard a deep voice chuckle. Oh no. Not some romantic interlude in the kitchen. What misdeed was Lulu being punished for?

Lulu peeked out cautiously and saw Tristan push the man away. "What in the Sam Hill do you think you're doing, Loren? For heaven's sake." Tristan had her hands on her hips, staring angrily at a tall man with dark hair and a love-struck expression.

"You know exactly what I think I'm doing! And you used to be all happy about it, too, Tristan. What's going on with you? You don't return my texts or my phone calls. It's time to do some catching up." He pulled Tristan roughly toward him again.

She jerked back and straightened her dress. "It's *not* time, and it's not going to *be* time. It's over. The end. Get over it. And—get out of my benefit."

The man said angrily, "No, I don't think it *is* over—" but he was cut off by a shriek of absolute fury that made Lulu jump.

"I *knew* it! Knew it!"

Lulu peeped through the crack at the door hinge and

saw another woman there—a woman who, judging from the look on her face, must have been the man's wife. She was dressed in a sweat suit, wore no makeup, and didn't look like she'd planned on being at a party.

The woman picked up a glass of white wine and threw the contents right at Tristan, who cursed loudly. And the man, Loren, was hearing it from both of them now. Tristan's voice was icy as she wet a wad of paper towels and said, "You're welcome to Loren—I never want to see him again. I should have known that when you lie down with dogs that you'll wake up with fleas."

The man with the dark hair was stomping out of the kitchen with his wife berating him as they left. "I knew you were up to no good! Telling me that you were going out to the coffeehouse to work all these nights. But no, you were sneaking out to see somebody who doesn't even *like* you. And who thinks I'm not even good enough to join her club! Wasting your time!" This, then, must be Pepper. Cherry had said they'd both been upset at being banned from the Memphis Women's League.

As soon as the two were out of earshot, Tristan abandoned her futile attempt to clean up her dress, and Lulu heard her heels quickly tapping off in the direction of the staircase. Lulu quickly left the kitchen right as the caterers were coming back in with stacks of dirty dishes.

Cherry sidled up to her. "Honey, I'm sorry; I just gave up on that food. I figured you must have started talking to somebody and forgot about the spices. I think the caterers took your plate away, too. I was talking to Sara and the next thing I know, your plate was AWOL."

Lulu's stomach made protesting noises over the missing food. "It's okay—I'll load up on dessert." She was still thinking about the scene in the kitchen when she heard the auctioneer calling for everyone to gather for the auction outside.

"I'm sure," said Lulu to Cherry and Sara, who'd come up to join them, "that the Back Porch Blues Band is more than ready to finally take a break. That woman has run them into the ground."

Sara made a face. "Where is Tristan, speaking of the devil? She's usually a whole lot more on top of the party than this. I haven't seen her for a while."

They walked out into Tristan's heavily landscaped yard. "I think she *may* be changing clothes," said Lulu innocently.

Sara's eyes widened, "You've got some insider information? What happened?"

Lulu didn't think this was the place to get into it. All she needed was to have Tristan come up behind her right when she was demonstrating the way the wine had splattered over her. Instead she said, "She spilled something on her dress." Then, looking around her, she said, "Isn't this the most beautiful yard you've ever seen? I just love all these flowering bushes everywhere."

"This yard?" asked Cherry derisively. "*I've* got a nice yard myself right now."

Lulu knit her brows. "You know, I drove by your house a few days ago and it *was* really nice. I don't remember you being such an avid gardener, Cherry."

Cherry preened. "I've discovered the secret to gardening."

Lulu said, "Well, spill it—I sure would like to hear the secret. Is it choosing native plants? I keep hearing about these invasive plants that are trying to take everything over. Or planting heat-resistant plants? Mine keep turning brown faster than you can shake a stick at them. I'm about to order myself a load of cacti."

Cherry shook her head. "It's none of those things. No, girls, the secret to gardening is plastic flowers."

Sara blinked. "Don't you mean silk?"

"No, I mean *plastic*. Silk would ruin out there in the sun and rain. No, plastic is the way to go, and it's amazing how lifelike these flowers look. You'd be amazed. My next step is Astroturf. I'm amazed by how real *that* looks. And just think—I wouldn't have to worry about mowing ever again!"

Cherry looked triumphant, as if she couldn't imagine Lulu and Sara doing anything but wholeheartedly agreeing with her. However, Lulu couldn't imagine not seeing Cherry ripping around her yard at a tearing speed on her riding mower with her Elvis helmet firmly in place. It simply wouldn't be the same.

Cherry said, "Now I'm not one to gossip . . ." Lulu bit her lips to keep from smiling, "but have y'all seen Steffi tonight? I know her mama didn't invite her to come to this party. And she's been looking pitiful. That girl is so messed up, y'all. I hate to say that about anybody, but it's the truth."

"She's got a lot on her mind right now, that's all," said Lulu. "Think about it—she just moved out of her mother's house, she's living with someone she doesn't really know"—Sara rolled her eyes, and Lulu hurried on because she knew Sara thought that her being a bleeding heart was going to come back to bite her later—"and she's learning how to wait tables and hasn't done a lick of waitressing in her life. To top it all off, her mother throws a huge benefit, and she's not even on the guest list. I don't blame her for gate-crashing. She rode with Sara and me tonight."

Cherry said, "I gate-crashed this soiree myself. Who cares? I paid the money for the ticket and wanted to support Sara—I decided I didn't need a personal invitation.

And I still say Steffi's a mess. She's been floating around this event like some ghostly creature—face pale, eyes big, not smiling. There is no expression on her face, and *that's* a face that needs all the expression it can get to help it out. I'd like to grab her and give her a makeover."

"Do you think it would help?" asked Sara in a hushed voice. "I'm not trying to be ugly, but I think that makeup and a more flattering haircut would only go so far to help Steffi."

Lulu sighed. "Bless her heart."

Sara looked a little queasy, and Lulu didn't think it had anything to do with the unseasoned food. "Sara, what's wrong? You getting butterflies about the auction?"

Sara fanned herself with her auction catalog. "Does it show? I've done shows before and sold some paintings at those, but an auction is really different from a show. You've got a painting that you spent a lot of time on put in a spotlight and then having bids called out for it—it's nerve-wracking."

"But Sara, Tristan wouldn't have asked you to be part of the art auction if she thought your paintings weren't going to sell. And the people here seem really responsive—I've seen them previewing the art, and the buzz is sounding good."

Sara said, "I think I'm also having second thoughts about giving the auctioneer that portrait at the end to sell. I know it's silly—I mean, Tristan *did* renege on the deal and I did put a ton of work into it."

"Exactly." Lulu nodded.

"But she *has* been nice to set up this auction and give me all this exposure."

"Sara, she's not finishing paying you for something you created especially for her. You're using the opportunity to sell the painting and make a little money for yourself as well as the charity. I wouldn't worry about it."

Sara twisted a spiraled lock of red hair around her finger. "I know that. But she really seemed to *hate* the portrait. Like she was ashamed of it or something. She's going to be livid when she finds out it was unveiled in front of everyone."

Lulu said, "If you're going to worry about it, then you *should* ask her about it. Better to find her and tell her what you're planning. I'll go with you."

"Thanks, Lulu." Sara gave her a grateful hug. "So let's go track her down—she's got to be done changing clothes by now, right?"

"Oh, for sure. She's probably checking on the food and the band. I know the band is ready to take a break. . . . Actually, it sounds like they've stopped."

Sara frowned and listened for a moment. "Have they started the auction? But that was supposed to be at the end of the evening!"

Chapter
4

Sure enough, the auctioneer was already describing the first painting. Sara rolled her eyes. "Now my stomach really *is* doing flip-flops. And now I'm out of time to hunt her down and tell her I'm planning on putting the picture in the auction."

"Maybe it won't go as badly as you think. Tristan might not even realize it's being sold. That would really be the best outcome—for you to sell the portrait and for her not to be the wiser."

"Or maybe it won't sell at all," said Sara glumly. "You know? I wonder if there's a chance that Steffi will want the painting if no one offers to buy it. I know she and her mom had a big falling out, but it's a good painting—and I'd let her have it for free if nobody buys it tonight."

Lulu winced. "I don't know about that, Sara. This was more than a little falling out—I think this is a major break between them." She shrugged. "But maybe she would want

it. I'm sure she's got to miss her mother on some level."
Lulu scanned the yard. "I don't see her around, though."

It was easy to get caught up in the excitement of auctions, thought Lulu. The auctioneer flew through his clipped delivery, the paintings all looked beautiful, and the guests were attentive.

Sara should be happy, thought Lulu. Her paintings seemed to be selling really well and for higher amounts than the other artists'. But instead, she looked more anxious than anything else. Her mind was clearly on Tristan's portrait.

The auctioneer said, "Sold!" on the last item, and Sara hurried over to him, pointing at the covered canvas and talking quickly. Lulu turned to look behind her and saw Tristan, wearing a different dress, walking toward the stage, obviously thinking the auction was over and preparing to thank her guests.

The auctioneer nodded to Sara and walked up to the microphone again. "We've got one additional item up for bid, y'all!" He uncovered the painting and his assistant held it up for the guests to see. "Here we have a beautifully rendered depiction of our hostess . . ."

There was a shriek, and Tristan marched up on stage and spoke fiercely to the auctioneer for a minute. The auctioneer quickly said, "Sorry, folks! This painting has been retracted, since it's already spoken for."

"Spoken for, my big toe!" said Sara angrily as she walked up to Lulu. "It's not spoken for if she's not going to pay me for it!" She looked, thought Lulu, just as furious as Tristan did.

Tristan got off the stage, and Sara stomped over to her. Lulu watched as a red-faced Sara spoke angrily to Tristan, waving her hands around excitedly. Tristan's hands were on her hips, and her face looked coldly furious. When they noticed people watching them, they strode off inside Tristan's house, presumably to keep their conversation more private.

Cherry said, "You know, the *potential* was there for this to be a good party. It's too bad that *Tristan* was the hostess because she clearly doesn't know how to have a good time. The food is icky, and now Sara is all upset because Tristan is acting like such a troll. The people she invited are all on the snobby side. The only possible redeeming factor of the party is the band. The guys are really playing their hearts out," she said, as the Back Porch Blues Band resumed playing.

"Tristan won't let them take a break," said Lulu with a sigh. "And I don't think the auction counted as much of a break for them. They probably barely had time to make it through that long line for the restroom."

"So if the band goes on strike and packs up their stuff and *leaves*, then that'll sink the party even further." Cherry rolled her eyes. "Get ready to run for the escape hatch."

Lulu stood on her toes to look around the backyard. "Actually, I'm not sure where my escape hatch even *is*. I need to chase Sara down. She was supposed to take Steffi and me back home at eight o'clock. I know she and Tristan went inside for a heart-to-heart, but surely that's over. I think I'm ready to head back home and crash."

"She's probably inside somewhere, cooling off from the argument. Maybe *really* cooling off because it's starting to feel kind of humid out here." Cherry glanced around. "Here comes that Darling Dress Shoppe Dee Dee. Ugh. Sorry, Lulu. I know you like her clothes. That's my cue to find someone else to talk to. Good luck finding Sara."

Lulu managed not to laugh as Dee Dee's eyes widened

as she watched Cherry walk away. Apparently, Dee Dee wasn't impressed with Cherry's short, poufed, fuchsia and black plaid dress. . . . She didn't think she'd ever seen anybody look more perplexed.

"Dee Dee, did you see Sara inside?" Lulu asked.

"I saw her having a big argument with Tristan," said Dee Dee, penciled-in eyebrows raised. "Don't know what they were fussing about, but that was the last time I saw her. They probably went into a quiet room to squabble in privacy because people were staring at them."

"I'm going to find her," Lulu said. "I just want to make sure she's doing okay—she was pretty upset over the portrait. Actually, she should forget arguing with Tristan and come out and hand out her business card to everybody— they're all talking about her art."

"I'll join you," said Dee Dee. "I need to find the powder room anyway."

As they walked into Tristan's house, Dee Dee took the opportunity to tell Lulu a little bit about the new shipment of clothes at the dress shop. "I really had you in mind, Lulu, when I bought some of these things at Market. I knew you'd like them. . . . They look exactly like you. Not like Cherry's clothes—bleah. Where does that girl shop? Not that she's a *girl* anymore, either. . . . Maybe somebody should remind her of that fact."

Lulu had a feeling that Dee Dee would dearly love to be the person to remind her. "I'm not really sure. Maybe she gets some of it online? She does like her bright colors, and she looks better in them than most people do."

"I guess," said Dee Dee doubtfully. "If you say so."

Lulu scanned the room. She saw the caterers collecting plates, people drinking wine and carrying paintings to their cars, lots of people standing and talking in groups, but she didn't see anyone who looked like Sara.

Dee Dee and Lulu passed through the living room and down a short hall toward the bathroom. "Looks like somebody might be in the study," said Dee Dee, nodding at a cracked door.

"Hmm?" asked Lulu, distractedly.

"I *said*," bellowed Dee Dee, "that it looks like somebody might be in the study!"

Lulu gritted her teeth. One of these days, Dee Dee's assumptions over Lulu's deafness were really going to push her over the edge.

They walked over to it. "Sara?" called Lulu hesitantly. Maybe Tristan and Sara were still carrying on that argument. "Sara, it's time for us to head back home . . ."

"Sara!" barked Dee Dee, apparently thinking Lulu's voice was too soft-spoken to get the job done. Then Dee Dee held her hand up, signaling Lulu to be quiet. "Someone's in there, arguing," she said in a stage whisper. And she settled in to listen.

Lulu heard Tristan's voice. "Steffi, I just can't believe you showed up here tonight. Isn't the whole *point* of estrangement to be *apart*?"

Steffi's voice sounded determined but a little wavery. "I thought that maybe after you had some time to think about it . . ."

"I *have* had some time. And I've decided I don't need your negative energy around," said Tristan, harshly.

"Negative energy?" Steffi sounded bewildered.

"That's right. From the time you turned thirteen, you've argued with me and challenged me every step of the way. Clearly, you'll do better somewhere else, since we have so little in common." The ice in Tristan's voice shocked Lulu. It was hard to imagine that voice came from a mother talking to her only child.

"Okay, Mother," Steffi said in a low voice. She gave a short laugh. "Consider yourself de-mothered as of this moment on."

Lulu and Dee Dee hurried back from the door as it opened and Steffi came out, shoulders slumped.

Steffi looked so deep in her unhappy thoughts that she didn't even seem to register Dee Dee and Lulu until Lulu said, "Steffi? I was looking for Sara. I guess you haven't seen her?"

Steffi shook her head, and Lulu put a concerned hand on her arm and said, "Are you all right, sweetie?"

Steffi's lip trembled, and the next thing Lulu knew, she'd fallen into Lulu's arms and was crying as if her heart would break.

Lulu led Steffi off down the hall, away from some of the curious looks they were getting. She turned to ask Dee Dee to run and find a tissue for Steffi, but she was nowhere to be seen. Dee Dee must have really hightailed it to the bathroom, thought Lulu. But then, it was one of the first times that evening that there wasn't a huge line waiting to get in there.

Fifteen minutes later, Steffi seemed all cried out. Lulu blew out a sigh of relief. There wasn't too much comforting you could do in that kind of situation and up against that kind of cruelty. The child sure had a powerful amount of hurt stored up in her.

"Want to go out and hear Morty, Big Ben, and Buddy play?" she asked Steffi. "They're really doing an amazing job tonight—it might cheer you up a little bit."

Steffi gave a tentative smile. "Thanks, Lulu. And thanks for being here for me tonight."

Lulu was impressed by Buddy, Big Ben, and Morty's stamina. Lulu had always found the blues offered a salve to hurting hearts and wasn't surprised to see that Steffi seemed a little more relaxed as they ate some dessert (which was, fortunately, better than the main course had been) and listened to the band. Cherry joined them and was even able to bring a smile out on Steffi's face.

There was an ominous rumbling above, and Lulu said, "Mercy! Now we're in for a storm?" After the evening she'd witnessed so far—horrible food and a vicious argument, Lulu was starting to wonder what was going to happen next—fire and brimstone?

"I don't remember the forecast calling for a storm," Steffi said with a frown.

Cherry nodded and pulled her helmet on, knowingly. "They said 'scattered storms.' That usually means that they have absolutely no idea what's going to happen, but they want to make sure they cover all the bases."

The next clap of thunder was more than a rumble—and it came alarmingly right on top of a vivid strike of lightning that illuminated the yard. Suddenly, sheets of rain came down, and there was a mad scramble to bring the dessert, guests, and various paintings inside. Lulu quickly thought of the Back Porch Blues Band and hurried over to see if she could help move their equipment to a dry place. But they were busily putting down the sides of the tent they were in and holding it down between the three of them and a couple of other people who were helping them battle the wind.

Lulu and Steffi had just walked into the house when the lights went out.

"Oh, now this is really too much," groaned Cherry. "Having a huge storm blow out of nowhere at a big party

is one thing. Losing the electricity is taking things a step
too far."

Everyone at the party seemed to be trying to stand really still so they wouldn't run into anything. Buddy joined
them. "They've got the tent and equipment under control
out there, so I thought I'd try to help out in here. Especially
since I noticed that the houses on either side of us have
power. Think maybe having all the speakers and mics and
lights tripped the circuit breakers?"

"It's worth a try to look for the fuse box," said Lulu. "Or
else we could try to light a bunch of candles. I remember
there were a ton of candelabras in the dining room and living room."

"Which was all well and good back when people
*smoked* and actually had *lighters* on them," said Buddy in
a dry voice. "Nowadays, nobody's going to have a lighter.
Even if there are a couple of smokers here, they wouldn't
have brought cigarettes to a party like this one."

Lulu said, "Good point. I never thought I'd miss smoking even temporarily, but you could at least always count
on a lighter or some matches. Where on earth could Tristan
be? I thought she was a better hostess than this. Well, let's
go try to find the fuse box."

"I'll check the garage," said Buddy.

"I'll peek inside some closets," said Lulu. "And keep an
eye out for our hostess, who should be taking care of this
herself!" She turned on her cell-phone's flashlight and set
off for the back of the house.

Lulu had no luck finding the fuse box. She'd had high
hopes for a large coat closet near the front door, but after
moving around a lot of coats, she found nothing. The other
downstairs closets also yielded nothing, nor did the kitchen.
Finally she saw a cracked door at the end of the hall. Must

be a downstairs master bedroom, thought Lulu. She walked resolutely to the door and knocked hard on it. "Tristan?" she called. "You in there?"

Hearing no answer, she cautiously opened the door. She had no desire to view an encore performance of Tristan's love life gone wrong. But there was still no answer and no signs of movement as she held her cell phone's small beam in front of her.

Lulu headed to the master bedroom's closet and opened the door. The closet was like a room all its own, with gorgeous ball gowns in every color. And there was a shelf of crowns. Actually, Lulu remembered seeing beauty-pageant tiaras in glass boxes in the living room, too, so she guessed that Tristan had had at least one moment of self-realization that displaying twenty crowns might be a little showy.

And there, in the closet, was the fuse box. With relief, Lulu set down the cell phone where the beam would point on the box. Unfortunately, it looked like nothing had been tripped—that maybe the storm had actually knocked down a limb on a power line somewhere and caused the power to go out.

Her relief, though, quickly turned to shock when she backed out of the closet and saw a limp Tristan Pembroke, wearing a pageant tiara, and very clearly dead.

# Chapter 5

Pink was with the policemen who quickly arrived on the scene.

"Lulu," he said, "we've got to cure you of this body-discovering habit you've fallen into."

"I tell you what!" said Lulu, shaking her head. "Seems like some weeks I can't go outside the house without finding some poor soul out cold."

Pink said, "But the question of the day is, was Tristan Pembroke some poor soul?"

"She couldn't have been all bad," said Lulu, but she doubted she was speaking the truth.

"Well, she sure rubbed somebody the wrong way," said Pink, nodding toward the back of the house.

Lulu shivered. "You can say that again. Getting murdered is bad enough, but then they made fun of her, too, by putting that tiara on her head." Lulu's stomach pitched at the memory. "It all seems even wickeder than an ordinary murder—it was so thought out. I guess that brass candle-stick near her body must have been the murder weapon."

Pink said, "That's something that forensics will have to confirm, but it sure looks that way."

"Murdering Tristan at a huge party meant that there was lots of noise for a cover," said Lulu thoughtfully. "And there's lots of commotion and maybe no one's paying a whole lot of attention to people coming and going. And then the lights go out, creating all kinds of chaos. Although I can't imagine for the life of me why someone would want to murder somebody in the dark. What if you missed?"

"I think," said Pink, rubbing a sandy eyebrow, "that the killer probably killed Tristan *before* the lights went out."

Lulu snapped her fingers. "I see. So the power going out was a cover to get the murderer back in with the other guests and escape detection. But then the killer would have to be someone who knew the house well enough to know where the fuse box was."

"Actually," said Pink, "we've discovered that the lights went out completely naturally. When the storm blew in, there was a car out on the main road that skidded and hit a transformer and knocked out the lights. It looks like even luck was on our killer's side."

Lulu nodded. "Especially if the lights going out corre-sponded to the moment the murderer needed to leave the scene of the crime. Getting out of that room could have been tough because there was a line for the restroom not too far from Tristan's bedroom."

"There are definitely some folks I need to talk to," said Pink, standing up and giving his khaki pants a hitch up. "Like Colleen. She sure was breathing fire about Tristan at Aunt Pat's. She definitely thought that Tristan was doing Pansy wrong."

"True," said Lulu, "but Colleen wasn't even invited to the party, for that very reason."

"That may be so," said Pink smoothly, "but there's also such a thing as party *crashing*. So I'm not going to let Miss Colleen completely off the hook."

Lulu suddenly felt a great longing for her brass bed and comfy quilt. "Pink, hon, is it okay for me to slide out of here now? I think I'm ready to grab Sara and go back home."

Pink was just telling her it was okay when the man in charge of the case, a wiry, middle-aged detective named Freeman, said quickly, "Absolutely—I have one more question to ask you. Do you have any reason to want Tristan Pembroke dead, Mrs. Taylor?"

He certainly believed in getting to the point. Lulu shook her head. "No, killing people isn't my way of solving problems, Detective. I didn't have a whole lot of respect for Tristan, and she did rile up a few people I knew, but that was just her way."

"We'll get in touch with you if we have any more questions," the detective said in a clipped voice. Pink shrugged at her. Lulu guessed that as the person who discovered the body, she shouldn't be surprised by getting a few questions.

"Oh, and where are the rest of the guests now? I know y'all needed to clear everybody out so you could protect whatever evidence was here."

Pink said, "We ended up blocking off the street and have them all out there. We needed to ask some of them questions and asked all the guests if they saw or heard anything that might help us out. You rode here with Sara, you were saying?"

"I did. And Steffi did, too. I'll look for her outside, then," said Lulu, picking up her pocketbook and feeling proud that she had the presence of mind to get it, considering all the events of the evening.

"Actually," said Detective Freeman quickly, "Sara Taylor is one of the guests we're most wanting to talk to. When you find her, please send her our way."

Lulu felt that queasy stomach sensation again. "That doesn't sound good. What do you want Sara for?"

"I got some witness accounts of an altercation between Sara Taylor and Tristan. I need to ask her a few questions about it," he said.

Pink's normally sunny face looked a little worried. "Say, Lulu, were y'all in Sara's car? That yellow minivan she usually drives?"

"We sure were. Why?"

"Because I didn't see it out there. And I looked for a few minutes when Detective Freeman said he wanted to talk to Sara."

Lulu said in a more confident voice than she felt, "Oh pooh. Sara's not going to have gone off and stranded me somewhere. I'll go track her down. I'll be sure to send her your way before we take off for home."

That ended up being easier said than done. Lulu had no luck finding Sara in the group of party guests who hadn't gone home yet. Cherry hadn't seen her. Steffi hadn't seen her. And Lulu didn't see hide nor hair of that yellow minivan.

Lulu decided to call Sara. Maybe she'd realized she was running low on gas or something and had gone to fill up while Lulu was being questioned. Lulu pulled out her cell phone and punched in Sara's number. There was no answer, so Lulu left a message. Now she was worried.

Cherry came over and gave her a hug. "Still can't find her? Don't worry, Lulu, we'll figure out what happened.

I'm sure it's some really ordinary explanation that we'll all be laughing over. Why don't you call Ben and see if she's just gotten in a fog and forgotten y'all rode together? Maybe she went home and turned off her phone and went to bed."

When Lulu rang Ben and Sara's house, though, he hadn't heard a word from her. And he was just as alarmed as Lulu.

Although Cherry had offered to drop her off by the house, Lulu stuck around at Tristan's house until Ben came. Together they drove around the area until they found a very frustrated-looking Sara struggling with the car jack and a flat tire.

"Sara, you scared the life out of Mother and me!" fussed Ben as he lumbered out of the car. "We didn't know what had happened to you. And why in Sam Hill didn't you answer your cell phone when we were trying to call you? I thought that's the whole point of carrying one—for emergencies."

Sara sat back on her heels away from the tire and pushed a sweaty tendril of curly red hair out of her eyes with irritation. "I know! It was all so stupid. Tristan and I had this big blowup over the portrait. I was so furious that I actually saw red—and I thought that was just a figure of speech. I was worried what I was going to say or do, so I decided to get out in my car and go for a quick drive . . . and get out of there. I promise I wasn't planning on abandoning you and Steffi, Lulu. Then, naturally, Murphy's Law—I get a flat. And this tire just did *not* want to change. As far as the cell phone goes, I left my purse at the party by accident. The cell is on vibrate, anyway. So I don't even have my driver's license with me. Good thing the police didn't stop by and try to be Good Samaritans."

Lulu thought that maybe Sara was going to be in far worse trouble with the police than driving without a license. "Unfortunately, sweetie, your night isn't over yet. I didn't even have a chance to tell Ben yet, either, because we were both so worried about you."

"Tell me what?" demanded Ben, frowning.

"Tristan was murdered during the party," said Lulu. "The police heard about Sara's argument with her—and they want to talk to Sara. I think it'll be much worse if we go back home; they'll probably think Sara's trying to hide something. Besides, we've got to go back and get Steffi."

Sara groaned. "Can this night get any worse? And— Tristan's *dead*? I promise, y'all, she was alive and kicking— practically literally—when she and I were having our big fight. Whoever murdered her, it wasn't me. In fact, I was probably out here driving around when she was killed."

"I believe you, honey—and let's keep our fingers crossed that the police will, too."


Lulu dragged herself around the house the next morning, getting ready. Ordinarily she'd call herself an early-morning person, but after the night she'd had, six hours wasn't enough sleep to recuperate.

The police, reflected Lulu on the drive over to Aunt Pat's, weren't as understanding as you'd think. Oh, Pink had winced and nodded sympathetically, but clearly this wasn't his case. It was that Detective Freeman's. And he had this look of complete disbelief on his face during Sara's entire story. Hadn't he ever met anybody who needed to cool off after an argument? Or had a flat tire? Or known somebody to forget her cell phone and not be reachable? Where was the portrait that had caused such a ruckus?

How could a big painting like that go missing? It made Lulu grouchy just thinking about it—and Lulu was rarely grouchy in the morning. Her grouchiness made her even grouchier. On top of it all, she wasn't feeling all that alert, so after she unlocked the door, she made herself some coffee at the restaurant, first thing.

She blinked in surprise as Steffi Pembroke came in through the back door. "Steffi? Honey, what are you doing here? Did I wake you up this morning when I was trying to get ready? I'm sure I made enough noise to wake the dead—I was *that* tired and stumbling all over. I'm so sorry about what happened to your mom last night. And you certainly shouldn't be here working today! In fact, you should take this next week off altogether."

Steffi rubbed her eyes. "It was okay, Lulu—I couldn't sleep. I was up all night thinking about Mother. I know people hated her, but . . ." she shrugged, her voice breaking off. "I feel terrible because she and I had that big argument, and now she's dead. I hate that some of our last words to each other were so cold." Steffi's shoulders sank.

Lulu's heart hurt for Steffi. The poor lamb felt bad about acting ugly to her mama—but her mama had acted ugly to her for her whole life . . . even when she was just a baby. So Lulu was quick to say, "And your mama's last words to you?"

Steffi looked confused.

Lulu said, "I mean, was she all sugar and spice during that last conversation?"

"Not really," Steffi said slowly.

"Well, then," said Lulu with a sniff. "I wouldn't feel so bad about myself. It's not like your mama was taking the high road." But Steffi still looked worried and Lulu said, "Why not tell me a little about what happened last night, honey?"

Steffi walked into the restaurant's office and sat down. "Sorry. I'm so tired I think I need to take a load off my feet. Maybe I'm not fit for waitressing today, after all," she said with a short laugh. "I guess I should never have gone to the party last night. I'd just decided the best way to get back at Mother and really get under her skin was to show up at the party and kind of hang around. That was going to make her more unhappy than anything else."

Lulu said gently, "But you looked like the most unhappy person there, Steffi. I felt so bad for you."

Steffi's head hung down until her lank hair partially hid her face. "I know. That's the way it always is. I always think that Mother is going to care, and it ends up just being me who gets hurt. The way she was talking to the blues band, looking at me with her cold stare—I couldn't stand it. I should have remembered that it's impossible to hurt *her*. But still . . . I hate that we ended our relationship on that note. I never wanted anything more than to get along with her."

Lulu reached over and gave Steffi a hug. "You know, I bet your mother felt the same way, deep down. It's such a shame that y'all were never able to have it become a reality. Tell you what? Why don't you head back to the house? It'll be nice and quiet there today since I'm here, working. Just lie back on the sofa and read a book or watch a little TV. I made a peach cobbler yesterday that I bet you'd love. Or maybe take a couple of naps—I know you need to catch up on your sleep."

Once again those intense eyes of Steffi's caught her off-guard. "Please don't send me home, Lulu. I don't feel like being by myself today. I know it makes sense to rest, but I can maybe leave a couple of hours earlier than my usual shift, right? I'm sure I'll be tired out in another six hours—then I'll be ready to crash. And eat some peach cobbler."

"Of course, honey," Lulu said quickly. "Whatever you need to do."

The back door to the restaurant opened again, and Ben and Sara were there, looking about as tired as Lulu felt. "Seems like I was just here," muttered Ben. "Wonder if lack of sleep makes mental time warps?"

Sara opened her mouth to make, Lulu was sure, a sharp retort when she suddenly noticed Lulu and Steffi in the office. "Oh mercy," she said, coming up and giving Steffi a hug. "I am so, so sorry." Sara gave Lulu a confused look. "Isn't Steffi taking the day off?"

Chapter 6

Lulu was sure that everyone who came to Aunt Pat's that day wondered why Steffi didn't have the day off. But although Lulu had wondered if sleep would have been the better solution for Steffi, the waitressing seemed to work out just fine. It ended up being a big day at the restaurant, with lots of tourists stopping in for a bite, so Steffi probably didn't have enough time to think about anything but keeping orders and tabs straight and checking up on her tables.

Steffi was about to shift off for the day when Lulu noticed a handsome man with dark hair coming through the door of the restaurant. Her breath caught a little. It was the man from last night—the one that Tristan had been pushing away from her. Loren.

Sure enough, he didn't want to be seated when the hostess asked him how many were in his party. Instead, he said something short to the hostess as his narrowed eyes combed over the restaurant.

Lulu hurried over to the door. "Can I help you with something, sir?"

Up close she could tell how pinched the man's features were, as if he were completely exhausted. "Is Sara Taylor here? I wanted to speak with her."

Lulu nodded. "Yes, she's here. But she's got her hands full with customers right now—there's four or five of her tables that are trying to get their checks. Tell you what— why don't you have a seat in the office for a few minutes; then she can come join you." Lulu planned to be joining the two of them, too. After seeing what happened in Tristan's kitchen yesterday, Lulu had no intention of letting him have private time in the Aunt Pat's office with her daughter-in-law.

It took a good fifteen minutes for Sara to be able to pull away from the dining room. Lulu had half hoped that he'd have given up and headed back to patch things up with his wife. But part of her did want to hear what he had to say— particularly if it was about last night. She couldn't for the life of her imagine what kind of business he'd have with Sara.

Sara walked into the office, pulling her apron off and laying it on her lap as she plopped down on the sofa. "Sorry it took a while to wrap everything up, Mr. . . . I'm sorry; I don't think I know you." Sara's freckled face looked completely perplexed.

"I'm Loren Holman. I was at the party last night—the one at Tristan Pembroke's," he added, as if Sara would have been at more than one party that night. Lulu noticed that his voice caught a little on Tristan's name.

Sara absorbed this information, and then shook her head. "I'm sorry—have we met?"

The man shook his head and cleared his throat. "No, we didn't actually meet at the party. But I saw the portrait you did at the auction—the one of Tristan. I was wondering . . . well, I was wondering if I could make you an offer on it."

Sara frowned at him in confusion.

"I was friends with her," he said in a halting voice. "I'm interested in having the portrait to remember her by." He suddenly broke down with harsh sobs.

Sara looked at Lulu helplessly, and Lulu shook her head in amazement. "There, there, Mr. Holman," said Lulu, reaching out and squeezing the man's hand. "It was a shock, wasn't it? What a horrible night." And Lulu knew the full story of how rotten the night had been for him. Apparently, being rebuffed by Tristan and condemned by his wife wasn't enough to end his infatuation. Although she'd have thought that death would have been.

As if things weren't uncomfortable enough, the sobbing in the office caught Steffi's attention as she was walking past the door. She peered around the side of the door and saw the man. "Loren," she said in a startled voice.

He looked up and saw Steffi, and the expression on his face made her break down, too. In a couple of seconds, she was hugging him and crying right along with him. "Can you believe it?" she said, sobbing. "I'm so sorry, Loren!"

Lulu pushed back her chair and stood up. "I think what this room needs is some food," she declared. She vacillated a second between bringing in some comfort food like corn muffins and baked beans and something sweet. Then she remembered the double chocolate layer cake she'd baked yesterday. "It needs *chocolate*," she clarified. And Lulu hurried out the door for cake, plates, and a pitcher of milk.

"I'll help," said Sara quickly, following Lulu to the kitchen.

"Do you have a better idea what's going on in there than I do?" asked Sara as they pulled together a tray of food.

"I might know a little bit more than you do about what's going on," said Lulu. "I overheard something last night that I wasn't intended to. It's nothing too complicated—that fellow had this major crush on Tristan Pembroke, and they had an affair. Then, after she wasn't interested in him anymore, she dumped him. Except he wouldn't dump. And now he's *still* interested in her, and she's dead! He has a wife and everything, too," said Lulu, clucking.

"And Steffi?"

Lulu shrugged. "You got me, sweetie. I'm guessing she just feels sorry for him. Maybe we'll find out a little more once we pump them full of chocolate and cold milk."

As they walked back in the office, Lulu heard Steffi saying, "I know you loved Mother, Loren. She was such a hard person to love because she totally resisted any signs of love or affection at all. I feel bad for you—you deserved more. And she treated you just as bad as she treated everyone else . . . and me."

Steffi's voice cracked a little, and Lulu quickly said with cheerful determination, "Cake, anyone? I think a little bit of chocolate will make everyone feel better, at least for a little while. Sometimes it helps to chase our sorrows down with a little sugar." She laid down the tray on the small table.

"And y'all are going to love this cake," said Sara staunchly. "This isn't just an ordinary chocolate cake—it's *double* chocolate. And it's so moist you won't even believe it. I had some this morning right when I came into Aunt Pat's—started off my day with something sweet."

The cake seemed to be working, thought Lulu. She even saw a hint of a smile on Loren's face a couple of times as Lulu had told them all a story about something funny that had happened at the restaurant the week before.

After the cake was reduced to a few chocolaty crumbs,

Sara said slowly, "Getting back to the portrait, though. Loren, you were interested in buying the portrait of Tristan as sort of a memento." She spread her hands out helplessly. "That's fine with me. The only thing is that I have no idea where that portrait is right now."

Loren's eyebrows came together to give his face an even darker expression.

"The portrait was up at the auction, which is where you saw it, I guess. Then Tristan and I ended up having an argument over it. She wasn't a huge fan of the painting," said Sara with a flush. "After our argument, I left. I came back later to talk to the police, and I looked around and didn't see it. That doesn't mean it wasn't there, though," she said quickly. "It could have been in another room. And the police had the house pretty locked down, so I wasn't really free to look."

"Where *should* it have been?" asked Lulu. "I know the auction was outside."

"That big storm blew in, and people were grabbing paintings," said Steffi. "Everyone had to rush all the paintings inside—even the ones that had already been bought. So it probably would have been with the other ones in the living room."

"I didn't see it," said Sara again. "I'm sure that once the police have sorted through everything at the house that they'll want the guests to come collect the paintings—and have me pick up anything that didn't sell."

Loren's look of exhaustion returned. "Thanks. I guess I'll wait for you to hear from the police, then. If you don't mind giving me a call when you get the portrait back? I'd really like to talk to you about it." He handed Sara his business card. "Could you call me at my cell number?" He pulled out a pen and circled the number.

"Loren, I'll walk you out to the car," said Steffi. "I was on my way out anyway."

As the two of them walked out the restaurant's back door, talking, Lulu sank back onto the sofa. "Mercy!" she said, grabbing the newspaper from the table beside her and fanning herself energetically. "Thank goodness that's over. That's more crying than I've seen for a long while. Of course, it was good for Steffi to cry—the poor thing. But having that cheating husband crying on top of everything? Enough!"

"I get enough drama from the twins," agreed Sara.

"What I don't understand," said Lulu, "is what he's planning to do with that portrait. I mean, that's a good-sized canvas. Not huge, but good-sized. It's not like he's going to be able to hang it up in his living room or anything."

Sara knit her brows. "Why not? It wasn't the prettiest thing in the world, I have to admit, but I'd think he could put it up wherever he wanted to."

"I forgot! You don't even know the full story. He's *married*, believe it or not. Certainly doesn't *act* like he's married, but he is. His long-suffering wife followed him out to Tristan's party last night and caught him trying to canoodle with her in the kitchen. I think it's Cherry's neighbor who's been wanting to join the Women's League—and Tristan had been blackballing her and Cherry. Tristan wanted nothing to do with Loren, either—Steffi was right about that. I wonder if Tristan Pembroke really *was* allergic to love—and she felt that need to push back whenever someone started getting too close."

Sara said, "You know, I hope that portrait turns up. If Loren had Tristan's cold eyes following him around his office or wherever he's planning on sticking that portrait, it might be enough to cure him of his infatuation for life. I don't know if his wife will want him back, though."

The office door swung open and Lulu's granddaughter Ella Beth, Coco's twin, stuck her head in, ponytail swinging. "Granny Lulu? There's a man out in the dining room who's asking to talk to you."

Lulu frowned. "*Another* man needing to talk? This day is getting on the gabby side."

Sara said slowly, "Ella Beth, did the man say what his name was?"

"I can't remember the last name he said, but his first name was Gordon."

Sara closed her eyes briefly as Ella Beth went back out of the office, and Lulu said, "What? Do you know who this man is, Sara?"

"I don't *know* him, Lulu, but I think I know who he is. Ben was telling me about him yesterday, and with everything going on, I forgot to give you a heads-up." Sara took a deep breath. "Your son is setting you up on a blind date. *Real* blind, apparently, since he didn't even tell you that you were going to be meeting this guy."

"*What?*" Lulu's stomach knotted up with the horror of it all. She believed she felt sicker over this than she had over finding Tristan's body.

"Ben thought it was the best idea ever," said Sara with a sigh. "This fellow is supposed to be some big food blogger."

"A *what?*"

"He has some sort of online magazine that he updates every day with pictures and recipes and people's restaurants. A whole bunch of people read his posts, apparently. He just moved to Memphis, he's single, he's your age, and he likes food. I guess that was enough for Ben to think y'all would be smitten with each other."

Lulu got up quickly and grabbed her pocketbook.

"What are you doing?" asked Sara.

"Honey, I'm getting the heck out of Dodge, that's what! I don't want to be going on any blind dates. Ben probably didn't even notice if this guy is nice looking or likes women or anything. I'm going to hightail it out the back door while the getting's good. If you could cover for me and tell him that I left early for the day—that I had a headache coming on after all the craziness last night."

It was too late. There was a light tap on the door, and then it swung open again. Ben was there in the doorway, blocking it, thought Lulu furiously. He said in a hearty voice, "There's someone I would absolutely love for y'all to meet. Sara and Mother, this is Gordon McDonald. He's our special guest at Aunt Pat's today. Mother, remember how I told you about Gordon visiting and how excited you were?" Ben gave her an innocent look, which only succeeded in making Lulu more furious with him.

Still, years of using good company manners couldn't really be disregarded, no matter how hard she might try. "Mr. McDonald, it's nice to meet you," Lulu said stiffly, holding out her hand.

There was really nothing wrong with the man, thought Lulu. It was just the high-handed way that Ben had set this up that set her teeth on edge. Gordon looked like a perfectly nice man. He had a neatly trimmed white beard and white hair. He had a pleasant smile and a small tummy that spoke of years of enjoying good food. It was a shame that she was dead set not to like him.

Before she could say anything else, Ben added cheerfully, "I've got a wonderful red-velvet cake that Mother made this morning, Gordon. How about if I bring you out a slice?"

Gordon's eyes widened. "You sure do believe in southern hospitality here, Ben. Sure, I'd love a piece of cake. I've heard a lot about red-velvet cake, but would you believe that I've never had any? I've heard that it's traditionally a groom's cake here in the South."

Lulu couldn't repress a small shudder. Oh no—was he going to be one of those pushy kinds of suitors? And—would this day ever end?

Chapter

7

The day that had started a little too early for Lulu and had involved a too-long conversation and snack with Gordon finally came to a close. Lulu drove home with a huge feeling of relief. The red-velvet cake that Ben had baked and attributed to Lulu was delicious, of course. Through the years, Ben had become an amazing cook. Lulu was worried. If the way to a man's heart was through his stomach, and Gordon thought Lulu had been the one to make the cake, then he was probably well on his way to falling head over heels with her.

As she arrived home, Lulu blinked at seeing an older-model Volvo in her driveway, right next to Steffi's car. Visitors? Would this day ever be over? Lulu knew that she wasn't going to be able to resist the urge to pull out some food for her company, whoever they might be.

A tall brunette with high cheekbones and a familiar face stood up as Lulu walked through the kitchen door.

"Lulu? Hi. . . . It's Marlowe. Marlowe Walter, Tristan's sister. Steffi's in the bedroom, packing—I offered to let her stay at my place until everything settles down with her mom's house."

"So good to see you again, Marlowe! It's been years, hasn't it?" Lulu shook Marlowe's hand and then said sadly, "I'm sorry about your sister. It must have been such a shock when you found out."

Marlowe sat back down at the kitchen table. "It really was, actually. I'd gone out of town for a few days for work, and Steffi called my cell phone to give me the news. I can't imagine Tristan allowing herself to be murdered," said Marlowe with a short laugh. "I'd have bet on Tristan against any attacker."

Lulu felt a little ill at ease. It had been awkward listening to Steffi and Loren mourn Tristan earlier, but somehow hearing her referred to in such a harsh tone by her sister was just as bad. She said slowly, "Tristan was a difficult person sometimes, wasn't she?"

"You can say that again. Fortunately, though, my sister and I had worked around that difficulty. Through estrangement."

"Oh, I'm sorry. You and Tristan weren't on speaking terms?" Lulu couldn't imagine not talking to a member of her family. They were tripping up over each other on a daily basis.

"Not anymore. I finally got tired of being Tristan's emotional punching bag. She was determined to mess up my life as much as she possibly could. It was a lifelong habit of hers." Marlowe reached absently for her pocketbook beside her before dropping it back down on the floor again. "I quit smoking a month ago," she said ruefully, "but the habit of reaching for a cigarette is still there."

Lulu really couldn't help herself. She was *compelled* to

bring out some food, even though all she'd done all day long was put food in front of people. "You know what's good for that? A little snack. I have some of the most delicious spinach-cheese dip—I got the recipe from one of my good friends after she made some for this party we were at . . ." and before she knew it, Lulu had pulled out plates and napkins and some melba toast and had heated up the spinach dip and put the steaming food in front of them on her red and white checkered tablecloth.

Lulu asked, "Did you say that Steffi was packing her things?"

Marlowe spread some of the dip on her melba toast and took a big bite. "She is. I hope that's okay?" She paused in midbite, as if that were a scenario she hadn't thought of. "I really appreciate your taking Steffi in for me. She and I have always been close. . . . I hate that I was out of town when she needed a place to go. Thanks so much for being there for her."

"Oh, I was happy to help her out," said Lulu quickly, "and of course she should be with you now that you're home—especially until everything gets straightened out with Tristan's house."

Marlowe nodded. "I'm sure Tristan must have left all her things to Steffi. It's a matter of the will being settled, I guess."

"There was no one else that Tristan would have willed her property to?" asked Lulu.

Marlowe took a big sip of milk, then said, "No one else. Our parents have been long dead; she couldn't stand her ex-husband, and they've been divorced for fifteen years, anyway. And, as I mentioned, she and I weren't even on speaking terms."

Lulu had learned that sometimes she got more information from people if she didn't say anything—just nodded and waited. Sure enough, Marlowe kept talking.

"It always was that way," she said sadly. "It used to really bother me that she and I couldn't get along. Seemed like every time I turned on the TV there was a sappy greeting-card commercial featuring sisters as best friends. But she was always trying to get the better of me—even back in high school. She sabotaged my cheerleading tryout by mixing a laxative into my soda, and I spent the whole tryout in the restroom. She always flirted with my boyfriends and always managed to steal them away from me. You know her ex-husband? He was my boyfriend first."

Marlowe looked reflective. "The worst, though, was when Dad died. He'd willed the bottling company to both of us. It was a disaster from day one. Tristan kept pulling funds from the company for her living expenses—and we needed that capital for the business. A couple of weeks ago, she decided that we should sell the company. I hadn't spoken to her for ages, when she suddenly called me out of the blue and tried to browbeat me into agreeing with her. Sure, now that she's run the business totally into the ground she wants to sell it. Dad poured his lifeblood into that company—I wasn't going to let her unload it for a fraction of what it should have been worth. And what about all the employees who'd worked there practically their entire lives?" Marlowe's face was flushed.

"So what's going to happen to the business now?" asked Lulu slowly. "Will Tristan's share go to Steffi?"

Marlowe said, "Who knows? I'd imagine it would go to either Steffi or me. Thinking about it, I'm sure Tristan's share in the business would go to Steffi, since Tristan liked nothing better than to totally stymie me at every turn. She was furious that she had to consult me for things related to the company. But working with Steffi wouldn't be a problem at all."

Steffi walked into the room with a couple of bags on her shoulders. "A problem with what?" she asked, a frown creasing her face.

Marlowe waved a hand. "With the bottling company. I was talking about how difficult it was to deal with your mother with the business."

Steffi made a face. "I'm not going to have to deal with the business, am I? I don't know anything about it, and I don't want to."

"We have time to figure that out," said Marlowe soothingly, "but, of course, at some point soon we'll need to make some decisions to get the company on track again."

Steffi said anxiously, "I'd rather you handle all that, Marlowe. That sounds like something else to worry about, and I'm already overloaded."

"We'll see how things are listed in the will. If you end up with ownership, I can give you advice on what I think is the best course of action for the company," said Marlowe. "Every decision I've made for the bottling company is with your grandfather's dreams for the business in mind."

"Deal!" said Steffi, with obvious relief, as she shifted the bags on her shoulders. Marlowe stood up, "Here, Steffi, let me help you with that." As they started packing up the cars, Lulu cleaned up the kitchen and couldn't help thinking that Tristan Pembroke's death meant that life sure was a lot easier for Marlowe Walters. *Had* she still been out of town at the time of the murder? Could anyone vouch for her?

"Cherry," said Lulu the next morning, "I need your help."

"*Do* you?" asked Cherry. She yawned into the phone. "Right now? It's so early."

Lulu frowned and craned to see the kitchen clock. "Is my clock wrong? It looks like nine o'clock to me."

"You restaurant folks are such *early* birds," said Cherry sleepily.

"I'm sorry, Cherry! I thought you'd be up by now. Isn't today your Graceland day? I thought you'd be all set to spend your day with the King."

Cherry was one of a group of the restaurant's regulars called the Graces because they were Graceland docents. In fact, Graceland had actually had to start the docent program there because of Cherry and the other ladies—they were at the mansion so frequently and knew so much trivia that they were giving mini tours even without Graceland's blessing. They figured they couldn't beat them, so they might as well join them.

"Sure, it's my day at Graceland, but that's at one o'clock. So I usually don't even get up until ten. Just for future reference, you know." Cherry gave another yawn. "Don't worry; I'm going to get myself fixed up with some coffee. What can I help you with today?"

Lulu said, "I want to do some poking around. I thought you could be my partner in crime."

"Cool! So—this is industrial espionage or something?" Cherry sounded more alert. "Are we going to try to find the secret sauce recipe for Three Little Pigs Barbeque?"

Lulu clucked, "Oh no. The Aunt Pat's secret sauce is *much* better than the Three Little Pigs Barbeque sauce."

"Good point. So a different kind of snooping then? Let me guess—you want to take a crack at this new case. We're going to have to start calling you Detective Lulu soon."

"Pooh. No you won't, either. I'll admit to enjoying a little mental stimulation, but this time I have other motivation. I want to clear Sara from any kind of involvement."

"What? Nobody thinks Sara murdered Tristan Pembroke, Lulu. For heaven's sake. Just because Sara had this big blowup with Tristan over that portrait and just because Sara's feelings were hurt, and just because no one could find her for a couple of hours. . . . Oh." Cherry paused. "So what's today's mission?" Lulu could hear the sound of cereal hitting the bottom of a bowl.

"That day when I was shopping at Dee Dee's boutique? Tristan and Dee Dee had some kind of scurrilous business deal going on. I'm pretty sure it had something to do with the pageants—it sounded like Dee Dee was giving Tristan insider information on what some of her clients were wearing and what their talent was. I think Tristan was actually *paying* Dee Dee for those tips. Then Tristan, who coached these girls, would get her client to pick a talent that would blow away the other girl's. Dee Dee kept consulting this big binder of a notebook, and I want to take a look inside the notebook and see what I can find out."

"Sounds like a good plan," said Cherry. "How do I figure into it?" She was talking around a mouthful of food, but Lulu managed to make out the garbled parts.

"Distract Dee Dee for me. I'm going to take you in there and say you're wanting to change your look and I thought that Dee Dee would be just the boutique to handle your style makeover."

There was a spitting noise on the other end of the phone. "That'd be a makeover all right! No offense, Lulu, but Dee Dee's shop is all floral prints and froufrou, girly-looking stuff. There's not a flashy or cool-looking garment in that whole place."

"Which is *exactly* why you'll need so much help," explained Lulu.

"I won't have to buy a dress, will I?" Now Cherry really did sound pitiful.

"I think you could have a sudden change of heart in the dressing room," said Lulu judiciously. "You could tell her you need to sleep on it—that such enormous wardrobe makeovers need careful thinking out. I'll give you a signal when I've looked at the book and found out whatever I need to know. Let's see—what's a good signal for us?"

"Ooh! Ooh! I want to come up with the signal! That's the coolest part of the whole thing—acting like real spies," said Cherry. "Let's see. You could say . . ." There was a long pause on the phone while Cherry tried to wake up enough to come up with a signal. "Oh, I know! You could say 'Uh-oh! I think it looks like rain.'"

Lulu blinked. For someone as wildly uninhibited and colorful as Cherry, it was a strangely humdrum code for her to come up with. She'd expected something a lot more creative. "That's the signal?"

"Well," said Cherry with a sniff, "it's a good thing for *you* to say. If it were *me* giving the signal, then it would have to be something a lot more exotic."

Lulu thought a moment. "Actually, Cherry, it would be a good plan for *you* to have a signal, too. Just in case Dee Dee suddenly gets suspicious or makes any sudden moves toward the register. It would be a warning to me to stop snooping around."

"Good idea!" said Cherry. "My signal will be something to do with Elvis. Let's see. I'll ask Dee Dee if she knew that Elvis met Priscilla in Germany. Because who would guess that? It's such an amazing bit of Elvis trivia! Then maybe she'll be so interested to hear how they happened to meet in Germany that the signal won't even be necessary because she'd get distracted. Elvis will be like our guardian angel." Cherry's excitement was palpable.

Lulu's head started hurting.

Dee Dee smiled when Lulu walked through the dress shop door, but then looked none too pleased to see Cherry follow her. And Cherry had certainly not been thrilled to be there, either.

"Lulu," she'd said to Lulu sadly, before they'd walked into the shop, "you know now that I'd do anything for you. And I love that we're doing this spying. But it gives me the heebie-jeebies to even think about shopping for clothes at Dee Dee's Darling Dress Shoppe. It goes against my personal credo to ever shop at a place with 'shop' spelled with a p-p-e. It means that the store owner is trying to be *cute*. You know I fight *cuteness* with every atom of my being."

Fortunately, Lulu had been able to rally her troop and remind Cherry of the mission. That cheered Cherry up enough to be able to go inside. However, she did look around a couple of times to make sure no one saw her walk in.

Dee Dee quickly became all business as soon as she realized that Cherry apparently had every intention of redoing her entire look and wardrobe—apparently courtesy of Dee Dee's Darling Dress Shoppe.

Lulu said, "Yes, Dee Dee, when Cherry told me that she was ready to make a new start to her life and she wanted to display this change with a new wardrobe, I told her I knew just the place."

"This transformation was all of a sudden, wasn't it?" said Dee Dee, still a little grumbly about Cherry's reaction to the clothes days ago.

"Yes!" said Cherry quickly. "Yes, it was really sudden. Actually—I found God. Yes, I did. It was," Cherry's voice dropped down low as if the store was full of interested eavesdroppers, "Tristan's murder. She didn't even get a chance to redeem herself of all her sinfulness before suddenly meeting her Maker. I'm done with shopping at the Hipster Honey, with all their trashy clothing. With my newfound need to spend my spare time in the church, I really need a whole new wardrobe—of floral dresses. Just like Lulu." Lulu saw Cherry gulp as if the words were hard for her to say.

Dee Dee looked doubtfully at Cherry—garbed in a fluorescent-pink top, lime-green miniskirt, and wrist-to-elbow plastic bangles in a rainbow of colors. She gave a little shrug. "So, you're looking to tone down your look a little," she said slowly.

"Yes," said Cherry, and Lulu hid a smile at the bravery in Cherry's voice. It sounded like Cherry was steeling herself for a firing squad. "I want to tone it down a little."

Dee Dee said, "I'll get you fixed up, no worries. Yeah, Tristan's death came as a big shock. Quite a party, wasn't it? Uh . . . could you take that helmet off? That way I can get some ideas what goes well with your hair and eyes."

Lulu had a feeling that *nothing* really went well with Cherry's hair, which was a startling henna red. But Dee Dee seemed set to give it a try.

After a few minutes of pulling some dresses and tops and slacks off the racks, Dee Dee said, "Ready to try some things on, Cherry?"

Lulu quickly assessed the number of clothes that Dee Dee was holding. It probably wasn't enough for her to do excessive snooping. It might be enough to get her *started*, but . . .

"Could we find a few more things?" asked Cherry, who must have come to the same conclusion. "When I try on clothes, I want to try *everything* on. I don't want to put my street clothes back on, then find *more* clothes, then have to change *again*." She made a face as if the whole idea of changing clothes was distasteful to her.

They found a few more outfits, and then Dee Dee put everything in a changing room. "All right, Cherry. Let me know if you need another size or another color of something." She walked toward the cash register as if she were planning on waiting there. Lulu figured she was probably going to try to sell Lulu on a couple of things. Dee Dee knew that Lulu was an easy target for a sale—ordinarily.

Cherry said quickly, "Oh, that's not going to work, Dee Dee. You see, I'm used to a little more help."

"Help?" Dee Dee scowled before she managed to pull her face into a more ambivalent expression.

"Yes. Over at the Hipster Honey, they *assist* with the trying-on process. It's a collaborative event—sort of like you're being styled by a stylist. I've never picked out my own clothes before." Cherry blinked innocently at Dee Dee.

"I've never dreamed of trying to be like the Hipster Honey!" said Dee Dee in a voice that said she was appalled at the very thought of it. "But I guess, if that's what you're used to, I can help you out." This last was very grudging.

"I need some direction," said Cherry. "I need to know what works and what doesn't."

"Couldn't you just step out of the changing room and get Lulu's opinion, since you're looking to have the same kind of look?"

Lulu jumped in. "Oh no. I like it to be a *surprise*. I'd rather see the final picks at the very end."

Dee Dee shrugged. "Have it your way." And she and Cherry disappeared into the changing room—which, Lulu had to admit, must have been a little bit of a squeeze. Dee Dee wasn't the smallest person in the world.

Lulu hurried over to the counter and looked on the shelf that was under the cash register. Sure enough, there was the big black binder she'd remembered seeing the day that Tristan was in the shop. She opened it up, and the first thing she saw was a sort of spreadsheet with girls' names down one column and what looked like a list of dresses, "teal princess dress with low-cut bodice," and talent, "singing 'Nessun Dorma'!" or "jazz-dance routine." There were also little editorial notes in the margins, like "redhead and uses too much self-tanning lotion! Ugh!"

Lulu froze as she heard Dee Dee's voice say, "Let me grab that in a bigger size for you, Cherry."

Chapter 8

But then Lulu heard Cherry's voice saying stridently, "No! No, I want the dress tight. Yes, this is *exactly* the look I'm going for."

"For church?" Dee Dee sounded doubtful. "I know you're used to wearing clothes snug, but . . ."

"It's perfect. Ha! Perfect! So let's try on the next one, okay? Can you help me unbutton the back?"

With a relieved sigh, Lulu relaxed and flipped through the binder again. She paused on one page that looked different from the spreadsheets of the beauty-pageant contestants. Lulu cocked her ear for a minute to make sure things sounded settled in the changing room. She heard Cherry say, "I don't know, Dee Dee. What do *you* think looks better? The light-blue floral or the peach floral? Tell you what, let me try on the peach one again; then let's decide . . ."

Lulu held the page far out from her and cursed herself for forgetting her reading glasses. And for Dee Dee's horrible handwriting, which certainly didn't help. She finally deciphered the words "Tristan—affair." And there appeared to be notes, as if Dee Dee were keeping track of dates and times of trysts: "saw in car—Wednesday, 2:00." And an even more cryptic one: "by the hedge—not trimming it." There was also a picture—not a very good one—that seemed to be Tristan embracing some man. She couldn't really see the man's face—

Cherry suddenly loudly said, "Dee Dee, did you know that Elvis and Priscilla actually met each other in *Germany*? Ha ha! That's nutty, isn't it? Priscilla was only fourteen at the time . . ."

"Cherry, let me *go*. I need to get a tissue." Dee Dee's voice was cranky, and she pushed through the curtain on the dressing-room door. "For heaven's sake!"

Lulu didn't have time to shut the book and put it back where it belonged—she barely had time to jump away from the counter and over to the dress rack. She thanked her lucky stars when the shop's bell rang, creating another distraction. Dee Dee said, "Hi there! How are you all today? Be right back," before she went into the back of the shop, presumably for the tissue.

Lulu turned to look and saw Steffi and Marlowe in the shop. "Hi, y'all," said Lulu. "Who's doing the shopping today? Marlowe or Steffi?"

Marlowe said, "Hi, Lulu. I'm taking Steffi to do a little shopping. I thought she might want some new clothes."

"And shopping is a great way to cheer up," said Steffi, pushing her lank hair out of her face.

Poor thing needed some new clothes, thought Lulu. It was like Tristan had thrown up her hands and given up on the child. Steffi could look a lot cuter than she did. She wasn't a pretty girl, but she could at least look pulled together. And not wear all those baggy clothes she was so crazy about. If she *did* have a figure underneath all those clothes, you sure couldn't tell it to look at her.

Marlowe was already looking through the separates when Cherry called out from the depths of the dressing room, "Lulu? How's the weather looking out there?"

"Oh, it looks like rain I think."

Steffi looked at her with a funny expression on her face. "No, it's a beautiful day, Lulu. Marlowe and I were just outside. There's not a cloud in the sky."

"Isn't there? Silly me!" Lulu gave a forced laugh. She heard the emphatic nose blowing diminishing and decided it was a good time to get far away from the notebook. Lulu summoned a sudden great deal of interest in the accessories at the far end of the store and hurried over to look at them more closely.

Marlowe was saying absently, "Such a wide selection here. There are pageant-type things, then everyday-type clothes, too."

Lulu stole a look over her shoulder and saw Dee Dee's stormy expression as she quickly walked over to the counter and snapped the binder shut with a glare at Steffi and Marlowe. Lulu seemed to have completely escaped suspicion. Lulu supposed there were some advantages to being a mild-mannered older lady sometimes.

Dee Dee said abruptly, "Wide selection? Yes. Dee Dee's Darling Dress Shoppe has been a destination boutique for pageant contestants for twenty years, so I have a whole line completely devoted to that—gowns, casual wear, swimsuits, that kind of thing. But then I also have everyday clothes and dresses for my regular customers who are just looking for something pretty to wear."

"Mother loved this place," said Steffi, with a hoarse

laugh, and Marlowe looked at her quickly, frowning. Lulu could tell she was probably wondering if she should have chosen another store to shop in.

Cherry finally pushed through the dressing-room curtain wearing her startlingly bright street clothes and smoothing her hair down before putting her helmet back on. "Oh, hi, Steffi. Hi, Marlowe. Hope your shopping goes well."

Dee Dee tapped across the floor to Cherry. She looked, thought Lulu, just a bit confrontational. "Which dresses did you decide on?" she asked smoothly.

Cherry looked confused, as if she'd forgotten she was supposed to be picking out a new wardrobe. "Oh. Oh, I think I'll sleep on it. It's a big decision, you know."

"It's not! It's just dresses! You said you wanted to change your whole look."

"I do. But these things take *time*, Dee Dee. And perhaps some prayer," added Cherry piously. "But thanks for all your help."

Lulu thought that Dee Dee seemed to be gritting her teeth.


"Sara was telling me," said Lulu, in what she hoped was an appropriately horrified manner, "that *Tristan* had actually sabotaged Pansy's efforts for Miss Memphis."

It was lunch hour, and Colleen had eaten every last lip-smacking bit of her barbeque plate. She was reapplying some fire-engine-red lipstick when Lulu sat down across the table from her.

Colleen patted her lips with one of the paper towels that were on every table. "Isn't that the most wretched thing

you've ever heard about in all your born days? I declare
that Tristan Pembroke was one of the wickedest people I
know. The very wickedest!"

"Sara said something about the story actually making
the national news. You're not going to believe this," said
Lulu, "but I somehow completely missed that whole brouhaha when it happened."

Colleen's eyes scanned over Lulu's tidy appearance in
her floral dress and the apron on top. "I'd believe it, honey.
Following pageants isn't everybody's cup of tea."

Lulu mustered up a clueless expression as Colleen
leaned in to tell her story.

"So Pansy has a real crack at Miss Memphis. Her coach
was telling us that Pansy had some of the best talent he'd
ever seen—*real* talent, you know. And she's blessed with
flawless skin, and all the other girls in the pageant got
blemishes. So she looked to be the number-one pick for the
pageant. And you know that Miss Memphis leads right into
Miss Tennessee and then Miss America. And Pansy had a
shot at those titles, too."

Lulu would believe it when she saw it. She had to admit,
though, that Pansy *was* a pretty girl. But she didn't seem
exceptionally pretty enough to win a big title.

"It's the night of the pageant, and we're all backstage
with curling irons, butt glue, fake eyelashes, and ten
pounds' worth of makeup. I'm out in the audience to watch
the show. First of all was her talent competition—the dance
number. Pansy looked like she was struggling with the
dance. Honestly, I was wondering if she was sick or something. She looked like she had two left feet! Then I noticed
her shoes. They weren't hers!" Colleen sat back in the
booth and bobbed her head emphatically.

Lulu frowned. "She'd lost her shoes?"

"Someone had *stolen* her dance shoes. She had to borrow some other girl's shoes, and they were almost two sizes too small!"

Lulu wondered if maybe in all the backstage chaos Pansy hadn't just misplaced her shoes. "Isn't that a shame? What a pity she lost because of something like that."

"Well, and that's not the half of it! I haven't even gotten to the part about her dress yet."

Lulu said, "Somebody did something to mess up her dress, too?" That *would* be a little too much of a coincidence.

"Yes ma'am! Somebody had thrown loose powder at it. *And* drawn on the back with lipstick. It was the most shocking, cruelest thing I'd ever seen in my life. Pansy had *lived* for that pageant for weeks! Ate, drank, and slept it. All that work, down the drain."

Lulu shook her head at the sheer maliciousness of it all.

"So, when it was time for Pansy to do her evening-wear competition, her beautiful dress—the one we'd spent a thousand dollars on—was totally vandalized. I practically threw up when I found out. Looked like it had graffiti all over it."

"Did she go out in the dress?"

Colleen nodded. "She surely did. What else could she do? It wasn't like she could borrow one. But I've never been so proud of Pansy. She walked out on that stage with her head held high and a pageant smile on her lips the whole time! I was so proud." Colleen carefully wiped away a tear from the corner of one of her heavily lined eyes.

"Could the audience tell?"

"Oh mercy! Yes! They could tell. You should have heard the horrified gasp that rose up out of the crowd like a cry of pain. As soon as they laid eyes on that dress, they knew what had happened. And their hearts just hurt for her. But I think the judges were so impressed by her composure that she still ended up with first runner-up. Not that that was going to land her in the Miss Tennessee pageant and then the Miss America pageant or get her a big scholarship or anything." Colleen fumed for a minute, eyes spitting bullets at the very thought of the injustice.

Lulu prodded, "But then it made the national news somehow? I'm not sure how I could miss a story like that!" She gave a self-deprecating laugh, but she knew *exactly* how she could miss a story like that—because she wasn't the least bit interested.

Colleen tapped a red-enameled nail against the table. "That very day it got picked up on the news wire. It was such a tragic story, you see. One of those things that makes people wonder what the world's coming to . . . when a pretty and talented girl like Pansy loses a big pageant because of somebody being hateful. Yes, Pansy was on all the morning talk shows that next morning."

"And you," said Lulu in a low voice, "knew who that hateful somebody was."

Colleen didn't seem at all concerned about how loud she was talking, though. "For heaven's sake—she's dead! I'm not going to worry who hears me say it: Tristan Pembroke ruined Pansy's chances for the Miss America pageant. She was the coach for the winning girl, and she couldn't *stand* the fact that Pansy was favored to win. Tristan was backstage, and her contestant was right next to where Pansy was getting ready. Pansy and I had to go back to the car and get some things out, and I'm sure that's when the shoes were swiped and the dress was destroyed." Colleen looked broodingly out the window. "I'm not a bit sorry Tristan is dead. What an ugly person she was."

Lulu was hoping to get a little background on the rest of the family. Although she'd been acquainted with them for a while, she never really got to know them. "I've always felt so bad for Steffi," she said.

Colleen interrupted her. "*Oh*, yes. Poor lamb. See, Tristan and I were both on the pageant circuit when we were teenagers. Tristan was practically always the winner, every time." Colleen managed to note this without any amount of rancor, thought Lulu. It must just have been the way things were. "Tristan, when she was pregnant, kept talking about how she was going to enter the baby in every pageant imaginable. . . . She even planned on putting Steffi in the baby pageants. She had that baby's room dolled up like a princess was going to be living in there." Colleen broke off with a shrug.

"But when Steffi was born," said Lulu, "she wasn't quite the baby Tristan expected?"

"Not at all," said Colleen. "And Tristan was as mad as the blazes to find out that she wasn't pageant material. I think she blamed the poor baby for it and never forgave her for not being as pretty as Tristan planned for her to be. So, the next thing I know, Tristan is still keeping her involvement with pageant life but as a coach this time. That's how Pansy and Steffi ended up being friends—because Tristan used to coach Pansy, and the girls would play together backstage before the pageant would start up. They've always been as close as sisters, even though Steffi is a couple of years older than Pansy. Pansy *was* pageant material, but it never came between them." Colleen couldn't quite keep the smugness out of her voice.

Lulu was about to ask a couple more questions about Steffi and Pansy's connection with each other when Colleen suddenly noticed her watch. "I'm sorry to cut this short, Lulu, but I've got somewhere to be! Anyway, that's the basic story, so now you know."

Lulu was mulling over her conversation with Colleen as she walked back to the Aunt Pat's office to have a cup of coffee and think things through. She couldn't think for the life of her how a mama could reject her baby for her looks—and it seemed to Lulu that all Steffi had ever wanted was a show of love from Tristan. It was all such a shame.

Ella Beth stuck her head in the office. "Granny Lulu," she said, her freckled face serious, "the police are talking to Mama in the kitchen, and she shooed me out. Can you check and make sure she's okay?"

"Pink's talking to her?" asked Lulu, her heart jumping into her throat a little.

"No, it's not Pink—it's some other policeman." Ella Beth made a face. "He's not very nice looking, either. He looks kind of mean."

Coco, who had also apparently been shooed out, looked a little less concerned. She yawned and said, "Ella Beth, when will you learn that the police are just trying to figure out where everybody was and what they saw? It's not like they're dragging Mama out to jail or anything." Then she frowned for a minute and said, "They're not, are they, Granny Lulu?"

"Absolutely not!" said Lulu briskly. "They're just following certain procedures to help them investigate." She hoped she sounded more certain than she felt as she hurried to the kitchen.

Sure enough, Detective Freeman had settled his long, wiry frame on one of Lulu's bar stools and was leaning up against a counter, writing in a notebook. The fellow looked like he needed a good meal, but Lulu sure wasn't the one who planned on giving it to him. She didn't want him hanging out at Aunt Pat's any more than he already was.

Sara's freckled face was flushed, her hair was standing up wildly on her head as if she'd run a hand through it several times, and she looked flustered. She gave Lulu a small smile when she entered the kitchen.

"Detective Freeman, you remember my mother-in-law, Lulu Taylor, don't you?"

The detective nodded slightly at the introduction, then continued with his questions. "As I was saying, Mrs. Taylor, you didn't point out that you and Ms. Pembroke had a connection besides your commissioned painting of her."

Sara knit her brows. "And I was saying to *you*, Detective Freeman, I have no idea what you're talking about. Ms. Pembroke wasn't a regular at the restaurant, and I never spent any time in conversation with her at all."

Freeman pounced. "Except, perhaps, at the beauty pageants your daughter Coco competed in? And that Tristan Pembroke judged? Could it possibly be that Ms. Pembroke's votes prevented your daughter from advancing in pageant competitions? I know how hostile these stage mothers can get—of course, it would be understandable that you'd want your daughter to win," he said in a soothing voice that seemed designed to lure Sara into confiding in him.

"Now just hold on a minute," said Sara hotly. "I am *not* a stage mama. Half the time I'm not even *at* these pageants. My friend Colleen takes her, since I'm working at the restaurant. It's just an after-school activity that Coco enjoys—that *Coco* enjoys."

"But you didn't think to tell me that Ms. Pembroke was a frequent judge on the circuit that Coco was on? I'm sure that your daughter doesn't always win these pageants. It probably upsets her a lot. You didn't think to mention to the police the other night that you could be considered disgruntled?"

Lulu snorted. "Oh please, Detective. Sara doesn't care squat about pageants, which is exactly why it didn't occur to her to say anything about them. Sara, disgruntled?"

Unfortunately, Sara at that very minute, was the living embodiment of *disgruntled*. Detective Freeman smirked as if his point had been proven.

"Well, I'll be on my way, then, Mrs. Taylor. And please, if you think up any other way that you and Tristan Pembroke were associated with each other, do me a favor and let me know."

As he left, Lulu got the sinking sensation that Sara was the detective's favorite suspect.

Chapter 9

After Detective Freeman left, Lulu retreated to the restaurant's front porch. Besides the kitchen, the porch was her favorite place to go at Aunt Pat's. The Labs, B. B. and Elvis, snored gently; the sound of the ceiling fans was a relaxing drone; and Lulu could half doze in the rocking chair with the sounds of Beale Street as background noise.

In fact, the stress of Detective Freeman's interview with Sara must have tired her out more than she'd thought because she nodded off for a little while right there on the porch. She only woke when the sound of the screen door closing made her give a little jump.

"Oh, sorry, Lulu," said Buddy. "I didn't mean to scare you like that."

Lulu straightened up in the rocker a little. "It's no problem, Buddy. I can't believe I dropped off to sleep like that. Want to sit down and chat for a few minutes? I think a little hanging out with friends would be good for me today."

"Sure thing, Lulu. Morty and Big Ben are supposed to be meeting me to play a little penny poker and eat lunch, but I'm early."

"Let's go ahead and get you set up in a booth, then, before it starts getting busy. Y'all need to be sure to order the corn pudding today. It's Aunt Pat's old recipe and one of my favorites. That bit of sugar in it makes all the difference."

"Now how am I supposed to wait for the fellas to come before I eat?" complained Buddy with good humor. "I've got corn pudding on the brain now." He gave a sigh as if the weight of the world was on his shoulders.

"How's everything going?" asked Lulu.

"Hard times, hard times," said Buddy, shaking his head. "But doesn't life usually go that way? You think everything is the cat's pajamas, and next thing you know, you're singing the blues again. With feeling."

"Mercy! I must have missed something. Did something happen with you and Leticia?"

Leticia Swinger was Buddy's lady friend, and they'd been getting along well, Lulu thought. She sang in the church choir, and he sang for the band. They certainly had plenty in common. And Buddy was a handsome and spry octogenarian.

"No, no, everything is fine as far as my love life goes. You should ignore my ranting and raving, Lulu. I'm a little bitter over the Back Porch Blues Band's last gig."

"That's Tristan's party, right? Oh goodness. Y'all probably didn't get paid for playing that benefit, did you?"

"Nope. Not a red penny. And after all that trouble we went through! That woman wasn't letting us take a break for *nuthin'*. And we're old men, Lulu! In our eighties. If nothing else, we should've had restroom breaks." His lined face was thunderous.

"Y'all didn't get any money when you booked the event?" asked Lulu. "I was thinking you'd said you'd gotten something in advance."

Buddy said, "We did get a little money down. Ten percent, maybe?"

"Just ten percent?"

Buddy nodded sadly. "Yes, Tristan said she'd had bad luck in the past with bands skipping out on her. I guess, to be fair, she couldn't have known she was going to get herself killed during the party. And we wouldn't dream of asking Steffi to pay the bill," he finished glumly. "We'll write it off as a rehearsal. A really *long* and tiring rehearsal that I'm still trying to recover from."

Lulu said, "Well, I guess we know why she ended up as a murder victim. I'm starting to believe that there wasn't a single person at that party who liked Tristan Pembroke."

"Thinking back, though, it's probably a good thing she ran the band into the ground," said Buddy solemnly. "We had the perfect alibi. Otherwise we'd all be suspects, too! Because we were *that* irked at the lady."

Big Ben and Morty walked up to the booth. "What're y'all doing? Gossiping?" bellowed Big Ben. Lulu saw his hearing aid but had a feeling he didn't have it turned up. It was time for the gossiping to stop, if everyone in Aunt Pat's was going to hear Big Ben's booming voice repeating it.

"Let me guess—the murder," said Morty. "Definitely the topic du jour." He turned to Lulu. "Are you planning on doing a little poking around again? You've gotten to be the amateur detective extraordinaire!"

Lulu said, "Actually, I think I probably will." She lowered her voice and saw Big Ben finally reach to turn his hearing aid up. "Sara is one of the suspects, you know."

"Insanity!" said Big Ben in a lower voice, but one that still carried. "Sara wouldn't hurt a fly. Might *yell* at the fly, or cuss the fly out, but she wouldn't hurt it."

Lulu sighed. "Yelling is what got her on the suspect list. Tristan got all fired up at Sara for bringing that portrait out and putting it up on the auction block without her permission. And Sara wasn't going to sit back and take it. So they were both yelling at each other in view of several witnesses. Then Sara took off in the car to cool down . . . and had a flat tire. It all looked pretty suspicious to the police. And Sara didn't think to mention her pageant connection to Tristan because the pageants just aren't that important to her. I know Sara didn't have a thing in the world to do with it, but the police don't. I'm going to try to find out enough to put the cops on a different trail."

A waitress brought a big pitcher of sweet tea and took everyone's orders. Morty took a big sip of tea and mulled things over for a minute. "Besides the Back Porch Blues Band, who else at the party couldn't stand Tristan?"

Buddy gave a deep chuckle. "I'm sure there are plenty of people to choose from." He thought for a moment. "Lulu, do the police think Steffi's a suspect?"

"Probably, just because of her history with her mother. After all, Tristan was a horrible mother to Steffi her whole life and recently kicked her out of the house after another big argument they had. Steffi told me that her mother said she was going to write Steffi out of her will. The police are bound to think that money would be a big motive—that Steffi wanted to kill her mother before she had the chance to change her will."

Morty said softly, "She's not working today?" When

Lulu shook her head, he continued. "It sure sounds like a powerful motive to me. Isn't money usually the main reason behind most murders?"

"That's what I've heard. But I told the police that Steffi was with me during the murder. And she was—I think she was really starting to regret coming to the party at all. She and her mama had this big argument, and Steffi came out from it totally miserable. She spent the rest of the evening with me—well, up until the point that the police came. I guess she showed up just to make her mother feel uncomfortable, but really, *she* was the only one who felt that way."

"How about Tristan's sister?" mused Morty. "Seems like Steffi was talking at the restaurant last week about how great her aunt is—and how her mom and her aunt don't get along at all."

The food arrived at the table, and Lulu waited for a minute for everyone to get settled. "I've heard the same thing about Tristan and Marlowe. Sounds like Tristan has always found ways to mess with her sister and generally make her as miserable as possible—even when they were kids, they were at each others' throats. And then Marlowe was saying that Tristan practically ran their father's company into the ground—she seemed to really take it personally. Apparently, Tristan was pulling money out of the business for her own personal use."

Big Ben nodded, "I vote on Tristan's sister, then. As revenge. It's not as *powerful* a motive as money, but still a biggie."

"The only problem is that Marlowe was out of town on business that night. So she couldn't be a suspect."

Big Ben's face fell. "Too bad. It was the perfect solution, too. Actually, it's so perfect, Lulu, that I think you need to double-check Marlowe's alibi. Maybe she wasn't really where she said she was."

"You know who else didn't like Tristan?" asked Morty, wagging a finger in the air as he remembered. "Oh—what's her name? Eats in here a lot. Her daughter does the pageant thing, and it's all she knows how to talk about."

"Colleen Bannister," said Lulu.

"That's the one!" said Morty, beaming. "What about her? And I hope she's a possibility because you keep eliminating our best non-Sara suspects from the running."

Lulu shook her head sadly. "I'm afraid she's *not* a possibility. She wasn't even at the party. Which is no surprise, considering there was no love lost between Colleen and Tristan. Tristan wouldn't have invited that woman to her party if her life depended on it."

The three men frowned at each other. Then Buddy said, "Colleen—we're talking about the same person, right? Big hair? Lots of makeup? Kind of country sounding? Pretty daughter?"

"The very one," said Lulu.

Morty smiled victoriously. "Well, then we *do* have a possibility, Lulu. Because Colleen was at that party—and so was her girl. We saw them outside while we were playing. And they were having the biggest argument you ever saw. The girl ended up stomping off toward the house and the mama paced and waited for her to come back. Steam was practically coming out of her ears! But I could tell she didn't want to go into that party. She just waited there at the edge of the yard."

The next day, Lulu decided she had some fences to mend over at Dee Dee's Darling Dress Shoppe. She was fully aware that she was responsible for bringing Cherry into the shop, monopolizing Dee Dee's time, and then waltzing out without spending a dime.

Since Dee Dee's shop was really, exclusively, the only place where Lulu shopped for clothing, she decided it would be wise to make up. Besides, she had a couple of things she wanted to know about Tristan, and Dee Dee seemed to know everything about everybody.

Dee Dee looked up when the bell rang as Lulu walked in the store. She frowned but then quickly mustered a more pleasant expression. Lulu guessed that's because she was by herself, with no redheaded, motorcycle-riding, time-sucking friends along with her.

"You doing all right, Lulu?" asked Dee Dee in a loud voice.

It did grate on Lulu's nerves that Dee Dee was determined to believe that she was hard of hearing. As if she was that much older than Dee Dee! Why, there probably were only nine years between them. Lulu managed to swallow her irritation, though. "Doing fine, Dee Dee, doing fine. And I did want to tell you I was so terribly sorry about the other day. Honestly, I don't know what got into Cherry. She told me she wanted a whole new wardrobe to go along with her new soul. I guess change is harder than we think."

"I guess so," said Dee Dee in a doubtful voice. "Well, what can I do for you today, Lulu? You're shopping for yourself?"

"Yes I am. I think I'm probably good with dresses, but I was thinking I could use a pair of slacks—really casual ones. Black, maybe?"

Dee Dee and Lulu started going through the racks. "You know, Dee Dee, I've been shopping here for years, but somehow I didn't know exactly how connected you were with the pageant world! It sounds like you're the go-to shop for pageant clothes."

Dee Dee looked pleased. "I've worked hard on it, yes. And the business has really built up over the years. It wasn't an overnight success, but over time, things have definitely come together. The pageants have been really good for the boutique. I couldn't have stayed afloat all these years by selling separates and dresses to the Lulu Taylors of the world."

Lulu wasn't sure if she should be insulted or not but decided to give it a pass. "I guess I'm just unaware of the pageant world altogether. Sara has been filling me in, since she's been involved in it for a while because of Coco. She and I were talking about poor Tristan's *tragic* death, and Sara mentioned to me that Tristan was very involved in pageants. I guess you must have seen a lot of Tristan? She sent some customers your way?" Lulu asked.

"She did," said Dee Dee, pushing some clothes down the rack a little roughly. "She was a pageant coach—the girls' mothers hired her to help them figure out what to wear, and what their talent should be, and how to walk— that kind of thing. She was good to recommend that her girls visit me for dress fittings—that's really where the shop's pageant side started to take off."

Lulu looked sympathetically at Dee Dee. "It must have been hard for you, Tristan's death. Such a terrible shock!"

Dee Dee gave her hoarse, cigarette-smoking laugh. "It wasn't a shock at all, Lulu. Tristan did help me out, but she rubbed a whole lot of people the wrong way. Look at the argument we overheard at the party between Steffi and Tristan! And that was only one example of many."

"I did hear," Lulu said, fingering a pair of black slacks, "that Colleen blamed Tristan that her daughter lost the Miss Memphis crown."

Dee Dee rolled her eyes. "In Colleen's head, Pansy was

already doing the Miss America walk and wave. That's one reason Colleen's head is all messed up."

"Pansy didn't have that much of a shot at it, then?"

"Didn't have a shot in . . . uh. She didn't have a shot," said Dee Dee, censoring herself with effort. She apparently thought Lulu had delicate ears as well as deaf ones. "Don't get me wrong—she's a pretty girl. And she wore *my* dresses, which means she made the most of her looks for the pageants. But her talent is just so-so at best. She can sing . . . sort of. She can play a fiddle pretty well. And she does some great parlor-game kind of stuff. But she doesn't have the kind of talent or interview capabilities that would put a Miss America crown on her head—or even a Miss Memphis one."

Lulu frowned. "But Colleen sounded like she was certain Tristan had damaged her dress. And stolen her shoes? I know it made the news really big, too."

"The national media loves *any* story about beauty-pageant girls being ugly to each other. They eat those backstage-antic stories up with a spoon. People love hearing about that kind of stuff. So it *did* get picked up on the newswire but not because there was a single bit of truth to the story at all. And I can't imagine Tristan Pembroke doing anything to sabotage Pansy. The girl just wasn't that much of a threat to her client. I can tell you one thing, though—the other girls in the pageants never like Pansy. I've heard them talking about her right here in the store, and they really talked when she made the national news like that. Pansy always wants to be the one in the spotlight, and that's not the way to make friends. Besides, those kinds of things happen at beauty pageants all the time—the girls get upset with each other. Maybe Pansy got someone upset and she was getting back at her."

"It sounds like one of the other girls could just as easily have damaged Pansy's dress to get back at her for being such a pill," said Lulu thoughtfully. "Colleen sounded so *sure*, though."

Dee Dee walked briskly over to a dressing room and hung a few pairs of slacks on the hook in one. "That's because," she said in her raspy voice as Lulu entered the dressing room, "Colleen *believes* her theory. And there's no denying the bad blood between Tristan and Colleen—it dates back to their own pageant days as teens. But I know Tristan didn't think Pansy was going to win the Miss Memphis pageant. She wouldn't have worried a second over it. Maybe she could have destroyed Pansy's chances in order to get back at Colleen. *Maybe*. But that's the only reason I can see her doing it."

"I think, especially after the whole spy mission and nearly having to buy a prissy dress, that I deserve a sidekick spot. At least just for *this* case, anyway." Cherry and Lulu were on the front porch of Aunt Pat's, and Cherry was rocking her chair back and forth with concentrated determination. "The next time a dead body turns up, you can reevaluate everything."

"There won't *be* any more dead bodies turning up," said Lulu, in a voice with more conviction than she actually felt. "We're already swimming in murder. But I do appreciate the sidekick offer, Cherry. As long as you're not a suspect," she added teasingly.

Cherry snorted. "I'll have you know that I've been eliminated from the pool of suspects," she said. "I may have had the motive, but I didn't have the opportunity."

"What was your motive again?" asked Lulu, squinting as if she was trying to see the memory from a far-off distance.

"The way Tristan blackballed me from joining the Memphis Women's League," said Cherry darkly. "The witch. But now I've decided I don't want to be in it after all. Evelyn told me there was no barrier to my joining, and then she handed me the schedule of events and told me that they'd vote me in at the next meeting. But Lulu, that calendar was jammed full of fund-raising bake sales—and I don't bake or want to start now."

"Couldn't you pick up something from the bakery to put out?" asked Lulu.

"Sneaky Lulu!" Cherry laughed. "I wouldn't have expected a professional cook to say something like that. No, I'm not interested in doing that, either. It's not just the bake sale—there are also dances. A spring dance and a fall one. And you'd have to put a gun to Johnny's head to get him to even *go* to a dance. Even if you got him there, he'd be a total wallflower. He'd probably be hanging out in the parking lot and drinking."

Lulu couldn't imagine that the sight of Cherry's husband with a bottle of beer in his hand would go over very well with the Women's League. "So you're not so interested in joining anymore. Although you *were* at the time, so I guess we can't eliminate your motive."

"No, to be perfectly honest, we can't. We can eliminate my opportunity, though. Because I didn't have a chance to even slip off to the restroom at that party. I was with people every single second, and it was all accounted for. There were tons of snobs there, but also a few people that I knew. We were jabbering about how bad the food was and talking about art—I didn't have a minute to myself the whole time. I even found another Elvis aficionado at the party, and we talked forever about Elvis's big comeback concert. The police triple-checked my alibi with the folks I talked with.

So, my being a social butterfly really paid off—I think they'd have tried to pin it on me."

Lulu blinked with surprise. "How did the police know about your motive, Cherry?"

"That Dee Dee," said Cherry, knitting her brows. "Remember the day that Tristan was coming out of the dress shop while I was going in? I was complaining how mad I was with Tristan? Well Dee Dee, of course, had to spill all to the police. She makes me so mad! Now I'm pleased as punch that I wasted her time the other day with all that shopping for clothes I didn't want." Cherry looked mad enough to spit.

"Okay, Cherry, you've convinced me that you're not a cold-blooded killer. And there *is* something I think you can do for me."

Chapter 10

Cherry's face brightened. "More skulduggery? I just love being devious. I almost died laughing when we were tricking Dee Dee at her Dah-ling Dress Shoppe. She looked so bent out of shape and frowsy, trying to get me in and out of all those dresses and then lie about how cute I looked. And all the time you were reading her secret notebook!" She paused a second. "Hey! Wait a minute—you never told me what you saw in that notebook! I got so carried away by the mission and our narrow escape and my almost having to buy a wardrobe of sweet little dresses that I never asked you what you found out."

"It was mostly her notes about what dresses each girl was wearing and their talent. But it also looked like she'd made some notes about gossip that the girls had mentioned. I think she was feeding all that information to Tristan as sort of insider knowledge that Tristan paid her for."

Cherry made a face. "It couldn't be *that* important. Who cares what each girl was wearing?"

"Tristan might even have paid Dee Dee to make sure a few of the girls in a particular pageant were wearing the same color or the same style dress so that her contestant really stood out. Something like that. It could have been a *very* big deal, as far as pageants were concerned."

Cherry looked disappointed. "I thought it was going to be something a lot more exciting than that."

Lulu said, "Well, there *were* more than just the pageant notes. There also looked to be some notes about other gossip—stuff that didn't have anything to do with pageants. It made me wonder if Dee Dee was a blackmailer as well as a pageant double agent. She'd actually jotted down in that notebook that Tristan was having an affair. And there was a picture in there of Tristan with some man, but I couldn't tell who he was."

"Now we're getting somewhere!" Cherry rubbed her hands together. "Let's say Dee Dee was blackmailing someone. Blackmailing and murder always go hand in hand in those TV cop shows."

"But that's because it's the *blackmailer* who gets murdered," said Lulu. "Why would Tristan get murdered if it's Dee Dee doing the blackmailing?"

"Maybe Tristan wouldn't pay. She doesn't seem like the kind of person who really gives a rip what people think of her. Maybe she even told Dee Dee *she* was going to expose *her*—and tell people that she was in the pageant-espionage business. If everyone thought she was a blabbermouth, it would take Dee Dee off the pageant gravy train really quickly."

Lulu tried to follow her logic. "So you think that Dee Dee was actually more of a blackmail *victim* of Tristan's. It sounded friendly enough that day at the shop, though. Dee Dee gave Tristan some information. Tristan paid Dee Dee." But then Lulu remembered something. "But you know, Dee Dee did make some kind of reference to money. Like she thought maybe they needed to renegotiate fees or something. At the time I didn't know what she was talking about, but it makes more sense now."

Cherry rocked triumphantly in the chair. "Like I was saying—Dee Dee had a motive, too. And I bet Dee Dee cared a whole lot more about keeping her shop open and chock-full of pageant contestants than Tristan cared about losing face as a coach. Heck, it would probably make Tristan an even more popular coach—she gets down and dirty in the quest to have her girls win! Now tell me what the new mission is because I'm thinking it has nothing to do with Dee Dee. Especially since Dee Dee probably isn't speaking to me after the shopping incident."

"I'd like to talk to your neighbor, Pepper. I hadn't told you this yet, but Pepper really had a to-do with Tristan at the party that night."

Cherry's green eyes widened. "Pepper was at the party? And had a blowup with Tristan? When did that happen?"

"Remember when I went looking for some seasoning for all that bland food? Well, Pepper's husband, Loren, and Tristan were having a scene in the kitchen while I was there. Loren was all lovey-dovey, and Tristan wanted nothing to do with him. When Tristan was finally pulling away from him, Pepper saw them together and really lost it. Threw some wine all over Tristan's dress. So Pepper knew that Tristan was having an affair with her husband."

Cherry gave a low whistle. "I bet she blew her top— she's got a huge temper on her. She was a lot madder than I was about the whole Tristan blackballing incident, too.

Loren's affair with Tristan is probably like rubbing salt in her wounds. I didn't know anything about Tristan and Loren being an item. So Pepper had a *lot* of motive to kill Tristan. *She* was even more upset about getting blackballed from the club than I was. Plus the fact that Tristan had an affair with her husband on top of it all!"

Lulu nodded. "That's a whole lot of motive right there. Revenge and jealousy are powerful stuff!" She thought for a second. "Are you and Pepper pretty good friends? I don't want to mess up a close friendship between y'all or anything."

"Not so much," said Cherry casually. "We're neighbors, and that's really all. We talk to each other when we see each other out in the yard."

"Do you think you can get her to have lunch with you?" asked Lulu. "I'm trying to think of a natural way to ask her some questions, and I know she doesn't come to Aunt Pat's much to eat."

"Oh, sure," said Cherry, with a dismissive wave of her hand. "Piece of cake. I'll tell her that I've got the club schedule and wanted to talk to her about getting in now that we're not being blackballed anymore. In fact"—Cherry pulled out a cell phone with a rhinestone-studded cover—"I'll go ahead and buzz her right now. No time like the present. Besides, I'm starving."

Lulu knew that she hadn't met Pepper under the best of circumstances at Tristan's party. Her impression that night had been that Pepper was shrill and shrewish, although she definitely had cause to be. She'd also stood out at the party because, having just followed her husband when he left the house, she wasn't dressed for a party.

Pepper looked much tidier as she put away some barbeque at the restaurant. But she was just as shrill as she'd been at Tristan's party. She might be small, but her voice carried across the restaurant to where Lulu was coming out of the kitchen to join them.

Pepper was studying the calendar with interest when Lulu sat down at the booth. Cherry said quickly, "Pepper, I don't know if you remember Lulu or not. This is Lulu Taylor, who owns Aunt Pat's."

Pepper looked up with a smile that didn't quite reach her eyes. "Nice to meet you." She looked back down again at the papers in front of her. "So, Cherry, you were saying that these are the events the club has planned for the fall and spring, right? And Evelyn said that nobody else was standing in the way of us joining?"

Cherry swirled her iced tea around in her glass. "That's what Evelyn said. I did want to let you know, though," she said, clearing her throat, "that I'm not quite as crazy about joining the Memphis Women's League as I thought I was." Pepper's mouth dropped open, and Cherry said, "I know, I know, it's all we've been talking about for the last month. Looking at that calendar of events, though? Can you see me doing a bake sale? Or dragging Johnny to a dance? What would happen is that I'd start skipping meetings. Then I'd start skipping the different events. Then I'd conveniently forget to pay my dues." Cherry shrugged. "Before you know it, Evelyn would be furious with me that she stuck her neck out and got me admitted to the club . . . and then I didn't do anything. Better just to not join."

Cherry shot Lulu a panicky look when Pepper started fussing at Cherry to persuade her to join, so Lulu quickly interrupted the tirade. "Pepper, Cherry had been telling me about how y'all were trying to join the club and how Tristan was blackballing you."

This diversion seemed to work. Lulu guessed it had

been Pepper's favorite topic of conversation for the past thirty days. "She was such a pill, Lulu. I don't know if you knew Tristan or not, but count your lucky stars if you didn't. All she wanted to do was mess with people. She'd do her darnedest to figure out what it was that you wanted the most and then try her hardest to block it from happening. It was her hobby."

"Why didn't she want you and Cherry in the club?"

Pepper said in a harsh voice, "Simple. She didn't think we were good enough for the Memphis Women's League. Tristan thought that by letting us in, they'd be lowering the club's standards. That's what Evelyn told Cherry, anyway."

Cherry bobbed her head in agreement.

"Know what the funny thing is? Tristan thought that I wasn't good enough for her club, but she thought my husband was good enough to have an affair with." Pepper gave a grating laugh.

Lulu blinked. Pepper didn't seem to have any kind of filter to keep from talking about really private things. "I'm sorry, Pepper. I didn't know your husband was involved with Tristan." She saw Cherry hide a smile at Lulu's discomfort over fibbing.

"Well, I knew he was seeing somebody, Lulu. I didn't know it was Tristan until I followed Loren out that night of her party. I knew he had to be seeing somebody, but I didn't know who it was. He's cheated on me before, you see, so I don't trust him a lick. He was mooning around the house, acting all lovesick and distracted. . . . I knew *I* wasn't the cause of it. He'd always change the computer screen whenever I walked into the room and erase his text messages so I couldn't see who he'd been writing. And he started working late and running lots of errands on the weekends."

Pepper took a big bite out of her peach cobbler as if to

remove the bad taste from her mouth. "Finally, I had enough of his nonsense. When he told me that he was going out that night to meet someone from work, I followed him. He's never met folks from work at that hour before. Sure enough, he drove right straight to Tristan Pembroke's house. Now I know that she didn't want him there—that she was trying to dump him. Who knows why she started going out with him to begin with? Maybe she thought it was funny to screw up everything in my life." Pepper jabbed viciously at a big peach slice with her fork.

"Maybe he was going there to end things with Tristan. Maybe he'd gotten the message that she wasn't interested anymore, and he wanted to break off the relationship in person," suggested Lulu mildly. She wanted to find out exactly how much Pepper knew about what was going on between her husband and Tristan.

Pepper snorted. "More like the other way around. He would have been pleased as punch to continue their affair. When he was pleading with me last night not to dump him, he said that he couldn't bear any more rejection. That *Tristan* had been trying to end their relationship and hadn't been answering her door or his phone calls or e-mails. He'd even shown up at some of the pageants to try to talk to her! He said he couldn't *handle* it if I suddenly ditched him, too. However, that seems to me like something he should have thought about before he cheated. No, he'd still be trying to get Tristan to take him back—if she wasn't dead."

"So did you wait for him out in the car outside the party that night?" asked Lulu, trying to act as if she didn't know the answer to that question already.

"Absolutely not! I marched right in there and dragged his sorry rear end out the door. I gave Tristan a piece of my mind, too, which was *long* overdue. Threw a glass of wine at her, too. I was so mad! Of all the people for him to be messing around with—and he knew exactly how much I hated Tristan! I didn't care that I didn't have a spot of makeup on and was wearing my sweat suit. I was that determined to pull him out of there."

"So, obviously," said Lulu, "you weren't at the party when Tristan's body was found."

Pepper sighed. "Actually, yes, I was still there. But I wasn't inside Tristan's house then—I was out in the car yelling at Loren. We were going to drive home and finish our fight there, but that storm blew in, and it was raining so hard that I didn't want to drive in it. I just chewed Loren out while we waited for it to let up a little bit. I didn't even notice the lights had gone off at the house. . . . Cherry was telling me about that the other day. I was so focused on setting things straight with my husband."

"How did you find out that Tristan was dead?"

Pepper made a face. "The police came up with a flashlight and shone it right in the car window like they thought we might be in there making out or something. I rolled a window down, and the police said there'd been a murder at the house and the guests were supposed to go to some particular place on the grounds and they'd be asking questions. I asked who it was who'd been murdered, and he said it was Tristan. Then, as soon as the cop left, we started fighting *again* because Loren was putting up such a howling ruckus over Tristan being dead." Pepper shook her head and picked at her nail polish, which was already chipped to bits on her fingernails.

Cherry said, "Hmm. I wonder who could have done it."

"Tons of people! Half the town was at her house that night. And I can't believe she had any real friends. . . . She was too much of a backstabber. She was the type that couldn't keep a friend for more than a few minutes without talking about her behind her back. But, you know, in these kinds of cases, they always say they look at the family first." Pepper shrugged like she didn't really care who murdered Tristan—she was glad that somebody had stepped up to the plate.

"I thought," said Cherry, "that they always looked at the husband or boyfriend first."

Pepper's eyes narrowed to slits. "What are you trying to say, Cherry?"

Cherry knit her brows as if she was trying to remember what she *did* think—or what she was supposed to think. This, thought Lulu, was the big problem with lying—you ended up losing track of what your position was supposed to be.

"Oh. I don't know. . . . I was thinking about those cop shows and what they do when someone goes missing or dies. I was thinking it's usually the spouse—just on TV, you know . . ." Cherry spluttered as she tried to get back on solid ground again.

"As long as that was all you were thinking," said Pepper darkly. "Because Loren is a cheat, a liar, a coward, and a sorry excuse for a husband. But he's *not* a killer."

Lulu jumped in again. "You think Tristan's family is behind it? Who were you thinking of?"

Pepper blew out a sigh. "I don't know. Steffi, I guess, is the obvious choice. I know Tristan treated her as awful as she treated everybody else, and the poor kid put up with it for all these years. Who'd blame her if she finally blew a gasket and couldn't stand it anymore? I wanted to kill Tristan, and I only spent a tiny amount of time with her. If I'd spent a lifetime with her, I'd never have been able to keep myself from wringing her scrawny neck."

Cherry said, "I didn't even know you knew Steffi, Pepper."

"Oh, sure—I know all of them. Tristan's sister, Marlowe, is my age, and we went through school together. We always hung out in the same crowd. We were never best friends, but we had the same friends so we ended up doing a lot of the same stuff. So I knew Tristan and Marlowe growing up. And I paid attention when Steffi was born— felt sorry for the baby, actually. Marlowe used to go on and on when we were teens about how terrible Tristan was. And now I know she was telling the truth."

Lulu poured Pepper a little more tea from the pitcher on the table. "What kinds of things did Marlowe used to say about Tristan?"

"Well, growing up it was all kind of silly stuff, I guess. But it wasn't silly at the time—you know how everything feels so important when you're a teenager. Tristan would do things like steal Marlowe's boyfriends, or tell people something really mean about her sister . . . like a gross habit she had or something. I think she even pulled pranks on her at different times, just to make her feel like a fool."

Lulu said, "But you haven't spent time with her as an adult to know if Tristan was still doing things like that?"

"Oh, sure I have. Marlowe and Tristan's bottling company uses the accounting office where Loren works. I'm sure that's probably how Loren got to know Tristan—he probably was over there delivering the sad facts about the state of their business and then Tristan turned on the charm and snagged him."

Pepper looked across the restaurant, but Lulu could tell she wasn't seeing a thing. "I ran into Marlowe at the store not too long ago and asked her how everything was going. She sounded real, real bitter over the state of the company— said that Tristan was running their father's business into the ground and taking money from the coffers. I bet you that Marlowe is going to be delighted to take over that company again and get the money flowing."

"It certainly does sound like a good motive for murder," said Lulu, nodding. "The only thing is that Marlowe wasn't in town during the murder. She was out of town for business."

Pepper gave the grating laugh again. "Out of town for *what* business? They haven't been able to get any new accounts in forever, Marlowe told me."

Lulu frowned. "Well, maybe she meant it was a trip for personal business, then. Or maybe she was only trying to make contact with an old account and give it a little TLC. At any rate, she wasn't in town during the party."

Cherry's face was confused. "But she was. I was at the beauty parlor the morning of the party to get my color . . . uh . . . touched up," she patted her henna-colored locks, "and I saw Marlowe pulling into the parking lot as I was leaving. I've seen her at my salon before, so I wasn't surprised to see her. She was definitely in town that day."

Chapter
11

It was at Tristan Pembroke's funeral that Lulu became convinced that ghosts didn't exist. If they did, thought Lulu, then Tristan would have haunted that funeral of hers with a vengeance.

There were no over-the-top displays of wealth. No elaborate floral arrangements. This funeral was given by an apparently grudging Steffi Pembroke and Marlowe Walters—and really, thought Lulu, who could blame them for being stingy? The two women greeted mourners (and the curious) at the funeral home the evening before. They'd chosen an open casket and had Tristan's body put in a garish dress that Lulu was sure hadn't belonged to the deceased. Loren was very emotional and had to leave early. Besides him, the only visibly affected mourner was an old lady who'd worked at Tristan's father's company for many years and remembered Tristan as a child.

"Don't she look natural?" she sobbed. "I never have seen her look more pleasant."

The funeral the next day was a simple graveside service. Tristan's minister had insisted on giving a homily, although apparently no one had opted for a eulogy because Steffi and Marlowe remained silent. The minister had also brought along a soloist, who sang "Amazing Grace." There wasn't, thought Lulu, a damp eye anywhere. Except, of course, for Loren, whose eyes were red from crying.

After the short service, the mourners milled around a little outside the tented area where there were some tacky funeral sprays that Tristan would have despised. Most of those in attendance had likely come out of curiosity instead of any fondness for Tristan. Loren, however, hugged both Steffi and Marlowe fervently and talked about how much he was going to miss Tristan. Marlowe looked irritated, but Steffi talked to him quietly for a couple of minutes before spontaneously giving Loren a second, sympathetic hug.

Cherry walked up to Lulu and murmured, "This isn't anything like Queen Tristan would have chosen for herself, is it? Where are the roses? The choir of angels? The heart-felt eulogies?"

"It is kind of understated, isn't it? Really, though, wouldn't we have thought they were being hypocritical if they'd gone all-out and made it a funeral to remember? Neither one of them could stand Tristan at the time of her death."

"Look at Loren over there," said Cherry, nodding toward the tent. He looked to be blowing his nose into a handkerchief as Steffi talked with him again. "Maybe *he* should have been the one organizing the funeral, since he was the only one who gave a rip about her."

"I'm surprised that Steffi is so concerned about him," said Lulu in a musing voice. "After all, he was having an affair with her mother."

"But her mother screwed him over just like she screwed over everyone else in her life, including Steffi. Steffi probably feels sorry for him because he really *did* care about her mom, even if she treated him like dirt."

"Wonder what Colleen's doing here?" mused Lulu. "She wasn't exactly on best terms with Tristan."

Cherry snorted. "She's probably making sure Tristan is really dead."

Lulu sighed. "People are probably wondering why Sara is here, too. Seems like everybody knows about her argument with Tristan—but then, it was pretty public when Tristan got so furious about that portrait." She watched sadly as Sara and Ben walked over to join them.

"Ben, that was nice of you to come with Sara," said Lulu. "I didn't know you were going to come along."

Sara said, "I felt like people were going to be staring at me, so I asked him to bring me."

"Like Sara is going to get *that* upset about the portrait thing," said Ben with a laugh. "But who knows—some people are just bound to believe the worst about you."

"Oh, great—here comes my best friend," said Cherry glumly. "Why do I have the feeling I'm about to end up buying a whole bunch of goofy dresses? No offense, Lulu."

Dee Dee looked pretty melodramatic, thought Lulu. It made her wonder if she'd ever had a background in the theater because it sure looked like she was playing a part—of the perfect mourner. She wore a tailored black suit, which seemed to be straining at the seams, black hose, black heels, a black scarf around her neck, and lots of dark makeup. Her hair was sprayed within an inch of its life, and she held an embroidered handkerchief as if she thought she might need to sop up tears, or some of the excess makeup, at any time.

"Sad day, isn't it?" she said, looking studiously grave. Then her eyes narrowed. "Cherry, hon, I thought you were going to come back in and buy some of those clothes we tried on the other day. Weren't you going to have a fashion makeover?" She looked pointedly at Cherry's funeral outfit, which included a bright purple blouse (which, Lulu guessed, was the closest color Cherry had to black) with a dark purple skirt.

"Yes," said Cherry, looking miserably at Lulu, "that's what I said, all right. But then . . . well, then I ran out of money."

Sara said, "Ran out of money! Cherry, I'm so sorry. What happened? Are you okay?"

"We can lend you a little to tide you over if you need it," said Ben with concern. "I didn't know you were in such bad straits."

Cherry gave Lulu a desperate look. Fortunately, though, there was a sudden distraction in the form of Pepper, who strode briskly up to the sobbing Loren and pulled him away from Steffi. Steffi hurried toward their group as Pepper began, to all appearances, giving Loren a piece of her mind.

Cherry happily latched on to whatever diversion she could find. "Steffi? I'm so sorry." Cherry paused, apparently not knowing what else to say. "Nice service," she ended, lamely.

Sara gave Steffi a hug. "I know it's been such a tough day for you. And I just wanted to tell you that I'm so sorry about your mom."

Steffi started tearing up a little, and Sara gave her another hug. "I never did make up with her," Steffi said in a choked voice. "She and I ended up on bad terms. The very last time I saw her, we were having an argument."

"So did your mom and I," said Sara. "We had a really nasty argument, and that makes me feel horrible. And I know you feel bad, too. But we didn't know we were *having* a last conversation with your mom or else we'd have said something different. We just didn't know. And she didn't either because she said some really rude things back, after all."

Steffi sniffed. "Thanks, Sara."

Marlowe walked up. "I wanted to thank y'all so much again for coming. I know you're here to show support for Steffi and me instead of mourning Tristan . . . and I want you to know how much that means to me." Pepper's voice rose all the way across the lawn to the funeral-home tent, and Marlowe raised her eyebrows. "Well, maybe one person came to mourn Tristan," she said.

"Poor Loren," murmured Steffi.

Dee Dee's voice was harsh. "*Poor Pepper* is more like it," she said. "Here's Loren, grieving publicly over a dead woman. I don't blame Pepper for being upset. It was an inappropriate relationship to begin with, and it doesn't seem to have an end to it! And that's not the only inappropriate relationship surrounding this case, either." Which was a statement that made everyone knit their brows.

"Shh. They're coming over," said Lulu in a low voice. However, the silence that followed Lulu's warning was probably worse than the gossip had been. Lulu noticed that Colleen was also finishing up her conversation with the minister really quickly and looked to be hurrying over to join them. She looked like she was dying to hear what was being said.

Pepper apparently wanted to show that she had no hard feelings about Steffi or Marlowe. She hugged them both and said, "Y'all will be in my thoughts and prayers."

Colleen came up breathlessly and added, "Me, too. Pansy and I will be thinking about y'all."

Dee Dee gave a short laugh, which made everyone give her a puzzled look. "I was just thinking," she said in a silky voice, "that this funeral is jam-packed with hypocrites. Really, about the only people who were close to Tristan or friends of hers were Loren and me."

Pepper bristled at the mention of Loren and Tristan, but Dee Dee kept on talking.

"I'm giving everyone a heads-up—you're not fooling me. I know a lot more about what went on at that party than people know. I know about people who were messing around where they weren't supposed to be. I know about things that went missing. And I know that things aren't always what they seem. You're not fooling anyone." With that, Dee Dee flipped the black scarf off her shoulder and flounced off—if one can flounce in three-inch heels, thought Lulu.

There was a stunned silence after Dee Dee's departure. Then Cherry gave a low whistle. "So Dee Dee's elevator doesn't go up to the top floor. Wow. And we all thought she was just a mild-mannered boutique owner."

"Am I the only one who is totally confused right now?" asked Sara in a pleading voice.

Marlowe gave a dismissive wave of her hand. "Dee Dee acts like she knows everything. Ignore her. She's piqued because she wasn't getting all the attention."

"And I can debunk one of the things she said," said Steffi. "She was *not* a fan of my mother's. They just did pageant business together; they weren't friends. Besides, she's one to talk about suspicious actions at Mother's party—I saw her sneaking around that night looking guilty as sin."

Lulu knew that a funeral was no place to squeeze information out of the bereaved. But she needed to find out more from Steffi and Marlowe.

One thing that Marlowe and Steffi were surely unable to avoid was the food, thought Lulu. In the South, you could opt for a simple graveside service and you could ditch the home visitation in favor of one at the funeral parlor (although there'd definitely be some grumbling feedback from among the most elderly), but there was no escaping the lavish banquet that would appear at your house courtesy of the determined well-meaning.

Sure enough, Marlowe said wryly, "I think there are some ladies from my church who are at my house right now, organizing casseroles and setting up a feast. Would any of y'all like to come by and have a meal?"

Usually, just the family members would go to a postfuneral meal like that, but Lulu knew that the Walters-Pembroke family had shrunk quite a bit. Marlowe wasn't married and had no children, and Tristan had either divorced or alienated any of the family members who might have qualified to attend such an event.

Most everyone shook their heads, but Cherry and Lulu offered to go. "How about if we follow y'all back and help the church ladies serve food and store it?" Lulu asked.

Marlowe looked like she was opening her mouth to protest having Lulu come over to work, so she quickly added,

"And I can have a bite to eat, too, of course. I'm sure there's some excellent food over there. If there's one thing the ladies at the Memphis Land of Goshen Baptist Church are known for, it's the quality of their cooking. Why, I buy their church cookbook every single year! I look forward to it."

"If you really want to," said Marlowe in a doubtful voice.

"Besides," said Cherry, "I've got some food to drop by myself. Kept it in a cooler in my car. And actually *drove* my car, instead of my motorcycle, so you know I'm serious."


The church ladies, thought Lulu, were just a little bit cliquey. Instead of looking happy that Lulu and Cherry had arrived to help, they looked sort of put out. Still, they managed to put their feelings aside enough to let Lulu slap labels on the different zipper bags and plastic containers of food and write the date and the cooking instructions in a Sharpie pen. There was so much food that a ton of it needed to go straight to the freezer.

Dolly, one of the church ladies, seemed to be in charge. "All right, y'all, let's go ahead and make up plates for Steffi and Marlowe. It's time for our bereaved to have some sustenance. Lisa Ann, I've heard that Marlowe is a big fan of deviled eggs, so let's give her a couple of those. And I've a feeling that Steffi will love some of that tomato pie that Lulu brought over. And—what's this, Lulu? The other dish you brought?" Dolly lifted up the lid and gave an approving smile. "Why, I do declare! It's boiled custard, just like my darling mother used to make. I haven't had boiled custard for a million years. We'll make sure that both ladies enjoy some of that."

Cherry nodded her approval at the heaps of green-bean casserole, fried chicken, Virginia-ham-filled buttermilk biscuits, crustless pimento cheese sandwiches, macaroni and cheese, fruit-filled Jell-o, and bacon pasta salad on the plates. "Nothing makes a body hungrier than a funeral," she mused, putting another sticker on a container of chicken divan. "Wonder why that is? The only thing that would make this better is a bottle of wine."

The church ladies blinked at her.

"It's practically medicinal, y'all. Remember, they're *grieving*." Cherry looked in the fridge and found an open bottle. "Actually, it'd just be Marlowe drinking—I keep forgetting that Steffi is underage. I reckon I should have a glass with her. . . . I'm sure she'd rather not drink alone."

Lulu suppressed a giggle, and Cherry said solemnly, "Lulu, will you share a glass with Marlowe and me? To offer up in Tristan's dearly departed memory?"

Lulu agreed, and she and Cherry headed to the living room to join Marlowe and Steffi.

"I had to escape," said Cherry, shaking her head. "Did you see the *disdainful*—really, even *suspicious*— expression on their faces when they saw my chicken spaghetti? I thought that was disgraceful, to make fun of somebody's offering for a funeral buffet."

"I hadn't noticed," lied Lulu.

"You did, too. Of course, they were pleased as punch to see your tomato pie and boiled custard. Shoot, they're probably gobbling it down themselves now that we've left the kitchen and can't see them."

Lulu diplomatically ignored this.

"Thanks so much for coming in here to visit with us, y'all. Steffi and I feel like ladies of the manor having everybody in there working in the kitchen while we're just lounging around in here," said Marlowe. "This is a nice distraction for both of us. Though I feel so worn out after the day we've had, I probably just need to sleep."

Lulu agreed, "Sometimes sleeping is the best medicine. I know it really was a rough day for both of you, but the service was lovely."

Marlowe shrugged. "It was done. That was the important thing. It probably wasn't done to Tristan's exacting specifications, but at least we were able to have a service for her and get some closure, too."

Dolly appeared with plates of food and a rather peeved expression on her face at the sight of the boozing. "Here's some extra food, ladies, to go on the side. The aspic on the iceberg is mine—it's the same recipe that my great-great-grandmother used to take to all the Colonial Dames luncheons. And the dollop of mayo on the top is homemade, of course." She smiled smugly.

Marlowe blinked at this. "Oh. Well, thanks, Dolly. I really appreciate it."

"Well, it was made with love, hon."

Marlowe rolled her eyes at Lulu as the door closed behind Dolly.

Steffi said, "I meant to ask you, Lulu, if Sara ever found out what happened to the portrait she made of Mother?"

Marlowe said, "I was wondering if maybe Tristan had destroyed it herself, considering the fit she threw when Sara put it up to auction." She took a big forkful of the tomato pie and then quickly took another.

"Oh," said Lulu, looking as innocent as she could. "I didn't know you knew about that, Marlowe. Since you were out of town for the party, I mean."

Marlowe hesitated a moment. "Yes, I was out of town.

But Steffi filled me in on what happened at the party. And she said Tristan's face was something to see."

Lulu thought Steffi looked flushed. Come to think of it, she didn't remember seeing Steffi around for the auction. That was when Sara had mentioned looking for her, and they'd both actually scanned the yard looking for her. So either Marlowe had seen Tristan's reaction for herself, or she was recounting someone else's story.

"No, the portrait hasn't shown up. It's all right. . . . She's not that worried about it. But I guess it's just another mystery from that night."

Steffi frowned. "If I come across it, I'll give her a call. I hate to think of her doing all that work and then having the portrait disappear like that." She looked blankly at her pulled-pork sandwich as she thought. "I wonder if Dee Dee took it for some reason. Maybe that's why she was sneaking around at the party."

"You said something about that at the funeral," said Marlowe. "Why did you get the impression she was acting suspicious?"

"She was actually looking over her shoulder a couple of times to see if anyone was looking at her. And she was kind of lurking around. It seemed suspicious to me," said Steffi.

"You didn't ask her what she was doing at the time?" asked Lulu.

"It really wasn't my place to find out what she was up to. It wasn't my house anymore, after all—Mother had kicked me out. Honestly, I didn't really care what she was doing. I figured, anyway, that it had something to do with the top-secret pageant stuff that she and Mother were always doing." Steffi smiled. "All the cheating they were doing."

Marlowe perked up. "Cheating?"

"She and Dee Dee had been throwing pageants for years. Girls would come into Dee Dee's shop and get fitted for dresses. And, like these girls do, they'd start to talk. They'd blab about their talent and what kind of dress or swimsuit they were going to wear. They'd talk about the other girls, too. Dee Dee would take notes and then Mother would pay her to give her the scoop. It was a nice little gig."

Marlowe said thoughtfully, "Insider information. I see. So what would Tristan do with the information?"

"It's really how she got to be such a successful coach. If she knew the other girls were all singing, she'd have her contestant dance—so she'd stand out. If all the girls were wearing short dresses, she'd choose a long one. She made sure that her contestants really stood out for the judges," said Steffi.

"Do you think," said Lulu carefully, "that Dee Dee could have had some reason to murder your mother?"

"The way I see it," said Steffi harshly, "Mother and Dee Dee were doing something crooked. Mother was using information that nobody else had to help her girls win. Maybe something started going wrong with their system. Maybe Dee Dee wanted to stop being the snoop. . . . People could have started catching on. She could have told my mother that she wanted out and then Mother could have refused and said she'd tell people what Dee Dee had done. Because, really, the person who would have been hurt most if it all came out would have been Dee Dee. She'd have lost all that business for her shop."

Lulu thought back to the tiara on the murdered Tristan's head. Did Dee Dee really feel that much hatred for Tristan? She hadn't seemed to. She'd have said that Dee Dee had a purely business relationship with Tristan and that if she had murdered her, it would have been in a very business-like and unemotional way.

"There was something else I wanted to ask you," said Lulu, trying to sound as gossipy as she could, "and then we've really got to get off this subject and talk about other things. But somebody was telling me that they saw Colleen and Pansy at Tristan's party that night."

Chapter
12

Marlowe laughed. "Sounds like somebody didn't have her contact lenses in! Colleen and Pansy couldn't stand Tristan. They sure weren't going to go to her house for a party. Tristan wouldn't have invited them, for one. And then they wouldn't have wanted to be closer than a mile to her, even if she *had* invited them."

Steffi smiled a little. "They've always been really supportive of me—they felt like Mother had done me wrong, and they were even madder at her than they usually were. In fact, Pansy had just written something that *day* on her Facebook page about Mother. She told me later that Mother had called her on the phone and made some kind of dire threat to get her to take off what she said. . . . One of the girls Mother had coached was friends with Pansy on Facebook and saw the comment and told her about it."

Lulu knit her brows. "Facebook. Right." Lulu had managed so far to totally avoid Facebook. But she knew enough to understand that when one person writes something on his or her Facebook page, all of that person's friends can read it. So Tristan would have been upset with Pansy. . . . Could she have made Pansy mad enough to crash Tristan's party to confront her about it? Maybe Tristan threatened to make Pansy lose more pageants?

Lulu decided it would be better to change the subject, since Steffi was starting to close up. "So, are y'all starting to get settled in now? I know Steffi was so glad to be able to move in with you, Marlowe."

Marlowe smiled. "Well, Steffi and I have always been pretty close. I was glad to offer her my home as her own."

Steffi's expression softened a little. "Marlowe is like the mother I always wanted."

There was another interruption as Dolly stuck her head in the door and studiously ignored Lulu and Cherry, the interlopers. "Now, y'all, you should be in pretty good shape, foodwise. We labeled and froze the things that could go into the freezer, and the rest is in the fridge. Y'all are on the prayer list for the next two weeks, although you can certainly ask Pastor Phillip to get that extended. You're also on the casserole rotation, so you'll get supper each day from the casserole committee. And Sue Ann couldn't make it today because of her rheumatoid flaring up, but she said to tell you that she's got one of her famous pound cakes ready to bring to you tomorrow."

Dolly frowned at Steffi's plate. "Eat some of the aspic, hon. It's renowned. As soon as I heard that Tristan had passed, I came straight home from my Circle meeting at church to cook it up."

Dolly quickly popped back out again.

"I think her girdle is on too tight," grumbled Cherry. "It's cutting off circulation to her brain somehow."

Marlowe looked to be trying to remember the thread of the conversation again. "So, yes, I think we've gotten into a bit of a routine. While I'm at work, Steffi has been trying to sort through some of her mother's things. I helped her last weekend—it's a big job with a house that size." A look of irritation passed over Marlowe's face as if the size of Tristan's house had been a sticking point between them in the past.

"I'm ready to go back to work at Aunt Pat's, too, if that's okay. Thanks for letting me have some time off," said Steffi.

"Oh, honey, that's no problem at all—I told you that you could take as much time as you needed. I know sometimes it helps to stay busy, but sometimes it's good to just take some time off, too," said Lulu.

Marlowe said, "So we're getting there, Lulu. Steffi has a new home, she's ready to go back to work—she may even have a boyfriend entering into the equation," she added slyly, and Steffi flushed. Obviously, thought Lulu, it wasn't something she was ready to talk about yet.

Marlowe must have come to the same conclusion because she said, "And once we get Tristan's will sorted out, then we'll be even better. Not that I think there was a lot there to sort," she said, shaking her head. "Tristan was very good at spending money she didn't have."

"Maybe we'll be surprised," said Steffi quietly. "Maybe there'll be more there than we think."

"Or maybe," said Marlowe with a short laugh, "there'll be less."

Cherry hunkered over the booth at Aunt Pat's and said, "Okay, Lulu—give me the lowdown. Who's next on the suspect list that you need to talk to?"

"I haven't met with Pansy yet," said Lulu thoughtfully. "So she should probably be next on my list. And I probably need to talk to Colleen again, too."

Cherry shook her finger thoughtfully. "Know what we should do? We should beard the lions in their den. We should go over to a pageant and really sit down and talk to them. You're probably not going to catch up with Pansy anywhere else—Aunt Pat's is Colleen's place to eat but not Pansy's."

"*We*?" asked Lulu. This sidekick thing was really starting to get out of hand with Cherry.

"It'll be perfect, Lulu. I'll distract one of them while you question the other one. Sara could tell us which pageant they'll be in next. Or Coco could—she's always telling everybody about the pageants."

"Whether they want to hear about them or not!" agreed Lulu. "But Cherry, you've never expressed any kind of interest in beauty pageants. What kind of an excuse can we give for you being there that won't make us look suspicious?"

Cherry said, "I'll just say that after hearing so much about pageant coaches that I thought it would be something I could try to get into myself."

Lulu said slowly, "So you're planning on telling everyone that you're interested in becoming a beauty-pageant coach."

"Yes!" Cherry beamed.

"But honey, you haven't had any pageant experience, have you? Won't they have expected you to have done pageants when you were young or something? What will you say when they ask you what your talent is?"

Cherry waved her hand in the air. "Oh, I'll make it up as I go along. It's not like they're going to know one way or the other whether I was in pageants as a teen or not. I grew up in Mississippi, remember? I could say I was Miss Mississippi, and nobody's going to know the difference. Besides, I was in sort of a pageant once."

"You were?"

"I was prom queen," said Cherry. "Back in the day."

Lulu blinked. "Somehow I'd never pictured you as prom queen, Cherry. That's such a conventional kind of thing, and I see you as really eclectic and colorful and . . . you."

"That's the thing—everybody was ready for something different. Something fresh. And maybe that'll be the case in the beauty-pageant world, too. Maybe those folks will be tired of the Tristan Pembroke–type of coach—all snooty and unapproachable. Maybe they want a new sheriff in town . . . fresh, and funny, and a real straight-shooter."

Cherry was really warming to her subject. Lulu was starting to wonder if maybe she'd really end up as a pageant coach by the end of the case. "Sounds like a great idea. But I think the next pageant was supposed to be out of town—Coco was fussing about it because Sara didn't want to drive her."

Cherry clapped her hands together. "Even better! We'll look even *less* suspicious. You'll be the good grandma, taking Coco to the pageant, and I'll be along for the ride and learning more about becoming a pageant coach. Can we check real quick and make sure she can still sign up as a late entry?"

"And Cherry," said Lulu, in what she hoped was a stern voice. "Let's be really, really careful. We're poking around an awful lot, and somebody out there is a killer. Pretty soon that murderer might start putting two and two together—we don't want to be victims two and three."

After Cherry left, Lulu rocked awhile in the front-porch

rocking chair and spent a little time thinking about the case. At least there was no shortage of suspects. She really would have been worried if Sara was the only one the police were investigating.

The Labs, B. B. and Elvis, were snoozing on the front porch. The warmth of the afternoon and the sound of the ceiling fans clacking above her all conspired to make Lulu drowsy. Before she knew it, she had dropped off to sleep.

She woke up to the sound of the screen door slamming and the Labradors jumping up to greet a new guest. Lulu rubbed her eyes to clear the dreams from them and sat up to see, to her horror, Gordon McDonald.

"Taking a little nap?" he asked with a smile. "Ben called me and told me that it was so quiet over here that you were snoozing on the porch with the dogs. He thought this might be a good time for you to show me around Memphis."

Lulu had dark thoughts about her son.

"He also mentioned, since food is a big interest of mine, that you'd cooked up a southern delicacy for me to try."

Lulu's thoughts turned more to the murderous side. Clearly Ben was cooking for her and claiming that Lulu had concocted it just for Gordon. And Ben was a darned good cook, too. If the way to a man's heart was through his stomach, then whatever Ben had cooked up was surely going to make Gordon head over heels with her. Drat him.

"Well . . . yes. There's a southern delicacy for you to sample back in the kitchen if you want to head back there. Ben is getting things ready for the supper rush, so you're free to go in there. And—sure, I'm happy to drive you around a little bit and kind of give you an overview of Memphis." It just wasn't in Lulu to be rude to the man—or anyone, really. Old habits—and old manners—died hard.

"If you don't mind my asking, what's the delicacy? That you cooked?"

Lulu answered sweetly. "Why don't we have it be a surprise? You could take a bite and see what you think? You might know what it is after you eat it." Who knows what Ben cooked up in there? He might have gone the sweet-and-sugary route or he might have really done some off-the-wall but interesting southern dish.

Ben popped out on the porch, saw Gordon with his mother, and looked pleased. "Oh, good—you made it by," he said quickly. "And just in time—I think Mother's shrimp and garlic cheese grits is ready to be savored. It's so creamy and delicious that you won't believe your mouth, Gordon."

Ahh, thought Lulu. Shrimp and grits.

"Mother, why don't you take Gordon back and show him the famous Aunt Pat's kitchen? I know Gordon will love seeing it, but I've got to get ready for the evening rush. Do you mind doing the honors?"

Lulu was seriously thinking about creative ways to murder her son. He was absolutely bent on making sure she spent as much time as possible with this man. But out loud she said, "Of course. Come on back, Gordon." She managed to squelch her irritation. It wasn't Gordon's fault, after all.

As usual, when Lulu was showing off the Aunt Pat's kitchen to a visitor, she warmed to her subject.

"Aunt Pat," she explained to Gordon, "was the wonderful lady who raised me. She brought me up with lots of love, laughter—and the most savory food you've ever put in your mouth. Aunt Pat was the most talented cook I've ever come across. She'd take a basic southern dish, like fried chicken, and make it magical. Every day I'd come straight to the restaurant after school and plop down on the wooden stool and tell Aunt Pat all about my day while she chopped vegetables and mixed up the rub for the barbeque. This kitchen is my favorite place on earth." She looked around with satisfaction at the shiny copper pots hanging on the pegboard and the long counter where Aunt Pat taught her how to cook.

Gordon sat down on one of the wooden stools while Lulu put a good-sized helping of shrimp and grits on his plate. "You're not going to believe this," he said, "but I've never even *eaten* grits before. I could only find the instant kind at the stores up north and thought that I'd be short-changing myself if that was my introduction to the food."

"You're a wise man," said Lulu, nodding. "I think you're really going to enjoy your first experience with grits. It's a lot like your polenta, I think—I know y'all eat that up there. It's great as it is, but it's also a really tasty base for other things to be mixed in there. Garlic cheese grits is really delectable, especially if you run it in the oven for a while and bake it. Plain old grits with butter or cream cheese is also tasty. And of course, there's the famous shrimp and grits." She put the plate down in front of him and watched with a smile as he let a forkful cool for a few seconds, then put it in his mouth.

Gordon's eyes closed. "Delicious," he said. Or at least, that's what Lulu thought he said. It was hard to tell with his mouth so full of food. He swallowed and said, "And the grits taste so creamy! I wasn't expecting that."

"Oh, we're all about adding cream and butter here at the restaurant," said Lulu with a laugh. "It's comfort on a plate."

Lulu could tell that she wasn't going to get out of being a tour guide. It wasn't in her to be rude, even though she hadn't signed up for any of this. Ben, on the other hand, would definitely have some rudeness directed his way some time in his very near future. "Where were you interested in going, Gordon? I know Ben was saying that you were brand-new to Memphis, but have you had a chance to look around at all?"

"Not at all, Lulu," said Gordon, still working hard at eating up his shrimp and grits. "But I've read a little bit online about Memphis. And, of course, I've seen Beale Street—that was one of my first stops. I mean, *really* seeing it, not just coming to Aunt Pat's. I don't want to wear you out, Lulu, by having you go all over town in one day. I was thinking that maybe we could see Memphis in several days and focus on a few things a day—like Graceland one day, Sun Records another, Mud Island one day, etc."

"Great," said Lulu. She was afraid her voice might have been the teensiest bit sarcastic, but Gordon didn't seem to notice.

"Today I'd love to start out by going to the famous Peabody Hotel," said Gordon, his face lighting up. "I saw some pictures of the lobby, and it looked amazing. All that dark wood and the fountain right in the middle of the lobby . . . and the bar and restaurants."

"Then that will be our first stop," said Lulu with more enthusiasm than she actually felt. "Although our timing is a little off—we won't have a chance to see the duck parade."

"Shoot. Oh well, we can still see them swimming in the fountain, right? And then we can go up and see the royal duck palace?" he asked eagerly. "You can tell that I've done some research. They have their own little palace, right?"

"They surely do—right on the top of the roof. Maybe the royal duckmaster will also be there, and we can talk to him. He's always an interesting fellow to talk with."

The Peabody was bustling when Lulu and Gordon arrived. The bar was packed, the ducks were happily swimming in their fountain, and people were browsing in the shops adjacent to the lobby. Gordon was busily taking pictures and jotting down notes. Lulu discovered that Gordon was very interested in the restaurants in the hotel—interested enough to go find the chef of one of the restaurants. "If it's okay with you," said Gordon to Lulu, "I'm going to order a meal here and take some pictures of it. I told the chef I wanted to feature his restaurant on my blog, and he was thrilled."

Lulu gaped at him a moment before remembering to close her mouth up. She was taking time out of her day to show him around Memphis and he was planning on featuring another restaurant on his blog? He was going to order dinner and not offer to buy her any?

Before she could make a pointed mention of the fact that she was hungry herself, she noticed Marlowe Walter sitting by herself near the bar. She turned to tell Gordon that she'd be over in the bar when she noticed that he'd gone. Typical.

Marlowe was happy to see her. "Oh, good—I was getting bored waiting for this potential client to show up. I'm still trying to find some extra business for the bottling company, you know. I guess this guy is running a little behind."

Lulu sat down next to Marlowe, and she talked a little

bit about how the clearing out was going at Tristan's house. "You wouldn't have thought that Tristan would have been such a pack rat," said Lulu, shaking her head.

"She sure was, though. Every closet was crammed with stuff. That's part of what makes me so mad while I'm clearing out her house. She was spending money that she didn't even have—that was the bottling company's money—on things that she didn't even need or use. Some of the stuff she'd bought was still in its original boxes and obviously hadn't been used."

Lulu hesitated a moment. "Marlowe, there's something I wanted to ask you. Somebody told me that you were actually in town the night of Tristan's murder. But you told everybody that you were out of town on a business trip. Even Steffi thought you were gone and had to end up staying with me when her mother kicked her out of the house."

"I *was* out of town on a business trip when Tristan kicked out Steffi," said Marlowe with a sigh. "I was trying to scare up some new business for the company. We'd been losing accounts right and left. So, no, I wasn't available when Steffi needed a place to go. And I feel bad about that."

"But you came *back*," said Lulu. "Were you back in Memphis the day of the murder?"

"The scheduled late-afternoon meeting on the last day fell through—they had something come up on their end, and they rescheduled the meeting for a couple of weeks out. I actually told the folks back at the office that I was going to stay at the hotel that night instead of driving back." Marlowe shrugged. "But then, at the last minute, I decided I'd rather head back and sleep in my own bed. Besides, I'd been meaning to run by the salon for a while and hadn't had time to do it. I got the last appointment of the day and slid by to get my hair cut. Then I went home."

"Not to your sister's benefit?" asked Lulu.

Marlowe snorted. "No way. Remember, I was trying to *avoid* running into Tristan. My idea of a good time after a long trip wasn't to go see my sister. Besides, I was furious that I'd spent all that time and energy trying to build up the company when all she did was tear it down and make bad business decisions."

"So you decided not to say anything about being back in town," said Lulu.

"It didn't make any sense to. I knew I'd end up being a suspect right away. Everyone knows how much I love Dad's company and how angry I've been that Tristan has run it into the ground. Plus the fact that apparently Tristan was too lazy to update her will, despite all her posturing that Steffi and I were being written out of it. Steffi gets the estate, which we know was in terrible shape, and Tristan had a ton of debts, and I get the business, which is also in horrible shape and really worth nothing. But the police will say that Steffi didn't know about her mother's financial problems and so she still had a money motive—especially with Tristan threatening to write her out of the will. And the police will say that I wanted to get control of the company back so it wouldn't go completely bankrupt. So I was a natural suspect. And—I knew I hadn't killed her, so I was saving the investigators some time and keeping them from chasing a red herring."

Lulu said, "You don't have any idea who *did* do it, though? I've been trying to make sure that Sara's name is cleared. The police keep on coming back to question her—and I believe with all my heart that *that's* a red herring for the police, too. I know you want this settled just as much as I do. Is there anything you can think of, Marlowe?"

"Honestly, Lulu? I think most of the people who Tristan knew wanted to kill her. I'm harder pressed to think of someone who *didn't*."

Chapter

13

Marlowe's client showed up right after that, and Gordon finally emerged from the Peabody restaurant. He seemed oblivious to the fact that he'd left Lulu to her own devices all that time.

"So, what's on the agenda for tomorrow?" asked Gordon eagerly. "It looks like it's going to be a gorgeous day, so how about spending it outdoors? We could take the monorail to Mud Island. I want to see that scale model of the Mississippi River that they've got there. And there's a couple of places to eat there, too, so I could review the whole experience on my blog."

Lulu was feeling a little sour about Gordon's blogging now. She was spending all this time with him—and he wasn't even covering Aunt Pat's.

"Gordon, I'd love to," she said as sweetly as she could muster, "but my friend Cherry and I are planning on going to a beauty pageant tomorrow—out of town. My little granddaughter Coco enters them, so we thought we'd go support her."

Gordon, to Lulu's horror, looked fascinated. "Now *that* is some real southern culture right there. Beauty pageants!"

"Well, not so much," demurred Lulu. "Only for those who are interested. Pageants, I think, are sort of their own separate culture."

"Will there be any food there?"

Lulu sighed. It just wasn't in her to tell a whopper on the spur of the moment. "Not usually. But I saw online that since this pageant is around lunchtime and is in a ballroom at a hotel, people are allowed to bring food in. It's probably going to be a Crock-Pot city."

Gordon brightened. "Lulu, if you don't mind, I think I'll join up with y'all. I'll take my own car and meet you there, since I might want to leave after lunch. But—it sounds very interesting!"

Lulu was glad to make her escape from Gordon before the rest of her week got planned out with him.

The next day dawned early—and rainy—as Lulu picked up Coco at Sara and Ben's house, then got Cherry, and headed out of town to the pageant.

"Coco, honey, I'm so glad to see you!" When they arrived, Colleen swooped down and gave Coco a pecking kiss on the cheek, leaving a red lipstick smear, which Colleen expertly removed with a tissue. "I didn't think you were able to come. Did your Granny Lulu bring you, then?" Colleen gave that funny grimacing grin of hers at Lulu and Cherry. "And Cherry, I'm absolutely *stunned* to see you here today. I had no idea you were interested in pageants."

Lulu half listened as Cherry prattled off on her spiel on

her sudden and intense interest in being a pageant coach as Colleen made little cooing noises of delight. "And I suppose you'll probably start off with little Coco as your first *protégée*?" Cherry looked a little confused at Colleen's Frenchified handling of the word. "I'm just saying that Coco will be the first girl you're planning on coaching. Right? 'Cause I know she's had very limited coaching. And not really from a professional coach, at that." Colleen looked at Lulu reproachfully.

"Yes," said Lulu quickly. "I was a little surprised that Sara hadn't gotten Coco set up with a real coach, seeing as how Coco is so interested in pageants and . . . well, in winning."

Coco actually seemed to have some major reservations about her "Aunt Cherry" coaching her. This was something, thought Lulu, that they should have discussed with her in the car. Except that the whole thing was completely made up anyway. "Aunt Cherry will be coaching me?" she said, tilting her head doubtfully. "What kind of talent does she have? Mrs. Pembroke was a great voice teacher, and she also knew how to play the piano. Can Aunt Cherry do anything?"

Cherry looked a little put out at the fact that Coco had basically labeled her untalented. "Oh, I have *lots* of talents, Coco. We'll talk about it all later; how about that?" She changed the subject real quick, as Coco was opening her mouth to ask some more pointed questions. "Where is Pansy, Colleen?"

"She's off getting ready. It takes forever, you know. You should go catch up with her because Tina—that's Pansy's coach—is giving her some last-minute tips before she goes on. The last year or two, Pansy has gotten real serious about being a contestant. So you'll hear that reflected in the advice she's getting from her coach."

"Before I go talk to Tina, Colleen, could you do me a big favor and answer some questions for me?" asked Cherry in an enthusiastic voice. "I'm just *fascinated* by pageant life. Tell me about Pansy's talent and how you developed it."

Colleen preened a little. "Well, we're lucky because Pansy is sooo talented," she answered. "She's this fantastic actress, you see. She can play *any* part in *any* type of play—Shakespeare, Neil Simon, Arthur Miller, you name it. She plays the violin just beautifully. And she's a fantastic impersonator, too! We have a lot of fun with that if we're doing a comedy routine. She can do *any* voice. And she wants to go to this expensive performing-arts college— and we *know* she'll get in. It's just, well, it's expensive. So the pageants are helping with the scholarship money, if we can get enough. So, Cherry, you're not looking at a *career*; you're looking at a way to help connect girls with an education! And a successful future!"

Poor Cherry, thought Lulu. For a second, she'd looked like her stomach hurt.

"I know it's probably time to go get ready," said Lulu. "Coco, honey, let's go backstage, and I'll give you a hand."

"Uh, Lulu," said Colleen with a whinnying laugh, "There's a gentleman walking up to us with a determined look on his face—and I do believe he only has eyes for you!"

Lulu felt a sinking sensation and looked up to see Gordon making his way across the ballroom. "Yes, Gordon is a . . . um . . . food blogger. He's new in town, and Ben asked me to show him around a little bit. He was real curious about pageants for some reason."

Cherry said under her breath, "Isn't that a little odd? Men and pageants, I mean? I just can't see my Johnny all gung-ho to see teenagers in sparkly dresses singing 'Dixie.' Especially driving all the way out of town into the country on a nasty, rainy, windy day." She gave Lulu a coy look. "Or maybe it's true love, Lulu!"

Colleen looked a little hurt. "Cherry, I can't believe you would say such a thing! Pageants are a lot more than that, like I was just telling you. Besides, many of our judges are men, and we couldn't do all this without them."

"I agree," said Lulu quickly. She certainly didn't need Colleen to start acting all cool around Cherry and her. "I think the mention of food also interested Gordon. He's trying to discover real southern cuisine, or so he says."

Gordon walked up to the group, and Lulu quickly introduced them. "I hate to leave," said Lulu, "but I've got to get Miss Coco backstage or else she won't be ready for the competition."

"Yes," said Colleen, "you better rush, since the little girls go up first."

As Coco and Lulu walked out of the ballroom to the room next door that served as a backstage dressing area, Lulu heard Colleen completely in her element, giving Gordon and Cherry the lowdown on pageant talent, the different categories the girls would be judged in, and what might be inside the Crock-Pots along the back wall of the banquet hall. Colleen seemed to be tickled pink by Gordon and looked to be laughing at everything he said. Lulu was glad to have Colleen completely absorbed. She would have a chance to talk to Pansy in private for a few minutes without her mother hovering over her and editing everything that came out of her mouth.

Somehow, Lulu had thought that backstage would be a lot more organized and a lot less chaotic than what greeted her and Coco as they entered the big room that served as a dressing room for the pageant girls. There were bags of makeup everywhere—makeup in every conceivable color, too. There were dresses and shoes and bathing suits and curling irons . . . and lots and lots of hairspray. The girls all looked at themselves with fierce concentration in mirrors as they applied mascara, adjusted straps, and controlled wayward bits of hair.

"Let's sit next to Pansy," said Coco, clearly enamored with the older girl.

"Coco!" said Pansy sweetly and stood up to give her a hug and an air kiss. "Sorry, got my makeup on already. I didn't know you were going to be here today. And with your grandma, too!" Pansy smiled prettily at Lulu.

"Is it okay if we sit beside you?" asked Lulu. "I don't really know the ropes at all. Sara couldn't bring her today, and Coco was dying to come, so I volunteered for the job. But now I don't know what to do."

Pansy nodded at Coco as she ran off to say hi to a friend. "You're lucky then because Coco knows exactly what to do. She's a real pro at this. Besides, she's not doing the glitz competitions—Sara's got her staying in the natural ones. So hardly any makeup or styling. Natural—but pretty. And she loves every minute of it."

"I hope so," said Lulu a little sadly, "This isn't something I'd want her to do if she wasn't crazy about it."

Pansy's mouth curved. "That's what makes you a better stage parent than my mom. I had to compete in pageants, no matter what."

Lulu frowned. "I thought you loved it! Your mama made me think that this was your favorite thing to do."

Pansy shrugged. "It's okay. But it wasn't *my* choice. I started competing in pageants when I was only a baby— and nobody can ask a baby if that's what she wants to do.

When I was Coco's age, I spent my backstage time playing Barbies on the floor with Steffi Pembroke while our moms got furious with us." Pansy laughed.

"I didn't know that Steffi was in pageants," said Lulu slowly. She sure hadn't won any, if that was the case. Bless her heart.

"No, Steffi wasn't *in* the pageants. But her mom was there coaching girls or judging, so Steffi got dragged along."

"That's right," said Lulu, nodding. "I remember now that your mom mentioned that y'all had hung out at the pageants together."

"Steffi and her mom would have gotten along a lot better if Steffi *had* been able to be in pageants. But Steffi wasn't really pageant material." Pansy said this in a very matter-of-fact voice. "It ended up making for some big problems between Tristan and Steffi."

A very thin woman with her hair pulled tightly back walked briskly up to Pansy. "Pansy, hon, you don't look like you're on your game today. You're not ready. You're white as a sheet—you definitely need some more self-tanner." The woman, who Lulu assumed was Pansy's coach, Tina, looked closely at Pansy. "Did you put that hemorrhoid medication under your eyes last night, like I told you? 'Cause you're looking like you've got some bags there." Tina rummaged through Pansy's makeup bag. "Here—put some Vaseline on your teeth so your lips won't stick onto your teeth."

Pansy rolled her eyes. "Mrs. Taylor, this is Tina—my coach."

"Don't get exasperated with me, young lady. I'm trying to make you the very best Pansy you can be. Now remember, when you're doing your walk out there, I want you to act like you've got that huge crown on your head already. Got that? Just keep your head up like you're balancing the crown up there. Look those judges right in the eye. . . . Be confident!" And as quickly as she'd come, she dodged back out again.

Coco came back and started expertly brushing her hair. Pansy looked at herself in the mirror and sighed.

"Wouldn't your mother let you quit now if you wanted to?" asked Lulu.

"Now I really *can't* quit," said Pansy, sounding a little bitter. "I missed so much school by attending pageants that I fell behind and never really got caught up. What I want to do the most is become an actress. I have a shot at it, too—I've had acting classes, I can sing pretty well, and I can act. But the performing-arts college that I want to go to is pretty expensive . . . and I've booted myself out of the running for an academic scholarship. So now all I can count on are some pageant scholarships."

Lulu said, "Your mama was telling me a while back that she thought you were totally cheated out of the Miss Memphis crown. She was upset because that was supposed to have some great scholarships."

"Not only that, but then I would have been able to be in the Miss Tennessee pageant. If I'd won *that*, then I could have gotten *those* scholarships. Then, of course, is Miss America. And this is all much bigger money. Without this pageant money, I don't have a hope in . . ." she edited herself, looking over at Coco, "I don't have a hope to go to that school."

"She said it was Tristan who was responsible."

"Tristan ruined my dress and stole my shoes. She was bound and determined that the girl she was coaching won the pageant. And she did! As soon as I was out of the running, her girl was the clear choice to win Miss Memphis. And she knew it. Tristan was right there backstage, and my hanging bag and shoes were right next to her girl's stuff. She had plenty of time to mess with it while I was onstage for the casual-wear part of the competition." Pansy stopped putting makeup on and looked at herself broodingly in the mirror.

"Granny Lulu, can I have some quarters for the drink machine?" asked Coco in a pleading voice. Lulu fished around in her pocketbook for some loose change, grateful for the chance to ask some questions about the murder without having Coco listen in.

Lulu cleared her throat. "I didn't know Tristan very well, but it sounds like she was the kind of person who made a lot of enemies. Do you have any idea who might have done her in?"

Pansy shrugged a thin shoulder. "Plenty of people. Everybody was always talking about her—even the girls she coached. She was just a mean person. She was always nosing around for dirt on pageant people . . . and there were lots of pageant people at the party. So I heard, anyway," she finished quickly.

"Pansy, were you actually at the party that night? I have to ask because somebody I know was sure she saw you. But I didn't think you or your mother were there."

Pansy flushed and looked around Lulu real quick to make sure no one was close enough to listen in. "Mother doesn't want anyone to know we were there," she said in a hushed voice. "I did go—I was furious with Tristan, and Steffi had told me she was having a party. Tristan had been treating Steffi like a dog again, and I was sick of it. I wrote something on my Facebook page about Tristan, and I guess one of her girls told her about it. So she called me up and was insulting me and my mom—said I couldn't act and I wasn't pretty enough to win pageants and I was wasting my and my mom's time. And she was planning to block me from any pageant wins she could."

Pansy shrugged. "I really just went there to bug her. I wanted to see if she was going to throw me out or not—if I could force her to make a big scene at her fancy party. But then Mother showed up pretty fast, yelled at me for being there, and I took off for the house to see if I could at least show my face to make Tristan mad. Mother wouldn't even go in, so she waited for me outside. I wasn't in there long because I didn't see Tristan. Mother was furious with me—she hated Tristan as much as I did, but she always said we couldn't confront her or else she'd be sure to slam me if she was judging one of my competitions."

"What I don't understand," said Lulu, "is how Tristan could be a coach *and* a judge. That's a huge conflict of interest."

"She only judged when she didn't have a girl in the pageant. But she'd hold a grudge against certain girls, so it still wasn't fair. She wasn't impartial." Pansy started putting another layer of mascara on her eyelashes. "And Steffi says she cheated, too, by getting information from Dee Dee on what the other girls were doing."

Lulu said, "So you think pageant people at the party might have been upset enough with Tristan to kill her."

Pansy shrugged again. "It's possible. Plus, Dee Dee was there. I don't think she liked Tristan much. But you know who else I saw before Mother pulled me out? That guy Loren and his wife, Pepper." She paused with the mascara application and looked seriously at Lulu.

"And they would have wanted to kill her?"

"There's this whole crazy history with them. Loren is

creepy. I guess Pepper was there trying to keep an eye on her husband." Pansy saw Coco walking up with her drink, and she said quickly, "Ask my mom about it. She can tell you."

"Pansy?" asked Coco. "Can you help me with my dress? I always have trouble tying my sash."

"Sure, sweetie," said Pansy. And she and Coco walked off to a changing area with hanging bags everywhere.

"Psst!"

Lulu looked around, bewildered. Then she heard it again and saw that a young teenager, probably only fourteen, was trying to quietly get her attention.

Lulu pretended to be studying Coco's bag very closely, since stealth seemed to be in order. "Is there something you wanted to tell me?" she asked, without looking in the girl's direction.

The girl, very thin and blond, said quietly, "I heard what Pansy was telling you, and it's a bunch of hooey. Tristan didn't have anything to do with Pansy's dress being ruined and her shoes missing. I was at that pageant with my cousin and was hanging out backstage. I saw Pansy mess up her own dress with the lipstick. I guess she did the same thing with her shoes, too."

"*Pansy* did it?" Lulu's voice rose with surprise, and she spoke more quietly. "Why would Pansy do something like that? It messed up her chances to win the Miss Memphis pageant and to get that scholarship money she was looking for."

The girl said in a derisive voice, "Pansy wasn't going to win that crown. She's not that good! Not that pretty, even, compared to the other girls. She was hoping the judges would feel sorry for her or think she was being really brave by going out there with a ruined dress and borrowed shoes that didn't fit and *give* her the crown." She snorted. "She knew she was going to lose, so she decided to go for the pity votes."

"Did her mother know about this?" asked Lulu, looking to make sure that Pansy was still totally focused on tying Coco's sash.

"I don't know. Probably not, though. Pansy's mom wouldn't understand why she'd do something like that, since she thinks Pansy is perfect."

Suddenly, the girl snapped her mouth shut and started curling her hair with a curling iron with intense concentration. Lulu turned to see Pansy and Coco walking over and Cherry coming over to join both of them.

"Pansy? Just who I wanted to see!" said Cherry, with a big smile. "Your mama said you can give me the scoop on coaching and pageants and everything else I needed to know about."

"Cherry is planning to become a pageant coach," explained Lulu. Pansy must have thought this explanation was just as confusing because her brow stayed wrinkled.

"And Coco, maybe you can show me what you need me to do to get you all prepped. That's something else I need to learn about," said Cherry. Coco looked troubled that this process needed any kind of explanation.

"I'll slip back out to the audience so I won't be underfoot back here," said Lulu. "Good luck learning the ropes!"

"Thanks!" said Cherry. But Lulu thought her perky smile looked like it was starting to fade.

Colleen was a fidgety mess, decided Lulu. She couldn't seem to sit still. She'd perch on the edge of her seat, then she'd jump up and talk to someone, then she'd sit down again and start texting on her phone. She looked like she wanted desperately to be backstage instead of sitting with Lulu.

"We nearly had a disaster of momentous proportions while you were backstage," said Colleen. "Imagine if you had gone out in this nasty weather to the middle of no-where and the girls had gotten all dressed up and excited and there wasn't a pageant! One of our judges fell sud-denly ill and called to say she couldn't make it. Now, or-dinarily, that would mean we'd have to cancel the event unless we could scrounge up some last-minute judge from the town. But your friend Gordon, God bless him, was happy to step in."

"Gordon? Gordon knows how to judge a beauty con-test?"

"Well, no, of course he doesn't. But he's getting a crash course right now in it. Another emergency diverted. By the skin of my teeth." She frowned a minute and looked at Lulu as if trying to gauge if she might be upset that her friend had been drafted into service. "By the way, he's happy as a clam right now. Once he'd saved the day, all the moms were stuffing plates of food into his hand—probably trying to butter him up. So he's eating Sharon's chili and Cindy's pineapple and pork chops—and there's someone's chicken soup that he's raving about. He sure seems like a nice guy." She hesitated. "Are y'all . . . seeing each other?"

"Not a bit. I'm just showing him around Memphis, since he's new to town." She was a little worried about the chicken soup, though. That was supposed to be Lulu's and Coco's lunch. She hoped he wasn't cleaning out the Crock-Pot because all this investigating was getting Lulu hungry.

Colleen was still jittery and glancing nervously at the stage area, where they were messing with lighting and the sound system. "Don't you want to go back there?" asked Lulu. "Just to check and see how everything is going?"

"Honey, I'd love to, but Pansy has practically banned me from going backstage lately. Says that I act too much like a stage mom. Ha! I'm not nearly as bad as some of these moms," she said, leaning in real close to Lulu. "They'd walk right out there on stage with their girls if they could. You look in their purses, and all you'll see are extra sets of fake eyelashes and padding and tape. All they *think* about is their girls. I'm not quite that bad, but I make Pansy nervous, she says, so I'm trying to stay busy out here."

She sure didn't look busy to Lulu, but at least she wasn't running backstage.

"How did Pansy seem?" she asked Lulu anxiously. "Did she act like she had bad nerves?"

"Not at all," said Lulu. "In fact, she was doing a great job helping Coco get ready on top of getting herself ready. And she was even telling me all kinds of entertaining stories about pageant life."

Colleen gave a nervous laugh. "Oh, there's always a bunch of stories. I already told you what was going on with Pansy and Tristan, and that's just part of it."

"She also told me to ask you about Loren and Pepper. I didn't even know that y'all would know them at all. . . . I know Pepper a little bit through Cherry."

"Oh, Cherry knows them?" Colleen rolled her eyes.

"Cherry is their neighbor," said Lulu. "She and Pepper were trying to get into the Memphis Women's League—but apparently Tristan had blocked them from being able to join."

Colleen snorted. "Probably because Tristan thought

they weren't good enough to join her club. I'll have to ask Cherry what she thinks about Pepper and Loren, especially living next door to them. Because the impression that I got is that they're totally crazy. Well, I shouldn't say that—I don't know Pepper. But if she knows about the running around he's doing on her and she's *staying* with him, then she's crazy, too."

"I'm gathering that Loren and Tristan were an item?" asked Lulu.

"Or something." Colleen gave a shrill laugh. "All I know is that one day Loren showed up for a pageant and tried talking to Tristan. She totally blew him off, and he left, completely dejected."

"You knew that they were having a romantic relationship? It wasn't just business somehow? I've heard his accounting firm handled the books at her company."

Colleen said, "It was hard to tell what was going on that first time, although everybody here was talking about it and trying to figure it all out. But he came *back* to the next pageant. And that time I could overhear what he was saying. He was complaining because she wasn't taking his calls or coming to her door when he rang her doorbell."

Lulu shook her head. "Mercy! And what did Tristan say to him?"

Colleen looked gratified to have such a rapt audience and warmed to her topic. "Lulu, she was an ice queen. Really, she didn't even answer him. Didn't even acknowledge that he was there at all! She just walked away."

Lulu felt a little disappointed that there hadn't been any more drama than that, and Colleen hurried to add, "But then he came back *again*. And that time he cried. It seemed like it made an impression on Tristan—because even though she was still trying to ignore him, I saw them later making up in the parking lot. In Tristan's car."

Lulu blinked. "Oh my."

"But then I guess she went right back to not taking his calls and ignoring him. So he came by another time and read some really bad poetry to Tristan—all the girls were laughing. It really was ghastly." Lulu noticed that Colleen couldn't hide a smirk, though. "So *this* time Tristan pulled him a little ways away from everybody to really let him have it."

"Too bad she pulled him away from everybody," said Lulu sadly.

"Oh, honey, I couldn't *help* but overhear," said Colleen in a triumphant voice. "Tristan said she was sick of him showing up at pageants, and she thought she was becoming the butt of a lot of jokes. And she threatened to tell his wife about the two of them! I thought that was really a stroke of genius on her part. Of course, he said that Tristan didn't even know his wife, and she said she *did*—because Pepper was dying to join Tristan's club. So then he said he *still* didn't care. He didn't even care if Pepper knew or not—all he cared about was being with Tristan. Which is crazy right there, because nobody even *likes* Tristan! He got even crazier when he said that he was going to kill himself or even both of them if she didn't take him back."

Lulu drew a quick breath. "What did she say to that?"

"Tristan was as cold as ever. She said he was free to kill himself if that's what he wanted to do, although she figured he was being melodramatic. She was all scornful and said that *she* wasn't going to be a victim, but he could victimize himself if he wanted to. So maybe he did kill her. Or maybe Pepper killed Tristan, for revenge. Although why she'd

want that cheating husband is beyond me." Colleen rolled
her eyes.

"So it might have just been this love-triangle murder,"
said Lulu thoughtfully.

"Do we even really care who killed her?" asked Colleen. "Honestly, the world is a much better place without
Tristan Pembroke in it. At least poor Steffi isn't undergoing
daily persecution from her mother anymore. I mean, Steffi
was a huge disappointment to her mom, and Tristan sure
let her know it."

Lulu felt another wave of sympathy for Steffi. "Not that
she could help it, poor thing."

"But she *could* help who she hung out with. When she
started dating their yardman, I thought Tristan was going to
go through the roof! I mean, if Tristan was going to be picky
about Pepper getting into her women's club, what was she
going to think about her daughter dating the yard guy?"

Lulu had a feeling Tristan wouldn't have thought much
of the idea. Maybe that's what the final argument was
about—the one that resulted in Steffi moving out.


Coco, thought Lulu, was cute as a bug during
the competition and had even placed and gotten a sash.
Pansy, on the other hand, had definitely had an off day. Tina
was making all kinds of profane grumblings from next to
Lulu as Pansy came out on stage. And she certainly *had*
acted like a crown was already on her head—but she kept
her head so high that she tripped over her own gown and
caught herself right before she hit the floor.

She made the unfortunate choice of a leopard-print
dress ("I didn't even know that horrid thing was in her

hanging bag!" said Tina), and when the pageant director conducted Pansy's interview, Pansy's portion was full of perplexed looks, mumbles, and uhs.

As the division winner smiled through her tears, Lulu wondered if maybe Pansy *had* sabotaged her own dress. Because, as little as Lulu knew about pageants, Pansy sure didn't seem like much of a contender.

## Chapter 14

The next day, Lulu was in the Aunt Pat's back office when Sara stuck her head in the door. "Guess who's here again?"

"Who?" asked Lulu.

"Loren Holman. I have a feeling he's looking for me or Steffi about that portrait again. And I can't even look at him the same way again after all you told me about him yesterday when you dropped Coco back home."

Lulu sighed. "Well, I think he's a very sad, sad man. If you think about it, it's a tragedy. He finally found true love—with someone who didn't love him back. To make matters worse, now he can't even worship her from afar. *And* she had a violent death, which makes it even harder for him to have any kind of closure. No, he shouldn't have been cheating on his wife. And he shouldn't have been practically stalking Tristan. And he really went off his rocker when he threatened to kill Tristan and himself. But still—there's something kind of pitiful about him."

"Do you think he could have gone through with his threat and murdered Tristan?"

Lulu tilted her head to think about it. "I don't know. I guess, in his state of mind, he could have done it—but he sure seems to regret it now, if that's what happened."

Sara leaned back out of the office to check the restaurant. "He's just standing there. I guess I'm going to have to go out and talk to him. Want to come along? I can't handle any melodrama today."

"Sure, honey, I'll join you. Maybe he'll want to talk to Steffi, too. She came to work thirty minutes ago, if you want to grab her. Let's have him sit in a booth with us. I really don't want him making a scene standing in the middle of the restaurant."

As expected, Loren was in a state. He had beads of perspiration on his forehead as he asked Sara, "Has the portrait turned up? The one of Tristan?"

As if he'd be interested in any other portrait, thought Lulu.

Sara said, "Loren, I'm sorry, but I don't have any clue where that painting is. Steffi, has it turned up at all in your mom's house?"

Steffi shook her head. "No, I haven't seen it. I looked for it before I went through some of Mother's things. But I couldn't find it anywhere. I'm thinking that it's not at the house at all."

"How could it have left the house?" asked Lulu. "It was a big painting. Seems like someone would have seen someone leaving with it."

Sara said, "But if you think about it, lots of people were leaving with big paintings. After the auction, some of the folks went ahead and put the paintings in their car and went back to the party. Some of them ended up having to collect theirs later on, but there were still plenty of people who took their paintings out early."

Loren rubbed his palms across his red eyes. Lulu didn't think she'd seen anybody look so tired or dejected.

Steffi said quickly, "Loren, maybe Marlowe has seen the portrait—she's taken the day off from work to help with Mother's things. We could call and ask her."

Loren gave her a grateful look and then wiped a hand across his face again. "Y'all must think that I'm totally nuts. Who knows—maybe I am. My whole life is falling apart around me. Pepper has kicked me out of the house because I can't put Tristan out of my mind . . . even though she's dead." His voice was so quiet that they had to lean forward to hear him.

"Where are you staying now?" asked Lulu with concern.

"I'm staying at a hotel for a little while until I can find a place." He sat still for a moment. "I can't blame Pepper. She's got to be hurting pretty bad right now. But I just can't seem to help myself." His voice cracked on the last words.

Steffi leaned forward and impulsively squeezed his hand. "Why don't you come over and have supper tonight with Marlowe and me? Then you can ask her about the portrait. And, if that's missing, I'm sure we've got a couple of photographs of Mother that you're welcome to take home with you."

Loren's face brightened. "Steffi, I'd love to come. What time should I be there?"

"Well, I'm leaving Aunt Pat's around six o'clock, since I'm only working a half day. So maybe six thirty? I know Marlowe is going to be starving after spending the day working in Mother's house. And Lulu, why don't you come, too?" Steffi offered. "I never really got a chance to thank you for putting me up for a few days and for giving me the time off I needed."

"Only if I can bring some food," said Lulu. "Because no thank-yous are necessary—you're my friend. But if I can bring supper, I'm happy to come. And I've got all the ingredients for a chicken pot pie right here at the restaurant." Steffi looked like she was going to demur, and Lulu said, "Otherwise you're going to have to cook as soon as you get home, or else Marlowe is going to have to. And I'm right here with an industrial kitchen at my disposal."

"And Lulu cooks really well," said Loren, looking at Steffi persuasively.

"In that case," said Steffi with a shrug, "how can I refuse?"

Lulu knew that Marlowe and Steffi still had a ton of Dolly-approved casseroles in their freezer, from after the funeral. But there was nothing quite like a freshly baked chicken pot pie.


Loren appeared to have made an attempt to look a little bit nicer. He looked showered and better dressed than he'd been earlier at Aunt Pat's. Best of all was that he didn't look like he'd been crying or was about to cry.

At least, he didn't until Marlowe walked in the door from having spent the day at Tristan's. Lulu hadn't thought until that moment how much the sisters had looked alike. And Loren obviously hadn't thought of it either—his face looked blank with shock when he saw Marlowe, then he clearly struggled to keep from tearing up again. Lulu guessed that when he'd seen Marlowe briefly at Tristan's funeral, his eyes had been too full of tears to see Marlowe all that clearly.

Marlowe greeted Loren but looked too distracted to really notice how emotional he was. "Steffi, I brought some pictures back from the house. . . . You said Loren wanted a couple? The portrait never made an appearance." She put down the pictures of a smiling, carefully posed Tristan on the table. "We have *lots* of pictures of Tristan," Marlowe added dryly. "She sure didn't mind having her picture taken." She looked a little grouchy. "And not a bad picture in the bunch."

"Oh, Mother didn't believe in having bad pictures taken," said Steffi breezily. "That was my job. But I *do* remember seeing one or two not-so-great pictures of her . . . for about two seconds. That's how long it would be before those pictures were torn up and put in the trash can."

Loren smiled a little. "Thanks so much for the pictures, Marlowe. I appreciate it."

"Seriously, you can have as many as you like. I don't know what Steffi and I will do with them all. I've put them in a big box for now, and I guess we'll decide about them later." Marlowe shrugged. Lulu noticed that she wasn't trying to act as if she were bereaved at all—she had no problem showing her dislike for Tristan.

It seemed to make Steffi uncomfortable, though, and Lulu remembered how guilty Steffi had felt that morning after Tristan's death. It was only natural that a daughter would feel that way, after all. Steffi said quickly, "Lulu, thanks again for bringing supper to us."

"It smells amazing," said Marlowe, her expression brightening.

"I wouldn't ordinarily ask somebody to supper, though,

and then make her bring it with her." Steffi looked a little abashed.

"Pooh. I insisted on bringing it, remember? And everyone can tell you that I'm very stubborn when I make up my mind to be. It's ready whenever y'all are—I just put it in the oven to keep it warm."

It turned out that they were all ravenous, so it was a good thing that Lulu had made such a large pie and brought side dishes of spicy corn muffins and coleslaw from the restaurant. Otherwise, there wouldn't have been enough food to go around. As it was, Lulu skimped on her own plate to make sure everyone got a big helping. Loren ate like he hadn't had anything in his stomach for days (and maybe he hadn't), Marlowe was wolfing down food like all the work at her sister's house had given her a huge appetite, and even Steffi was plowing in instead of pushing it around on her plate like she usually did.

Loren's mood seemed to change after supper was over, though, and he seemed more reflective. He picked up one of Tristan's pictures and looked at it broodingly. "I just can't believe she's gone."

Steffi and Marlowe gave each other an uncomfortable look. Marlowe said, "Sudden deaths are always like that, aren't they? But things always get better with time."

Loren shook his head with frustration. "But this was a totally unnatural death. It wasn't her time to go. I wish I knew who did it." He put the photograph carefully back down on the table. "You know who was there that night? That girl who was always picking at Tristan. Tristan was always talking about her. And her mother was there, too."

Steffi laughed. "Oh no. Mother would never invite Pansy or her mom to one of her parties. You must have seen one of the girls Mother coached and gotten her mixed up."

"No, I'm positive it was that girl. She stood out to me because she was in such a bad mood—not like someone at a party. I wasn't in a party mood myself, but she really looked like she was there to pick a fight. I thought that maybe I should stick around so I could jump in and rescue Tristan if the girl started making any trouble." He looked sadly down at the photograph again. "I had no idea how much rescuing Tristan was going to need."

Steffi said quietly, "I didn't even know that you were at the party that night until somebody mentioned it later. I think I was in my own fog."

"And there were so many people there," added Loren. "One of them killed Tristan. I bet it was that girl. Those girls acted like these pageants were life and death or something."

Lulu felt like they were all going in circles with the same information. She needed to do something to make things lively again and get some fresh information. Maybe if she could get everyone in the same spot again . . . and get them interacting with each other. She knew people were hiding information from her—and she needed a chance for them to lower their guard and start spilling their secrets.

Food was always what jumped into Lulu's head first— gathering around food was what she'd done her whole life. So maybe a party. Although wouldn't that sound like an odd thing to have, under the circumstances? Then it came to her.

"Steffi, this is a good time to tell you that I'm in the *early* stages of planning a special night at the restaurant . . . a fund-raiser. Seeing as how you're part of our Aunt Pat's family, we really wanted to do something to help you out. I thought I'd hold a fund-raiser for you—just as sort of an investment in your future, you know. The net profits from that night would go to you. We'll have food, and I can get the Back Porch Blues Band to play. And I'll get the word out—put flyers around the restaurant and in the menus."

Marlowe said warmly as Steffi teared up, "Lulu, that's so incredibly sweet. I'll help spread the word on my end, too." She hesitated a moment, glancing at Loren, but then added, "I don't know if you know this, but we've been finding out over the last couple of days that Tristan's estate was not in good shape."

Steffi gulped down her tears. "Mother was swimming in debt from living a lifestyle that she couldn't afford. I never knew. We always seemed to have plenty of money. Marlowe told me that Mother drove Grandfather's business into the ground, too, pulling money out of the business account to use for her personal stuff."

"Reality was coming crashing in on Tristan," said Marlowe in a brusque voice. "She wasn't going to be able to maintain her standard of living for much longer before the debt collectors came calling. It's unfair that Steffi . . . and I . . . have to pay the price. My father's business was really Tristan's and my only inheritance. It was what I was planning to retire on. And now it's on the brink of collapse, and I don't know if I can resuscitate it or not." An angry flush crept up Marlowe's neck. "Plus, Tristan's house is mortgaged to the hilt. We'll have to quickly put it on the market and auction off a lot of the contents. It's going to be a lot of work."

"I wish she'd told me her problems," said Loren wistfully. "I could have helped her."

Loren couldn't even help *himself*, thought Lulu. He was living in a Tristan-themed fantasy world. Lulu couldn't imagine that Pepper would have happily let Loren hand their money over (what little they had of it themselves) to Tristan Pembroke.

Loren added, "Well, I'm definitely coming to the benefit, Lulu. I want to help out, and besides, you've got the best barbeque in town. It'll be a pleasure."

"I don't know how to thank you," said Steffi shyly. "This is really going to help me get back on track." She turned and smiled at Marlowe. "Marlowe has been helping me, too, just kind of mentoring me to figure out what direction I should go in."

Steffi paused, and Marlowe prompted her, "Go ahead, Steffi. Now's a good time to ask Lulu about your hours."

Steffi colored. "Well, I hate to ask you now, when you're being so great about this fund-raiser. But when I was talking to Marlowe about my future, especially now that we found out that Mother had all these financial problems I've got to take on, we started talking about me going to college. The only thing is that my grades weren't so hot in high school. With everything going on with my mom and our relationship, I didn't put a lot of time into studying like I should have. Marlowe was thinking that I could start with a community college, and then, if my grades are good enough, I could transfer to a big school."

"So maybe she could just work nights at Aunt Pat's," said Marlowe, getting to the point. "That way she could go to classes in the morning, study in the afternoon, and work at the restaurant at night. She wants to make enough to move to a one-bedroom apartment."

"That's a fantastic idea!" said Lulu, beaming at them. "We can work your hours out around your schoolwork—that's no problem."

"Steffi, you might even be able to work in a little bit of a social life . . . with a certain someone," Marlowe teased.

Lulu saw Steffi's blush grow. "Maybe," she said, so quietly they could barely hear her.

Lulu said quickly, "It all sounds like a wonderful plan, Steffi. I know you're so glad to have Marlowe here to help you figure this all out. And I'll let you know all the final plans for the benefit when they come together. I'm planning on it being a really fun event. We'll make it a night to remember!"

Luckily, thought Lulu, she had plenty of experience in pulling events off at a moment's notice. Years of catering political fund-raisers, family reunions, corporate luncheons, anniversary parties, and football tailgates had given her the ability to plan and implement a party in no time at all.

This one was going to be especially easy. For one thing, it was going to be held on-site at Aunt Pat's, with their industrial kitchen right there. For another, she decided to make it a buffet. That way they wouldn't have to worry about cooking a large number of different dishes. Instead it would be a simple menu of pulled pork, grilled corn on the cob, baked beans, coleslaw, and corn muffins. Tea—sweet, unsweetened, and half and half—would be out in pitchers, and they'd have cobbler and banana pudding for dessert.

Buddy, Morty, and Big Ben marked the date on their calendars and volunteered to play for free. Ben made up some flyers, and the twins clipped a flyer onto every menu and on the doors and walls. And Derrick had put it all up on the website and Twitter and all that stuff that Lulu tried to keep away from. Ben, naturally, had been sure to let Gordon MacDonald know about the fund-raiser, too. While Aunt Pat's wouldn't be *making* any money from the evening, Lulu was actually feeling really good about what they were doing to help Steffi. Yes, it had started out as a scheme to get everybody in the same place again and see what kind of information she could get—but she also liked the idea of giving Steffi a little help.

Lulu's cell phone rang while she was in the Aunt Pat's office, and she answered it once she saw it was Dee Dee on the line. "Lulu? I just wanted to call you real quick and tell you that I got a new shipment into the store that I think you'll really like. Actually, I ordered it with you in mind," said Dee Dee in her croaky voice.

Lulu frowned. This case was starting to get really expensive. Every time she needed to talk to Dee Dee, it seemed like she ended up spending money. "I sure do appreciate that, honey, but is there anything else I really *need*? You know I bought a mess of dresses from you just a couple of weeks ago."

"But you haven't gotten any sweaters from me for a long time, and I was thinking they might be really useful for you to take your wardrobe into fall."

Lulu made a face. It was hard to even envision fall when it was still in the upper nineties in Memphis. She knew that fall was going to *come* . . . eventually. But it just wasn't something she was excited thinking about right now. Still, though, it would be another opportunity to talk to Dee Dee—and Dee Dee seemed to know everything about everybody. "Okay, you've got me interested," she said, biting back a sigh. "Maybe I can come in at the end of the week?"

"That sounds good. I've got them set aside for you. And no pressure, of course . . . you know me." On the contrary, thought Lulu. Dee Dee was actually a really good salesperson. And usually good salespeople knew how to pressure you.

"Oh, while I've got you on the phone," said Lulu quickly, realizing she'd forgotten to tell Dee Dee about the event for

Steffi, "I wanted to invite you to come out to the benefit Aunt Pat's is having for Steffi."

Dee Dee sounded surprised. "For Steffi?"

"Yes, the poor lamb. We thought her mother was doing so well, but come to find out she didn't have two pennies to rub together. So I'm trying to help her out at the restaurant, since she's part of the Aunt Pat's family. We're going to have a barbeque buffet and band and the profits from the night are going to Steffi to help her out with her education."

Dee Dee was quiet for a moment on the phone. "That's a real shock, Lulu. I thought that Tristan was doing great. She was always spending money all over the place."

Including, thought Lulu, in Dee Dee's shop, buying information. "Well, that's what we've just found out. I guess Tristan was spending it; she just wasn't *making* it. So we're trying to make a little money for Steffi. She's got a real plan now, and I'm so glad because she seemed so lost. She and Marlowe have been talking about Steffi's future and decided that it would be best for her to start at a community college and work at the restaurant in the evenings. She's even got a young man, apparently."

Dee Dee gave her rasping, cigarette-hoarsened laugh. "He's a young *something*. Young rascal, maybe."

"What?" Lulu meant that she didn't understand, but Dee Dee apparently took it as a cue to speak louder for Lulu's "hearing impairment." Lulu winced as Dee Dee's grating voice came through the phone even louder. She held the cell phone away from her face.

"He's a *rascal*!" She bellowed. "He's Tristan's yardman. And he's *my* yardman, too—that's how he ended up with the gig at Tristan's to begin with. He has the scruples of an alley cat, and all he cares about is money. He'd leave my yard high and dry if someone offered him a nickel more to cut theirs."

Lulu clucked. "So he's not a very loyal young man."

"He's a scamp! And that's not the worst of it. I saw him with my own eyes making out with Tristan one day. My own eyes!" Dee Dee sounded like she'd wanted to go home and rinse those eyes out with drops to cleanse them. It was pretty disingenuous of her to think this way, thought Lulu, considering she'd walked on the seamy side herself with blackmail and using her store to sell insider information on pageant contestants.

Lulu clucked. "Such a pity! So he and Tristan were having a relationship?"

Dee Dee said, "Honey, there was no relationship involved. I know you've led a sheltered life, but this was just a fling. I think Tristan wanted to hurt Steffi for going out with the guy to begin with. You know it must have made Tristan absolutely furious when she told her mother she was dating the yardman. All Tristan cared about was appearances, you know—how she looked, how her life looked."

"And it sounds like how her life looked was simply an illusion," said Lulu in a sad voice. "None of it was even true." Then she said briskly, "But young people seem like they can move ahead so much easier than us old folks. I'm sure this is water under the bridge for Steffi and this young man. I wanted to try to invite everyone that Steffi and Marlowe might know so they wouldn't be put in the position of asking their own friends to come and pay money at a fundraiser for Steffi, so I'll try to track this fellow down."

"No need to track him down, Lulu. Like I said, he's my yard guy. His name is David, and he mows Tristan's grass on Thursday mornings at ten—right before he comes to my house. So you can find him either place. And I'll be sure to make it to the benefit—of course I want to help poor Steffi out. Who all are you inviting?"

Lulu smiled. Dee Dee couldn't resist going anywhere where she might have a chance to do some wheeling and dealing. "Well, like I mentioned, I'm trying to reach out to all of Steffi's and Marlowe's friends. And Loren said he'd be there when I talked to him—Steffi seems like she's befriended him out of pity. And I know Colleen and Pansy will be there, since Steffi is one of Pansy's best friends from when they were little. Pink will be there. And of course all the Graces. I'm advertising it a lot, too, so I'm planning on a crowd."

"Lulu, I wouldn't miss it for the world."

Chapter
15

Thursday morning, Lulu parked her car at the end of Tristan Pembroke's long driveway and listened for the sound of the lawn mower. Sure enough, she heard a faint hum from the back of the house. Lulu stepped out of the car, straightened her dress, and started the trek to the backyard. What a shame, she thought, that Steffi was going to have to sell this beautiful place. If she *could* sell it.

When Lulu reached the backyard, she saw a young man about Steffi's age on a commercial riding mower. He had black sunglasses on, the reflecting kind. He'd somehow, thought Lulu, wrinkling her forehead, forgotten to put a shirt on. Lulu had a feeling that could be a favorite look for him because it showed off his muscled chest. And it was definitely muscled.

He was steering the mower in a curve when he saw Lulu and abruptly stopped the machine and turned it off. Lulu said, "I'm sorry—David, isn't it? I didn't mean to interrupt you."

He strode over to a wrought-iron table where the missing tee shirt was located, picked up the shirt, and swabbed his face and neck with it. "Sure you did. Otherwise, what would you be doing back here? You're not exactly on the beaten path." He snorted. "I'm not even sure what *I'm* doing back here. Tristan's dead, and who knows if I'm even going to get paid for cutting the grass or not."

"Yes, it's such a *tragedy* isn't it?" Lulu said with a hint of reproof in her voice. "I can hardly believe Tristan is gone."

"Me either!" he said, reaching down for a water bottle and taking a few healthy gulps.

"That's what I'm here to talk to you about," said Lulu.

He looked suspiciously at her now. "You with the cops? I already told them that I was just Tristan's handyman and yardman."

"Were you at the party that night?" asked Lulu. "There were so many guests there that I wouldn't remember you if I'd seen you, I'm sure."

He gave a short nod. "I was there. Not for long, though—not my kind of gig. I wasn't invited, but I showed up, underdressed, I guess. Everybody was snooty, and I didn't care jack about the art stuff. Steffi was all over me like a puppy dog or something. And Tristan was mad about seeing me there, so she asked me to leave." He shrugged. "So I cut out of there."

"Just like that? No hard feelings or anything?" asked Lulu.

"Not at all. I was more worried about keeping my job than anything else. Not worth losing a paying customer over." Lulu remembered Dee Dee's words about David's interest in money.

"You were saying you were only Tristan's yardman and handyman, but you were more than that, right? I heard you'd been seeing both Tristan and Steffi. And you said Steffi was like a puppy dog that night? So on the night Tristan was killed, you were back with Steffi?"

His dark brows drew together in a frown. "Now *who* did you say you were again? With the cops?" But once again he didn't give Lulu time to answer. "I already went through this all a million times with you people." He threw the shirt back at the table. "Steffi and I had been out with each other and then *Mrs.* Pembroke threw herself at *me* one day out of the blue. And I'm only human, ain't I?"

Lulu thought that was questionable but decided it would be prudent not to answer.

"So, when I thought I might have a chance with the lady of the manor, things sort of cooled between me and Steffi."

"On your side anyway," said Lulu dryly.

"That's right. Steffi didn't seem to get the message. And when Tristan kicked Steffi out of the house, I knew who was going to be the better Pembroke for me to be focusing my attention on."

Lulu felt a little nauseated at the idea of asking David to come to Aunt Pat's. What could Steffi see in him? Well, besides his obvious physical attributes. And maybe he was charming enough when he wasn't being honest. She bet he was a really talented liar.

"Except it didn't end up that way, did it?" asked Lulu with a forced sweetness.

David acted like his Machiavellian talents were being maligned. "Well, I couldn't have been expected to know that she was going to *die*," he said. "I mean, she was an older lady, but she wasn't old enough to *die*."

"So then you started going out with Steffi again after Tristan was murdered."

"That's right. She and I picked right back up where we'd left off. *Who* are you again?"

There was a small voice behind them that said, "She's Lulu Taylor. She owns Aunt Pat's Barbeque restaurant."

Lulu could see that David was trying to figure out how much Steffi had heard of their conversation. His face suddenly lit up, and he flashed a charismatic smile, and Lulu knew he'd decided to go with hoping she'd heard nothing of the conversation. "Hey there, cute thing! Are you getting along okay? I've been so worried about you." He reached out his arms and Steffi melted into them.

His eyes were piercing as he looked at Lulu over Steffi's head. "A barbeque restaurant? That's very interesting. She was interested in talking with me about the yard work. . . . Isn't that right, ma'am?"

Lulu wasn't in the mood to help him out. "Actually, no. I wanted to invite you over to the restaurant next week for the benefit I'm doing for Steffi. Since you're her friend, I thought you'd want to come, and I didn't want Steffi to have to bother with inviting people over."

David gave a short laugh. "Benefit? Like Steffi is even worried about money now."

Steffi turned her head a little on David's chest and looked at Lulu with pleading eyes. She clearly didn't want her to say anything to David about her mother's poor financial situation. Lulu said mildly, "Well, no matter how much money you have, it always helps to have easily accessible money before the will is probated." Lulu wasn't sure that what she was saying really made any sense, but David seemed satisfied with it.

"In that case," he said, giving Steffi a kiss on the nose, "I'll be happy to be there."

It was a good thing that Ben was prepared and did a lot of cooking for the fund-raiser, because the word really got out—through old methods like church bulletin boards and a blurb in the paper, and new methods like Twitter and Facebook—that there was going to be a fundraising buffet at Aunt Pat's. And the dining room stayed packed the whole night.

Fortunately, Lulu had brought in some extra kitchen helpers and servers for the night. Even though it was a buffet, the food still had to be brought from the kitchen to the buffet line—and it needed to keep coming. Sara and the extra hands were doing a great job keeping up with demand, which kept Lulu from having to spend the evening in the kitchen—and gave her the chance to talk to all the folks who had come.

Buddy, Morty, and Big Ben were playing better than they ever had out on the restaurant's front porch. Lulu thought they got better with age. Feet were tapping, and food was disappearing, and money was coming in hand over fist.

Lulu walked around and greeted the guests for a while, then decided to stay back a little bit and spend some time watching to see what happened next. That was one thing she wished she'd had at Tristan's party—time to absorb her surroundings and watch the guests to see what they did.

She'd done a great job getting everyone to the restaurant. Pink was there—because he was *always* there at Aunt

Pat's. Colleen and Pansy were some of the first to arrive.
Then Loren came in, straightening his collar and looking
self-conscious. Dee Dee arrived and immediately started
talking loudly to Lulu about the clothes she wanted Lulu to
see at the store.

Dee Dee also tried to talk to Sara about something
(Lulu guessed it was about a pageant dress for Coco), but
Sara was so busy lugging food out of the kitchen that she
shook her head at her and hurried off to the kitchen. Marlowe and Steffi were both there, frequently talking to people who came up to give them condolences and ask how
they were doing. Steffi looked a little stressed, thought
Lulu, but that's probably because she wasn't used to being
the center of attention. David spent some time hanging out
with Steffi, but he quickly seemed uncomfortable and
stepped outside to smoke a lot.

There was also a lot of movement in and out of the
restaurant—from the food at the back table to the bar, where
the desserts and beverages were set out. And then there were
folks who went out to the front porch to listen to the band for
a while. Of course, there were also customers who came in
straight from off the street to listen to the band and have
some food—the benefit part meant nothing to them, but they
sure were interested in the buffet. Lulu had already put the
Graces on notice to rescue her if she looked like she couldn't
get away from Gordon. So far, they'd played interference
with a lot of charm. Gordon looked pleased as punch with all
the attention he was getting. With any luck, thought Lulu,
he'd end up smitten with one of them instead.

Cherry sidled up to Lulu. "Did you see who just came in?"

Lulu squinted across the crowded room. "No—who?"

"Pepper! She's come to make Loren feel uncomfortable . . . and I think she's doing a good job at it."

Sure enough, there was Pepper, keeping in Loren's line of sight at all times and glowering across the restaurant at him.

Lulu sighed. "Looks like their relationship is on the rocks. But who can blame her? He's spending even more time chasing Tristan now than he did when she was alive!"

Lulu felt a light touch on her arm and turned to see Ella Beth's pixie face looking up at her with concern. "Granny Lulu, have you seen Mama?"

"She's around, honey, but she's busy keeping the buffet table filled. What's wrong?"

"Coco is in the office, crying."

Lulu stood up. "Is she okay?"

"I don't know. I think her tummy hurts or something. That's why I came out to find somebody—I know Daddy is busy cooking."

Lulu hurried to investigate and found that Coco did have an upset stomach. Whether it had something to do with the empty bag of miniature chocolates she'd found in the kitchen and eaten on the sly was anyone's guess. Lulu suggested she spend a little time in the restroom right off the office, then called Sara's nephew, Derrick. "Hi, honey."

"Granny Lulu?" Derrick asked. "Did you need some more help at Aunt Pat's?"

"No, I think we're good with the kitchen staff, but I could use your help with something else. Could you come and pick Coco up and take her back to the house and sort of keep an eye on her? I'm afraid we're all too tied up here to take her back."

"Is she sick?" There was a little trepidation in the teenager's voice.

"Well, she might be. But I think it's just a matter of eating too much chocolate candy. Either way, she sure doesn't feel good. And could you give me a call if you think she's feeling worse or if she starts to really get sick?"

"Will do, Granny Lulu."

Lulu stayed with Coco until Derrick arrived to pick her up. She was relieved when Sara's seventeen-year-old nephew walked in the door. At least, she *guessed* it was Derrick—his bangs had gotten so long that you could hardly even see his face. Of course, though, he didn't really meld into a crowd . . . not with all his tattoos and piercings. He quickly collected Coco, and they left the restaurant.

Pink noticed a green-faced Coco leaving with Derrick. "Uh-oh. Is Coco feeling puny?"

Lulu sighed. "I'm afraid so. And I didn't even tell Sara and Ben about it because they're slammed right now, and I knew they couldn't get away." She scanned the room for a minute. "How is everything out here? Is the food coming out fast enough?"

"Seems to be," said Pink, patting his stomach with sat-isfaction. "And I think you can call the fund-raising part of it a success—Aunt Pat's has been jam-packed with folks."

Lulu was pleased to see that Gordon wasn't one of the guests jam-packing the restaurant. Although he'd come in for a little while, he'd quickly left when things got crowded. "Good," said Lulu with a sigh. "A successful evening is exactly what I was hoping for." She looked around the res-taurant to try to find her suspects, but there were so many people that she had a hard time placing them. Things sure weren't going according to plan, but that was so frequently the way, thought Lulu.

She decided to take advantage of the opportunity she had at hand—maybe Pink would have a little information. "Pink, I was wondering if you had any more updates on

Tristan's murder investigation." He raised his eyebrows at her as he chewed a corn muffin, and she said quickly, "Of course I know you can't talk a whole lot about it, but I was just wondering about *in general*."

"In general, it's been a real hard case to nail down. There was a big party going on, so there wasn't exactly a pristine crime scene."

Lulu frowned, "There wasn't a big party in Tristan's room, though!"

"Whoever was in Tristan's room had thought ahead, I guess, Lulu. They used gloves, and they'd swiped a heavy brass candlestick that was easily visible and available to anyone who walked into the living room."

"Wouldn't somebody have noticed a person walking around lugging a big candlestick?" Lulu gave a little shudder as she thought about Tristan's body.

"It might not be as obvious as you think. There were lots of people coming and going. Guests were carrying paintings and other artwork around. It could pretty easily be concealed in a bag. Unless someone was acting really suspiciously, maybe they wouldn't even notice it."

"No one saw anyone going in or out of Tristan's room?" asked Lulu curiously.

"Well, but that was a major thoroughfare for the party. Not her bedroom itself, but the guests walked past her bedroom to get to one of the bathrooms. Anyone could have dodged in there really quickly, pulled the candlestick out of a purse or from inside a suit jacket, and clubbed Tristan." Pink held his hands out in supplication. "You can see it's not as easy as it sounds."

"Pink, that Detective Freeman doesn't really think that Sara's involved, does he?" asked Lulu, feeling a little sick at the thought. "He sure seemed like he was suspicious of her that night."

Pink gave Lulu a reassuring smile. "Lulu, if he was sure she did it, she'd already be in jail. That tells me he has no evidence to show the crime had anything to do with Sara. He's just making educated guesses and seeing what happens when he stirs up the waters a little. Sometimes that's a good way to get a suspect to confess or to tell an inconsistent story . . . that kind of thing. But you don't have to worry about Sara, obviously—she's not a killer."

Pink suddenly frowned and stood up. "Lulu—Coco and Derrick are back. And Derrick looks as sick as Coco does."

Derrick did. He was pasty white and shaking. Coco looked even sicker than she had before as they walked across the restaurant toward them.

"Oh mercy! Pink, I should have told Sara and Ben about Coco feeling poorly. She looks even worse."

"Want me to dial a medic, Lulu?" Pink had his radio out.

"Hold up—let's see what Derrick has to say first."

When Derrick went directly up to Pink instead of his Granny Lulu, Lulu knew something must really be wrong. "Pink. I parked in the parking deck off the alley—you know, the big one? I saw . . ." He looked over at Coco, who looked sick and confused, and then looked at Lulu pleadingly.

"Coco," said Lulu briskly, "let's go back in the office and let you rest for a minute. And get your Mama."

Cherry had walked over, looking curiously at Derrick and Pink. "Cherry," said Lulu quickly, "can you take Coco to the office and grab Sara—Coco's feeling sick."

"Sure thing. Let's get your mom, kiddo." Cherry bustled Coco off to the back of the restaurant.

Derrick gulped and then took a deep breath. "When I was unlocking the car door for Coco, I looked over and I saw something lying on the floor of the parking deck, in between a couple of cars. It was a dead woman."

Chapter 16

Pink radioed in for backup while Lulu took Derrick to the kitchen and gave him some brownies and iced tea and stayed with him while they waited for Pink to come back. Derrick really wanted to drive back home, but Lulu said, "Sweetie, they're going to have that parking deck totally sealed off until they have all the information they need. I'm sorry—we might be stuck here for a little while. I think that's probably where most of the people at the restaurant parked, too. . . . It's the closest deck to Aunt Pat's."

Derrick's face, which so often wore a tough expression, looked especially young and vulnerable. He rubbed his eyes, and Lulu realized how tired he was, too. "It was pretty bad," he said. "I mean, I didn't take a really long look because I didn't want Coco to notice what I was looking at."

Ben had stopped cooking for a moment to listen to Derrick. "What is this world coming to?" he asked, shaking his head. "Did it look like the woman had been mugged or something? Was there an empty purse nearby?" He rubbed the side of his face in agitation. "See, Mother, this is why I don't like you walking out of the restaurant by yourself at night." Lulu could tell he was still thinking happy thoughts of Gordon MacDonald being her personal escort from Aunt Pat's every night.

Derrick shrugged, uncomfortably. "I don't know if she was mugged or not. She'd just fallen facedown, it looked like, and there was a puddle of blood." He stopped, shaking his head. "And there was something else." He hesitated, like he didn't want to say the words. "There was a painting there next to her. It was all torn-up looking. It had lipstick or something smeared all over it, too. And it looked like one of Aunt Sara's portraits."

Lulu drew in a shaky breath and looked over at Ben. "It was ripped up?" Ben asked, confused.

"Yeah. I mean, it might not have been one of Aunt Sara's. But it looked a lot like one of the frames she likes using. I don't know—I only saw it for a second or two." Derrick stopped, miserably.

"What was it doing out in the parking deck?" Lulu felt like her head was whirling. "Derrick, you didn't recognize the dead woman?"

"I only looked at her for a second," he repeated. He looked as if he was glad he hadn't had to look at her for any longer than that. "I couldn't really tell."

"Here's Pink," said Lulu, with relief, as the door to the kitchen opened up.

"You okay, Derrick?" asked Pink in a gentle voice. "That was a rough thing for you to have to go through. You did a good job not letting Coco know what was going on. She'd have had nightmares for sure."

Derrick shrugged again, but his face flushed with color at the compliment.

"I'm afraid," said Pink with a sigh, "that the plot has thickened."

Lulu froze. "It wasn't just some random mugging gone wrong?" But she'd known it couldn't have been—she'd known that as soon as Derrick mentioned the portrait.

"No. It was Dee Dee."

"Oh no." Lulu stiffened. "Murdered?"

"Yes." Pink turned to look at Derrick. "I want you to think really carefully, son. Did you see or hear anyone leaving the parking deck while you were either arriving or when you were leaving with Coco?"

Derrick was quiet for a moment and looked like he was thinking hard. Reluctantly, he finally said, "No sir. I mean, yes, I heard people when I was arriving, but it was like a group of people partying or something. They were being loud and just sounded like they were leaving after having fun on Beale Street."

"Nothing else?"

Derrick shook his head. "I'm sorry, Pink. When I got to the deck, I was in a hurry to go to the restaurant and get Coco. Then when I had Coco with me, I was paying attention to her and trying to make sure that she was okay and not going to puke everywhere. Then, when I saw . . . when I saw *her*, I was just thinking about getting Coco and me out of there without Coco seeing anything. I didn't know if the guy was still around or not. And I didn't want to scare Coco. So I made stuff up, like I'd locked my keys in the car. Coco believed me."

Pink must have been able to tell that Derrick didn't know anything else—and didn't, as Derrick was able to assure him, even know the victim at all. Dee Dee wouldn't have crossed paths with a teenage boy, and she wasn't a regular customer at Aunt Pat's. "Thanks, Derrick," said Pink, patting the boy on the back. "I appreciate everything you've done. Why don't you go join Coco in the back office now?"

Derrick looked relieved to adjourn to the back office, where the TV was sure to be on, even if it meant hanging out with a nauseated little girl.

Pink rubbed the back of his neck like it was sore. "Here Pink," said Lulu, quickly pushing a stool toward him. "Have a seat for a minute." He plopped down and they looked at each other. "This is a mess, isn't it?"

"It's a mess. I hate to say it, Lulu, but chances are that one of your guests murdered Dee Dee."

Lulu nodded sadly. She'd figured as much. All of the suspects were there, and Dee Dee sounded like she'd been doing some snooping—and some blackmailing, too.

"Unfortunately, I had my face too deep into a plate of barbeque most of the night to be able to give a whole lot of information on your guests' comings and goings." Pink looked a little disgusted with himself. "How about you?"

Lulu thought for a moment. "The drama with poor Coco kept me from being able to notice anyone's movements really closely. I know I saw everyone here who I think is a suspect in the case. I talked to all of them—Loren and Pepper, Colleen and Pansy, Steffi and Marlowe . . . and Dee Dee." She took a deep breath and said, "But you know that Sara couldn't have done it. Even though it sounds like something weird is going on with the portrait that she made."

"Lord no, Sara couldn't have done it! She was busting it going back and forth from the kitchen to the buffet table all night. She's someone I *did* keep track of because I visited the buffet line every time she brought fresh food out."

Lulu released the pent-up breath she'd been holding. "Derrick couldn't be a suspect, could he? Even though he discovered the body?"

Pink said, "They'll ask him a couple of questions I'm sure, but why on earth would Derrick kill Dee Dee? To him, she was just some old lady who he didn't know. There's absolutely no motive there. Her purse wasn't stolen—her money is there. Why would he have killed her?"

"I wish I could help you out more with where people were, Pink. I hate to say it, but anybody could have left and come back in. People were moving around a lot—going out on the porch to listen to the band, then walking to their table in the dining room, then going to the buffet line at the back. It would've been easy for someone to have gone to the porch and kept on walking."

Pink said, "I think it would have been tougher for Steffi and Marlowe to leave, though, don't you?"

"I do think so. Every time I saw them, there was someone talking to one or both of them. Still, I guess it's possible. Surely they slipped off a couple of times to go to the buffet, or the restroom, or to sit down and eat."

"And why," asked Pink in his deep drawl, "do you think someone would have wanted to kill Dee Dee?" Lulu hesitated, and he added, "All I know about her is that she has a boutique and a lot of the pageant people shop there."

"And me," said Lulu. "She had clothing for . . . mature ladies there, too. I think she was simply trying to keep her shop afloat, so she had a little bit of everything there." Pink still looked like he was waiting for some sort of an answer, so Lulu sighed and said, "Dee Dee was snoopy, Pink. She liked to know what was going on in everyone's lives."

"And nosiness isn't a good trait to have when there's a murderer running around, trying to cover his tracks," said Pink with a matching sigh.

"Well, she wasn't *just* nosy. For Dee Dee, it was sort of a sideline business."

"Blackmail?" asked Pink, perking up. "How did you find out about this?"

Lulu winced apologetically. "From being a little nosy myself, Pink. I'd seen Dee Dee consult this black notebook when I was at her shop—she was messing with it one day when Tristan was over there. Tristan was paying her off for some pageant insider information, and Dee Dee was reading from her notebook, making sure she had the information right."

Pink frowned. "Pageants have insider information?"

Lulu put her hands on her hips. "Pink, pageants are a *big deal* around here! I didn't realize *how* big of a deal until I started going to them with Coco. Anyway, so I was dying to take a look at the notebook. Dee Dee had all *kinds* of information in there—not only what dress a pageant contestant was wearing and what her talent was, but other things, personal things that people probably wouldn't want to get out. And she even had some pictures in there, too—like evidence."

"She probably used the store as the meeting place to get money from the people she was extorting," said Pink in a grim voice. "And to show them exactly what she'd pinned on them."

"Right," said Lulu. "It wouldn't even look that suspicious because people go in and out of shops quickly all the time."

"So we need to search her home and business for a black notebook," said Pink, making a note in a notebook of his own.

"Her shop is the best place to look. It should be on that shelf under the cash register."

When Pink glanced up again, he looked reproachful. "Lulu, you should have told me about this earlier."

"Well honey, you didn't ask me! And that other fella was in charge of the case, and he's about as approachable as a cactus. That Detective Freeman." Lulu made a face.

"That's true. Okay. But if you find out anything else, would you please call me up and tell me? I don't want anything to happen to you. . . . Where would I go eat barbeque?" he asked teasingly.

Lulu smiled at him. "Oh, I'm sure Aunt Pat's would continue on without me. It wouldn't be as *fun*, though, would it?" Pink started leaving the kitchen, and Lulu said, "Any ideas how long before that parking deck opens back up? I've a feeling most of my guests are probably parked over there. And poor Coco needs to get home and in her bed, too."

Pink said, "That's going to end up being a problem. It depends on what level of the deck they parked on. Most of the folks will be able to leave unless they parked on the second level of the deck. If they parked on the second level, then it's going to be a while."

Ben piped up from in front of the pit. "We parked on the bottom level, so Sara should be able to scoot out with Coco, then."

"That shouldn't be a problem, no."

Lulu said, "Ben? What do you think we should do about everybody else? Keep putting food out there?"

"Mother, those folks have got to be stuffed. And really,

we're about at the end of what we planned on fixing for tonight. I think they should be okay with the band and just drinking sweet tea while they wait. Or they can check out some other places on Beale Street."

"But, of course, we're going to need to talk to a few of those people before they go, too—I'm going to need to nail down everyone's actions tonight." Pink yawned. "I think it's going to be a long night. Too bad, because I'm ready to hit the sack after all that barbeque. Oh, and do me a favor and don't mention anything about that painting of Tristan being at the crime scene. . . . I'm going to tell Derrick to keep it quiet, too. Is it okay if Detective Freeman and I use your office to do some questioning? It's usually better to figure out where people were as soon as possible and before they forget."

"Feel free," said Lulu. "I'm going to see if we can get Sara to take Coco home."

Pink hesitated. "If it's all right, Lulu, let me and Free-man talk to Sara for a few minutes before she goes. It's nothing important—it's just for the record. I know Coco needs to go home. And Sara can take Derrick home, also . . . I'm sure he'll be ready to get out of here, too."


The rest of the evening had seemed to go on for-ever, thought Lulu as she got dressed the next morning. On top of it all, she didn't learn any new clues. Everyone was tight-lipped as he or she waited to talk to the police, and even Pink hushed up and wouldn't talk. The suspects looked somber when they found out about Dee Dee's death as Pink was herding them to the back office—even Loren, who said that he didn't even know who Dee Dee was. Pepper, who had shopped at Dee Dee's boutique, was quiet; Colleen sniffed melodramatically into a tissue; and Steffi and Pansy gripped each other's arms as if they thought the murderer might be coming after them next. Marlowe seemed shaken and confused.

Everyone had left with relief as soon as the police had reopened the parking deck. Lulu had helped clean up at the restaurant and fell into her bed exhausted at almost two o'clock in the morning.

And she could tell it, thought Lulu with a grimace as she saw her reflection in the mirror. Especially with the circles under her eyes. She got out a little makeup to help cover them up.

Lulu jumped as the doorbell rang. She smoothed down the dress she'd just put on and hurried over to peep out the front door. She saw it was Cherry and opened the door. "Good morning! You're out bright and early this morning."

Cherry followed Lulu into her cheerful kitchen, where Lulu poured them both a cup of coffee. "Wow, Lulu, you look worn out." Lulu winced, and Cherry said, "Sorry, hon. I know it was a long night. I couldn't sleep last night myself, which is one reason I'm here so early. I finally gave up and pulled some clothes on and came on over."

"I'm glad you did because I didn't even get a chance to talk to you last night after everything started going downhill."

"Is Coco feeling any better?" asked Cherry.

"She's fine. Her tummy ended up getting upset because she ate a whole bag of miniature chocolates that were left over from last Halloween. Poor thing." Lulu knew she wouldn't be doing that again anytime soon. "With all that was going on with Coco, I didn't really get a good sense of what was going on in Aunt Pat's last night. Did you see anything?"

Cherry said, "Actually, I saw a lot. I figured you'd need me to be on sleuthing backup. I saw a lot of coming and going. *Everybody* walked out the front door and then came back in again later. I wish I'd taken a little more notice of when everyone left and came back, but I didn't know it was going to be important." Cherry looked put out.

"You found out more than I did, at least!" said Lulu. "So did it seem to you that most people were going out on the porch to listen to the music? Or were they joining friends that were out there so they could talk for a while?"

"Or were they going out there to murder Dee Dee?" Cherry finished wryly. "That's what we don't know, of course. But I did notice that Dee Dee had spoken to all the suspects. And that all the suspects ended up going outside at some point. *And*," Cherry looked smug, "she'd given them *all* some sort of a note."

Lulu frowned. "That *is* a little strange, isn't it? I wouldn't have thought that Dee Dee would have wanted to talk to all of them."

"Talk? I'd say Dee Dee was planning on blackmailing them or putting some pressure on them in some way. What do you want to bet that she was trying to squeeze some money out of all our suspects? It sounds like that was Dee Dee's special talent. Did you happen to notice when she wasn't in the dining room anymore? When you went off to take care of Coco, was she still in there chatting?"

Lulu pressed her fingers to her temples like she could conjure up the memory. "You know, Cherry, I couldn't say for sure. I was trying to keep track of everybody at the beginning of the fund-raiser, but then so many people came in from off the street that I just couldn't do it. I don't remember seeing her when I went to the back of the restaurant. But she could have been on the porch or in a booth where I couldn't see her."

"Okay," said Cherry briskly. "So we don't know for sure how long she was out there. But I *can* tell you that I never saw her after I saw her making the rounds to talk to the suspects. Not once."

Lulu said slowly, "Let's just say that Dee Dee came in, spoke to Steffi and Marlowe, had a little food, talked to me for a couple of minutes, noticed who was at the party, spoke to all of them, and handed them notes with times to come see her out in her car. Maybe she thought it would be the quickest and easiest way to try to extort some money out of people."

"She had money on the brain," said Cherry, with a bob of her head. "I could tell that she was practically salivating when she thought I was going to buy a whole wardrobe from her. She'd probably already spent it in her head."

Lulu frowned again. "I need a little something sweet to get my brain going this morning, Cherry. Want some coffee cake? I cooked it yesterday and can warm it up in the microwave in a jiff."

Cherry definitely wanted some coffee cake . After a few minutes munching on it, Lulu said, "I guess we should think about what people Dee Dee might have asked to see. The one that doesn't make sense to me is Loren."

Cherry said, "I don't see him killing Dee Dee at all. He wouldn't have gone to her shop, and I can't see what she would have known about him to make him a good target for blackmail."

"True. Still, though—Dee Dee was being pretty nosy the night of Tristan's murder. She could have seen something at the party that night that proved that one of the suspects had murdered Tristan. So I think we should still keep Loren in the loop on that."

Cherry looked glum. "That means that *everyone* is still in the loop, then. She could have seen any of those folks do something suspicious the night Tristan was murdered. I was hoping we could at least eliminate *somebody*."

"Let's think if there's anything else that Dee Dee might have had on these folks, besides anything she might have seen the night of the murder. Dee Dee said some pointed things at Tristan's funeral—remember? I recall thinking how odd it was for her to be behaving that way at a funeral service. Just real coarse."

"That's right!" said Cherry, brightening. "She *was* acting weird. She mentioned something about people messing around where they shouldn't have been and stuff going missing."

Lulu's eyes widened. "Cherry, what do you want to bet that she was talking about the portrait? She probably saw who destroyed it."

"I wonder how it ended up there with Dee Dee," said Cherry. "That's weird."

"Maybe Dee Dee was the one who took it home . . . after she saw it get ruined. Maybe she thought she could use it to extort money out of somebody. She could have swiped it when she realized Tristan was dead, realizing that whoever messed up the picture would look really guilty."

Cherry added, "Then she could have given that person a note last night to meet her and had the picture in the car to use as proof. Didn't you tell me that Derrick said there was lipstick smeared all over the portrait? I bet the police can easily figure out who the person who scribbled lipstick on the portrait was—there'd have to be DNA all over that picture from the lipstick."

Lulu said thoughtfully, "And if my recollection is correct, Dee Dee knew exactly who Loren was, and he knew her from the funeral. She even said something that made Pepper upset—claiming that the only people at the service who cared anything about Tristan were herself and Loren."

Cherry snapped her fingers. "That's right! I remember how uncomfortable everybody was when she said it, too. And Pepper was right there!"

"I think Dee Dee was just one of those people who liked stirring up trouble," said Lulu, with a shake of her head. "And she went a little too far this time. Do you remember that she was also talking about an 'inappropriate relationship'?"

"You mean when she was talking about Loren and Tristan?"

"No, she said that wasn't the *only* inappropriate relationship. And something about things aren't always what they seem."

Cherry looked admiringly at Lulu. "You sure do have a great memory! I can't remember half of what she was babbling about that day."

"I was trying to pay attention to all that—looking for some clues. But I remember thinking at the time that Dee Dee wanted to be the center of attention. You know, that she was just trying to draw attention to herself."

Cherry said, "I'm thinking maybe she was also tipping off some folks that she was onto them. Right? Then she'd have set the scene before she started asking them for money."

Lulu was quiet for a moment, thinking. "I'm trying to think what Dee Dee knew about some of the suspects. You said she spoke to Marlowe. Do you think she was just talking to her because it was a fund-raiser for Steffi? Like she was being nice? Or do you think that she was talking to her because she had something on her?"

"But Marlowe wasn't at Tristan's party," said Cherry. "At least—I don't think anyone saw her at the party. But she *was* in town, like I mentioned to you before. I saw Marlowe at the beauty parlor not long before Tristan's party started." Cherry snapped her fingers. "And that's Dee Dee's beauty parlor, too. She and I have a regular appointment there on the same day, but not exactly the same time. So it's possible that Dee Dee saw Marlowe driving into or out of the salon. The next day, that would have been an important point—that Marlowe was in town during the murder although she claimed to be on a business trip."

"I've already talked to Marlowe about it. I didn't tell her who saw her, don't worry. She admitted that she was in town because her business trip had wrapped up early. But she says that Tristan's party was the *last* place on earth that she'd wanted to be."

Cherry took another swallow of her coffee. "So here's what I was thinking. We'll go around and talk to all the suspects again. And I'll drop by your house from time to time like I did this morning, and we'll rehash what we've learned. That way we're not acting all secretive and suspicious over in Aunt Pat's or something. *We* don't want to end up murdered, after all!"

"No," said Lulu with emphasis. "We certainly don't. How are we going to talk to everyone without looking suspicious while we're questioning them?"

Cherry tried to look modest. "I had a couple of ideas about that. Really, we can make it pretty natural, I think. I could tell Colleen that you simply don't know what to do now that Dee Dee's Darling Dress Shoppe is kaput. You're inconsolable! And, since I know that Colleen has shopped in every shop in town, I'll ask her to give us a little tour of boutiques."

"You're coming along for that, too?" said Lulu with surprise. "I know you can't stand to shop, and these shops won't be the kinds of places you like to go."

"It's a sacrifice for the case," said Cherry with a small bow.

"Why don't we just ask her to give us some places to shop? I don't think we need to be dragged all over town to see the shops for ourselves. And that might give us a little more time to talk if we're at her house. We could claim that *we're* about to go shopping and decided to stop by for a little advice."

"Sure—it doesn't bother me to get out of shopping, that's for sure. If we're lucky, then Pansy will be there while we're talking to Colleen. I have some ideas about talking to the other suspects, too." Cherry bounced in her seat like she might fly off. "I think we have a good shot at cracking this case, Lulu! And before Pink even does."

Chapter

17

That afternoon, after Lulu had checked in at the restaurant to make sure everything was running smoothly, she and Cherry hopped in Lulu's car to take off for their "shopping trip."

In minutes, they were knocking at Colleen's door. She answered it, smiling, but looking a little confused. "Well, hey, y'all. What's up? Want to come inside?" Colleen held the door open for them, and they walked into her chintz-filled living room.

"We're only going to stay for a minute," said Lulu a little apologetically.

"We just had some quick questions for you," said Cherry, making a show of sitting down so that Lulu would follow. "Lulu is so devastated about Dee Dee's death."

Lulu was startled that she was suddenly supposed to produce a look of devastation on her face. She hastily managed at least a serious expression, since she'd still had her social smile on.

"Dee Dee's was *the* place where Lulu shopped. She'd been going to Dee Dee's boutique for the last twenty years and pretty much gotten the same type of clothing." Colleen and Cherry looked contemplatively at Lulu's floral dress.

"To cheer Lulu up," said Cherry, with an air of philanthropy, "I told her that I'd introduce her to a whole new world of stores. I want to open her eyes to all the different *kinds* of clothes that she could wear."

Colleen looked doubtfully at Cherry's tie-dyed top and skirt as if not completely convinced that Cherry should be a fashion ambassador, even for poor, unfashionable Lulu.

"As you see, though, I tend to shop at some pretty hip shops," said Cherry.

Colleen made considering noises as if assessing the truth of that statement.

"But as much as I love these shops," said Cherry sadly, "I don't think I can convert Lulu to shop them with me. I think she's gotten too used to shopping at Dee Dee's Darling Dress Shoppe. I told Lulu, though, that you'd be sure to know some good . . . transition stores for Lulu to shop at. Nothing too radical of a change, but *some* change. She has a gentleman friend that she's seeing now, too," said Cherry, blinking innocently and clearly ignoring the angry flush that Lulu felt spread across her face.

"A makeover!" said Colleen with a squeal. Lulu's heart sank. "If there's a gentleman friend, it's definitely time for a makeover!"

Cherry tilted her head to one side thoughtfully. "You know, we really should think big, Lulu. Although I don't know if you're *quite* ready for a major makeover. Since you're still in the grieving process for your old boutique."

"I'd welcome some small changes," said Lulu stiffly. The idea of doing any kind of a makeover made her wince. She'd gotten too used to the clothes in her closet. "Have you got any ideas, Colleen?"

Colleen clapped her hands together. "Makeovers are my favorite thing on earth, that's all. Showing women their full beauty potential? That's what I'm all about. It's a shame that Pansy isn't here or else she'd help us with some ideas, too. You know how great she is with fashion and beauty." She squinted critically at Lulu. "Yesss, I can see some definite possibilities." Her gaze zoned in on Lulu's precariously arranged bun. "Yes, indeedy. You've come to the right person, Cherry. I know all about shopping!" She gave her trilling laugh. "There are several places I can think of that would just love the business, and I think you'd look so precious in their things, Lulu! Be sure to tell them I sent you. Let me find a piece of paper, and I'll write down some ideas for you."

While Colleen was jotting down names, she said, "I know what you mean, Lulu, about getting all accustomed to going to *one* place or always buying one thing, then having it go out of business or be discontinued or whatever. It absolutely kills me when my favorite lipstick or eye shadow gets discontinued! Then I have to spend a ton of time trying to find the perfect thing."

Cherry shook her head mournfully. "It's awful, isn't it?"

"Yes, I do feel that way," said Lulu, with some surprise. The actual demise of the store really hadn't hit her until a few minutes ago and she really *wasn't* sure where she was going to do her shopping now. Cherry had come up with the perfect excuse, and the smug smile on her face showed that she knew it.

"But I also," said Lulu, determinedly bringing the conversation back in the direction it was supposed to be going in, "am upset about poor Dee Dee being murdered."

Colleen stopped writing and said, "Isn't it awful? What's the world coming to that a lady can't even go out to her car without being gunned down?"

Colleen, thought Lulu, clearly hadn't gotten an accurate news briefing on the murder. Or else she was playing dumb so it wouldn't appear that she knew too much. Surely Pink had given her the lowdown when he was questioning her at the fund-raiser.

"The police aren't treating this like a mugging, Colleen. They say that Dee Dee was murdered."

"Is *that* what they were getting at the other night?" asked Colleen with surprise. "I simply couldn't figure out why they were asking all those questions. I thought they were trying to see if any of us had noticed someone suspicious lurking around in the parking deck when we were going or coming."

Colleen's expression was carefully blank, thought Lulu.

"The police think that whoever killed Tristan also killed Dee Dee," explained Lulu.

"Why on earth would someone want to kill Dee Dee—on *purpose*?" asked Colleen. "It makes more sense for her to just be a random victim. A mugging gone wrong." Colleen looked away, and Lulu got the idea that Colleen knew perfectly well why someone would want to kill Dee Dee.

Cherry shrugged. "I'd gotten the impression that Dee Dee was pretty nosy," she said. "Maybe she knew too much and somebody decided they had to eliminate her."

Colleen gave a shrill laugh. "Cherry, you sound like somebody who's watched too many cop shows."

"Maybe I have." Cherry gave a sheepish smile. "But I do think that Dee Dee's nosiness probably got her killed."

Colleen wrote down a couple more dress-shop names but still seemed to be thinking about what Cherry and Lulu had said. "So the police wanted to know where we all were—those of us who were also at Tristan's party."

"That's right," said Lulu. "And I don't think they had an easy time of it."

"That's the thing! There were so many people there, Lulu. When you throw a benefit, you really throw one. The restaurant was crowded with people. If I'd been *told* to keep my eye on everybody, I still couldn't have done it. And everybody was moving around so much, too—getting food or going outside to listen to the band. As for me, though, I stuck around the food most of the night. I had a real long conversation with Marlowe, too, about Steffi."

"About Steffi?" asked Lulu. "Is she doing okay?"

Colleen snorted. "She's actually probably doing a lot better now that her mama is dead! I've worried about that child for so many years. Her mother always treated her like a redheaded stepchild."

"Speaking of Dee Dee being nosy," said Lulu carefully. "She was telling me that Tristan was having an affair with her yardman. And you'd said that the yardman was involved with Steffi."

Colleen sighed. "Well, he was involved with Steffi. But it should come as no surprise that he was also having a fling with Tristan. Who *wasn't* Tristan having an affair with? That woman had the morals of an alley cat."

"You don't seem real surprised about it," said Cherry. "I somehow can't really see her hooking up with someone like that—he wouldn't be high class enough for Tristan."

"Well, she wouldn't have *married* him—she was more interested in getting back at Steffi, probably. Hurting Steffi. Because he was Steffi's boyfriend—her first real boyfriend. And

Pansy had told me that Steffi is crazy about him. And, like I've always said, Tristan liked to find out what people wanted most . . . and then find a way to take it away from them."

"Did Steffi know that he was cheating on her with her mom?" asked Lulu.

"Oh, I'm sure that Steffi didn't know. And it was so mean of Tristan to do it—that was one thing that child didn't need . . . more hurt."

Colleen handed the paper with the list of shops to Lulu and said, "By the way, that was so sweet of you to hold that fund-raiser for Steffi. You could have absolutely knocked me down with a feather when I heard that Tristan was basically penniless. And in debt! She'd even grown up with plenty of money. . . . What a shame that she plowed through it the way she did and then had to put on some big act to show that she was fine. When she wasn't fine at all. Then to leave Marlowe and Steffi to pick up the tab on all her foolishness." Colleen looked irritated at Tristan's supreme thoughtlessness in getting herself murdered.

"The night of the fund-raiser," said Lulu with a studied carelessness, "I was so busy with poor little Coco—you know she was sick that night?—that I really wasn't able to even talk to Steffi at all. Did she look like she was having fun?"

Colleen frowned. "You know, I didn't see Steffi all that much that night. In fact, I looked for her for a few minutes to ask her if things were getting better for her—and I couldn't find her."

Derrick looked at Cherry with horror. "You want me to do *what*?"

Derrick, Cherry, and Lulu were sitting on the front porch of Aunt Pat's a couple of days later in the slow period in the middle of the afternoon. Lulu poured Derrick another glass of iced tea when it looked like he might choke on the blueberry muffin he was eating as a snack.

"I was thinking," said Cherry, "that you could help your Granny Lulu and me with our detecting. We need to talk to Pansy for a little while without her mama horning in. We were hoping she was going to be at home when we were talking to her mom, but she was gone. We *could* try to catch up with Pansy at another beauty pageant."

"Although I'd rather not have to do that," interjected Lulu with some determination.

"So I thought—hey! Derrick and Pansy are about the same age, and Derrick said Pansy was even in a couple of his classes. Derrick could ask Pansy to study with him over here one afternoon. You do *know* Pansy, don't you?" asked Cherry.

"Know her? Not exactly. She and I hang out with totally different groups. And she's in the really popular one with all the pretty people. I'm not even sure if she *does* study. Besides, I'm not sure my girlfriend would be real happy about me hanging out with another girl, especially a girl like Pansy, even if is to study."

Cherry looked peeved. "Rats. That would have been the easiest way to lure her over here. Y'all could have sat on the porch and gotten some work done, and Lulu and I could have quizzed her."

Derrick's friend Doug stuck his head through the screen door. "Hey, man. You ready to go?"

"Sure," said Derrick. He hesitated a minute. "How about Doug?"

Cherry looked startled. She looked more closely at Doug—his scruffy goatee, his long hair, his jeans with the torn knees. "Ahhh . . ." she said.

"How about Doug what?" Doug asked curiously.

Lulu said, "It's nothing, honey. Want a blueberry muffin?" When Doug shook his head and still waited for an answer, Lulu sighed. "Cherry and I needed to talk for a while to Pansy. We thought Derrick could maybe ask her to come over to Aunt Pat's and study with him one afternoon."

Doug plopped down in one of the rockers and stroked his goatee thoughtfully. "Only problem with that is that I'm sure Pansy doesn't study. She's a major slacker when it comes to school."

No wonder Pansy wasn't counting on an academic scholarship. It looked like she really needed the money from pageant wins to pay for school. "We gathered there might be a few problems with that plan."

"Lucky for you," said Doug, pointing a long finger to the ceiling, "that I have an even better plan." Lulu noticed that Derrick was already grinning as if he knew what that plan might be.

Cherry rolled her eyes. "Why do I have a funny feeling I know what this plan is going to be?"

"I'll ask Pansy out, naturally. It makes the most sense. I'll see if she'd like an early dinner at Aunt Pat's restaurant where I can get to know her a little better." Doug's smile grew as he considered the idea.

Lulu knit her brows. "I'm not sure I like this idea, Doug. I feel like we might be playing with Pansy's emotions, asking her out on a fake date. I liked the plan better when it was all about studying."

"A *fake* date?" asked Doug, putting his hand across his heart. "My dear lady, nothing is further from the truth. No, I've worshiped Pansy from afar for many years. It'll be my pleasure to ask her out."

"Well, then, I'm worried about *your* getting hurt," said Lulu, still feeling uncomfortable.

Derrick guffawed. "Granny Lulu, Doug won't get hurt. He's a cult figure at the high school. *All* the girls want to go out with Doug."

Doug pretended to preen, and Cherry knit her brows. "Really?" she asked with suspicious disbelief. Clearly, Doug's scruffy appearance had not given Cherry the impression that he was some Lothario.

"It's true," said Doug, with no attempt at modesty. "Perplexing, but true. I'll go ahead and give her a call." He raised his hand to stop Lulu as she opened her mouth in worried protest. "If she likes me and we hit it off, we've started a beautiful relationship. If I like her and she doesn't like me, I'll live. And I'm sure I'll like Pansy, so we're in good shape . . . Granny Lulu."

They watched as Doug proceeded to text a couple of different friends to find out Pansy's cell-phone number. Minutes later, he called Pansy. "Pansy? It's Doug James. This is last minute and everything, but I was wondering if you wanted to catch a quick bite with me tonight." He waited for a second, and then nodded, smiling, at Lulu and Cherry. "Great! Tell you what, let's make it early, since we have school tomorrow. Want to meet me over at Aunt Pat's in a couple of hours?"

Doug got off the phone and stood up to make a short bow while they all clapped.

Derrick said, "But what about asking her the questions? When will Lulu and Cherry have a chance to talk to her?"

"It'll be easy," said Doug. "I'll just get up to take a phone call. Derrick, you call me at six and I'll excuse myself and get up to take the call. Then Lulu and Cherry can fire questions at Pansy for as long as they need—I'll keep an eye on y'all to see when it looks like I should come back to the table."

Chapter

18

Doug was really laying it on thick, thought Lulu. But Pansy seemed to be eating it up. Pansy was a little larger than life herself sometimes, so maybe Doug's behavior seemed natural to her.

"Pansy, you look positively ravishing," he was saying, and Pansy was beaming and hanging on every word. "I'm the luckiest guy in Memphis today. Hey, I didn't mess up your plans for today or anything, did I?"

Pansy gave a happy sigh. "No, this is perfect. I'm glad you called me up."

"Well, you know, I've been thinking about calling you for a long while now. But I was too shy and worried I'd be rejected." He ducked his head and blinked up at her through his lashes. Pansy laughed and swatted him. "As if!" she said.

Cherry rolled her eyes at Lulu. They were sitting in the booth directly behind the couple, and it was still very quiet in the restaurant, since it wasn't even six o'clock yet.

"You *could* have turned me down, you know," he said teasingly. "You haven't even accepted my Facebook friend request yet. And I'm devastated over it."

Cherry put her head down on the table as if it was hurting.

"For heaven's sake, Doug! When did you make this request? A few minutes ago? I haven't even been on Facebook today." Lulu saw Pansy take her phone out and access the Internet there. She punched a few buttons on her touch screen. "There. We're friends."

"Good," said Doug, with a smile in his voice. "I feel a lot more secure now. *If* I believe you. Maybe you've blocked me or something, instead."

"Check and see for yourself!" said Pansy.

Doug took out his own phone and fiddled with it for a minute. "Okay, never mind. False alarm. We *are* friends." He smiled beatifically at Pansy. "And now I'm on your profile page and will find out all kinds of fascinating tidbits about you. See, this is how to make first dates go well— start finding out as much as possible about the person you're with." He paused while he scanned Pansy's online profile. "And you seem to be absolutely fascinating."

Pansy gave a tittering laugh.

"I see some wonderful pictures of you—are these pageant dresses? Wow. And you've got seven hundred friends listed! See, I'm out with the most popular girl around." Another pause. "Ooh! What's this now? Looks like you've been flaming some people, too."

Pansy sounded a little less cheerful. "What? Oh. You mean the note I put on there about someone cheating so they could win? Yeah." She gave a short laugh. "The pageant biz isn't all sweetness and light, you know. We have a whole lot of competition between girls, and all of us want to win really badly. It gets ugly sometimes."

Lulu worried for a minute that Doug was going off on his own investigative tangent, so she was relieved when his phone suddenly rang. "Typical! This is a call I really need to take, too—I've got a project I'm doing for Chemistry, and this is my lab partner calling. Could you excuse me just for a few minutes?"

Lulu and Cherry had decided that the best thing to do would be for Lulu to sit down with Pansy by herself. Lulu thought Pansy might get on the defensive if it looked like she was being ambushed. Cherry was just going to listen in (she was back to back with Pansy in the booth).

Lulu slid out of the booth and walked to the next table. "Well, hi there, sugar! I didn't see you come in. Do we need to order you up something to eat?"

"Hi, Mrs. Taylor. No, probably not yet. I'm here with a date, so I better wait on him to get back to the table before I order."

Pansy smiled as Lulu beamed and said, "A date! How fun. Is he a nice boy, I hope?"

"I *think* so. He's treating me pretty well so far, and he's making me laugh. I love to laugh."

Lulu clucked. "There hasn't been too much to laugh about lately, has there?"

Pansy shook her head. "There sure hasn't been. I couldn't believe it about Dee Dee!" Pansy gave a tiny shiver. "To think that could have been any one of us . . . in the wrong place at the wrong time. We all parked in that deck, after all. It could have been me or Mom or you that ended up getting mugged."

Lulu frowned. "You didn't know, then? It wasn't a mugging gone wrong at all, Pansy. It was murder. That's why the police were so interested in asking us all those questions."

"Really? I thought they were trying to figure out if we'd seen anybody who looked dangerous when we were getting out of our cars that evening." Pansy rubbed her forehead. "It's just too much. I hate it. Can't the police find who's doing all this and put him away?"

"I know exactly what you mean," said Lulu. "It's made it hard for all of us, hasn't it? So—did you see anything that night that would help the police out? What did you tell them that you'd seen?"

Pansy looked like she was trying to remember. "I didn't see anything in the parking deck," she said slowly. "Well, I saw a couple of people, but they were obviously just coming back from partying on Beale. Nobody was lurking around the parking garage. I guess they're wanting to know who might have left the party? But everyone that Tristan knew was still there when the police came!"

"They were," said Lulu in a soothing voice, "but someone could easily have left the fund-raiser, murdered poor Dee Dee, and come back again to the restaurant. I think that's what the police are thinking."

Pansy was quiet for a few moments. Lulu saw Doug out of the corner of her eye, watching them for a clue that they were done talking. Finally Pansy said, "I did notice that Pepper was there, then she left. Then she was there again. I was laughing about it to Steffi, actually. She obviously came that night just to make Loren feel really uncomfortable. I mean—Pepper didn't even like Tristan! And I don't think she knew Steffi. I figured she was going to go out and slash Loren's tires or something like that."

"I was surprised to see her there, too," said Lulu in a

musing voice. "I thought she'd want to stay as far away from Loren as she could. When I saw her there, I figured, like you did, that she was only there to get under Loren's skin. I couldn't keep track of her, though—poor Coco wasn't feeling well that night and I was tending to her."

Lulu really needed to ask the next question—she'd put it off for a while now. But it wasn't an easy one to broach. Finally she decided that the only way to ask it . . . was just to ask it. "Pansy, honey, I hate to ask you this. But someone suggested that you might have damaged your own dress and hidden your own shoes for the Miss Memphis pageant."

Pansy froze. "Why would I do something like that, and hurt my chances of going to college?"

"This person suggested that you didn't have a chance to win the pageant, anyway. And that you thought that you could get sympathy votes from the judges if you had some sort of disaster happen to you before you were supposed to go on." Lulu shrugged helplessly. But the truth flared in Pansy's eyes for a moment, giving Lulu all the information she needed.

"That's bull! And I bet I know who *suggested* that to you. One of the pageant girls, right? That's because they're all jealous of me. They're jealous of my talent and my looks and the fact that I'm doing well and beating them at competitions. We're in it for the same scholarship dollars, so of course they're going to feel that way."

Lulu reached across and gave Pansy's hand a quick pat. "I'm sorry, honey. I shouldn't have brought it up. It was bothering me and so I thought I'd mention it to you."

"Mrs. Taylor, do me a favor and don't say anything about it." Pansy's voice sounded stressed. "That's the kind of thing that could mess up a girl's pageant career."

"Consider my lips sealed," said Lulu quickly. She looked across the restaurant and gave Doug a quick nod. "Oh, here comes your young man. I hope your date is going well, dear."

Pansy relaxed. "You know, I think it is," she said in a confiding voice.

Lulu was relieved. As long as both the kids were enjoying themselves. She didn't like being ruthless.

Cherry and Lulu didn't have to cook up plans to talk to Loren. He showed up the next day at Aunt Pat's to see Sara in midafternoon, when it was quiet at the restaurant. As soon as Lulu saw him and realized that he wanted to talk, not eat, she ushered him to the back office.

He was fidgety and agitated until Sara joined him in the office. "I know you're probably sick of seeing me here," he started, "but I just can't get that portrait out of my head."

Lulu and Sara looked at each other. Lulu had told Sara about the portrait, and she promised not to let it go any further. The police apparently thought that keeping the destroyed painting under wraps might help them to solve the case. Sara took off her apron and sat down on one of the chairs. "Loren, I know where you're coming from, but the painting is missing. And—I have a funny feeling it might be missing for good. I'm sorry, but I think you should probably try to move past it."

Loren bobbed his head. "I agree with you about the portrait being permanently missing. It would already have turned up by now if it was going to." He leaned forward and looked Sara right in the eyes. "That's why I want to commission a new portrait of Tristan." He opened up the laptop bag he had with him, and Sara gaped as he pulled money out.

"I can pay for the portrait myself. I know, of course, it

takes some time to paint. I've got pictures of Tristan that Steffi and Marlowe were kind enough to give me . . ."

Sara gave Lulu a sort of sick look as Loren rooted around in his laptop bag for the pictures of Tristan that he'd brought with him. He was carefully pulling them out of a folder when Sara said, "I just don't know, Loren. I feel kind of funny about it. A commemorative painting, sort of? Won't your wife . . . ?"

Loren shook his head, and a lock of dark hair fell into his face. "She's not going to even know about it because Pepper and I have separated," he said impatiently. "But it sure would mean a lot to me if you'd paint another portrait."

"How about," said Sara hesitantly, "if I think about it?"

"I could pay more money for it, if you wanted—"

Sara said quickly, "It's not about the money, Loren. I'm just not sure if this is something I want to take on or not. The first one honestly didn't turn out all that well—Tristan certainly wasn't happy with it."

Loren looked surprised to hear this. "I thought it was beautiful," he said. Love, thought Lulu, is obviously blind. Tristan had had a decidedly peevish look on her face in the original portrait, beautiful as it was.

Sara sighed. "It brings back bad memories, Loren. I don't particularly want to look at a photograph of Tristan for hours on end. It'll make me think about the murder. And now we have another murder on our hands. Whatever could have happened to Dee Dee?"

"Probably somebody she crossed the wrong way," said Loren absently. "It could even have been Pepper. Pepper's been mean and vindictive lately."

Sara knit her brows. "You're thinking your *wife* killed Dee Dee?"

"Soon to be ex-wife," said Loren coolly. "And, yes, I do think she's capable of it."

Lulu wondered if maybe even *Loren* could have destroyed the portrait. He'd surely been mad enough at Tristan at the party. He'd been furious, upset, betrayed. Couldn't he have taken out all those feelings on the portrait and then regretted it when Tristan had ended up dead?

Loren was still mulling over the possibilities. "I worry more about what happened to Tristan. Steffi sure hadn't been happy with her mother at the time of the murder. Or maybe it was one of those pageant people . . . like Pansy. Tristan kept talking about how much the girl hated her."

Lulu said gently, "Loren, is there anything that you saw the night of Dee Dee's murder that could be a clue to who's behind all this? I didn't really get much of an impression of anything that night because Coco was sick and I was trying to work out a way to get her back home." Loren looked up, and Lulu said, "You know the police are thinking it was murder, right? Some folks still seem to think it was a mugging gone wrong."

"You know, Lulu, I've thought really hard about that night. I want to see Tristan's killer behind bars more than anybody, and I'm sure whoever killed Dee Dee killed Tristan, too."

He lowered his head and said, "But Lulu, my attention was diverted at the fund-raiser, too, just like yours was with Coco. Pepper was bound and determined to make my life miserable. I know the only reason she was there was to make me uncomfortable. Every time I looked up, she was staring at me with this hateful expression on her face."

"Was there anybody else that you noticed?" asked Lulu. She was beginning to think that they weren't going to get any information at all.

"Well," he said, a little reluctantly, "I did see that woman—the pageant woman—looking for her daughter at one point. I was talking to Marlowe at the time, and she asked Marlowe if she'd seen Pansy. So I guess at some point Pansy wasn't around. But that could have been because the room was so crowded. But I *did* notice that I had a break for a while. Pepper was gone for *quite* a few minutes and I had a wonderful break from all her glares. *And* she'd spoken to Dee Dee earlier in the party. Maybe there's some kind of connection." Loren looked positively cheerful at the idea. "Because it wasn't that she left Aunt Pat's for the night. She came back into the dining room to torture me some more later."

"Seems like she could have simply been visiting the la-dies' room," said Sara wryly.

Loren shrugged. "It's a possibility, I guess. But she sure was gone for a long time." He frowned. "I did also notice that Steffi wasn't around for a little while. I looked for her for a few minutes when I was ready to leave. Of course, though, she turned up a little while later, so maybe she was just in the restroom, too."

This time when Cherry popped over, it was almost bedtime. Lulu heard Cherry's motorcycle in the driveway and peeped out the door. She'd pulled out some milk and some praline cookies when Cherry knocked at the door. "You saw me coming!" said Cherry, looking appreciatively at the refreshments.

"More like *heard* you coming. Have a cookie?"

Cherry wanted *several* cookies, actually. Finally she gave a grunt and pushed the plate of cookies away from her. "Stop me! Those are addictive. Okay, I dropped by the restaurant a while ago because I didn't know you'd left early. Sara said you'd been investigating without me." Cherry's expression was a combination of hurt and curios-ity, but curiosity was winning out.

"Well, honey, I couldn't help it. Loren came right on into Aunt Pat's, determined to speak to Sara again. He's got a real bee in his bonnet over that portrait. Actually, it's more of a hornet than a bee. And he wasn't all that much help, anyway. Honestly, Cherry, I'm getting discouraged. The police don't seem to be making that many inroads, and we're running into dead ends, too."

Cherry said, "So tell me what Lover Boy Loren had to say for himself. Maybe there's a clue mixed up in there somehow."

Lulu filled her in on their conversation.

"It sounds to me like you found out a few things," said Cherry. "Pepper, Steffi, and Pansy weren't visible for at least part of the party."

"Or maybe," said Lulu glumly, "they were all reapplying their makeup in the ladies' room. Or out on the porch listening to the band."

Cherry said, "Or maybe they were killing Dee Dee in the parking deck! We just don't know . . . that's the whole point of an investigation, Lulu!"

Lulu perked up a little bit. "You're right. Let's work through it a little. So we've got Pepper who's looking suspicious—or is she? I'm wondering if Loren is angry enough right now to blame Pepper for everything he can think of. If she's locked up in jail, then she's out of his hair for sure, after all."

"Maybe," said Cherry. "But what about the others? Pansy sure didn't mention leaving the fund-raiser, and neither did Steffi. It's something to follow up on, anyway. And how about the information that Pansy gave you? She didn't see Pepper for part of the time, either! So maybe Pepper was the one who sneaked off. Maybe Dee Dee saw Pepper do something really suspicious at Tristan's party—something that the police could've used as evidence. And then Dee Dee tried to blackmail her and she killed her."

"It looks like Pepper might be the next person we should talk to," said Lulu thoughtfully. "Any ideas on how to do that in a natural way?"

"Bunko," said Cherry decidedly. "We'll invite some suspects, and I'll tell them that we're going to have a Bunko night to unwind a little bit. Everyone can bring something to snack on."

"I'm liking this idea already!" said Lulu, cheering up a little.

"And then we can play the game. Pepper lives right next door, you know, so I can maybe convince her to stay a little longer." Cherry thought a second. "I know! I'll ask her to stay and help me clean up."

Lulu laughed. "She'll *love* that!"

"It's the kind of flakiness that she'd expect of me, though. She's already fussing about my plastic flowers, but I swear you can't tell. The only reason Pepper knows they're fake is because I told her." Cherry looked miffed.

"As far as the Bunko goes, though—won't it take a while to set it up? To invite folks and get them to come over?"

"No, because I'm supposed to have it tonight—it's my month, anyway. But out of the twelve girls we're supposed to have, a whole bunch can't come because of some golf tournament or something. So it's perfect! I was going to have to call around for subs, anyway." She lit up. "I'll invite Colleen, Pansy, Steffi, and Marlowe, too! Let's have *all* the suspects there, then we can see what happens. Murder at Bunko!" Cherry, thought Lulu, looked way too enthusiastic by the prospect.

"Except for Loren," said Lulu.

"Well, but we couldn't invite *Loren*. Men don't come to Bunko. Well, maybe some do, but not in our Bunko club. Husbands never sub. And he'd hate it and hate us and would be upset at Pepper being there, and he'd storm out, or she would, and then we wouldn't be able to talk to *anybody*." Cherry looked dismayed.

"No, Loren doesn't need to be invited," said Lulu. "Okay. So call them up and see who can come."

They could *all* come. "That's because," said Cherry smugly, "Bunko is the most fun game ever. And they can all use some fun right now."

Chapter
19

Lulu had played Bunko with the Graces in the past, but then it got too hard to work her evenings at Aunt Pat's around them, so she decided to sub from time to time instead. Every time she played, though, she felt like she was missing out by not being a regular part of the group. This group was especially raucous, but they definitely knew how to have a good time. This group was even *louder* than usual. Wine was poured and drunk, everyone brought in a decadent appetizer or dessert, and each person put five dollars into the kitty to serve as a prize for the winner.

Cherry had set up three tables, and four people sat at each table. Lulu's partner for the night was Steffi, and Pepper was paired with Cherry. Steffi looked excited. "I'm glad to get out," she said to Lulu. "Everything I've done lately has been either planning a funeral or answering police questions or going through Mother's things. It's great to do something *fun*." She flushed suddenly and said, "Of course, the Aunt Pat's fund-raiser was fun, but that's been the only thing."

Lulu looked sad. "Actually, the fund-raiser *wasn't* much fun. It was *supposed* to be. But the way the evening ended really put a damper on the festivities. Poor Dee Dee couldn't help it, of course."

Colleen joined them. She had on a very loud jumpsuit sort of outfit that Lulu guessed was stylish, but it looked horrible on her. Her face was garishly made up, too, and made quite a contrast to her daughter's. Pansy looked pretty in a much more natural way. Colleen said, "Did you find some new clothes, Lulu? You and Cherry really looked so determined to go shopping the last time I talked to you." She stared at Lulu's faded floral dress.

Oops. Lulu had temporarily forgotten that she was supposed to be more of a fashion plate. "You know," she said, thinking quickly, "Derrick had told me . . . you know young Derrick, don't you? Sara's nephew? Derrick told me that I needed to think about Aunt Pat's branding." Colleen tilted her head to one side like she didn't totally understand where Lulu was coming from. "I mean, people think of Lulu as a sort of frumpy old lady with a fondness for floral dresses. Maybe I'd mess up the brand identification if I went shopping."

Colleen looked doubtful. "I don't think anybody thinks of you as *frumpy*, Lulu. Just maybe not all that daring with your wardrobe. But at least you could wear your new clothes when you weren't at work. It would give you a whole new lease on life."

Steffi said, a little roughly, "I think Lulu looks great. She's always neat and tidy and friendly and comfortable-looking. Lulu, you shouldn't change the way you look for anybody."

Lulu remembered how hard Tristan had been on her daughter. She could imagine that she'd probably tried to force her into wearing clothes that she really wasn't comfortable in, simply because they were stylish.

Evelyn, one of the Graceland docents that made up the Aunt Pat's group of regulars the Graces, walked over. "Y'all," she said, delicately sniffing the air, "I hate to bring this up, but does something smell funny to you?"

Lulu frowned. "Something's burning. Cherry, do you have something cooking, hon?"

"Oh snap!" said Cherry, putting a hand to her head. "The cheese dip!"

It had, thought Lulu, probably *been* cheese dip at some point in the cooking process. Before it had morphed into a charred lump in the pot, that is. It didn't help matters that the rubber spatula had been left by the careless Cherry in the pot. It had melted, and the smell of burning plastic was getting pretty strong.

"Too bad," drawled Evelyn, waving a bejeweled hand languidly. "I was sort of in the mood for some cheese dip. Luckily, Pepper brought some bourbon balls that I think I'm going to start indulging myself with."

Lulu hurried over to the sink and started washing her hands. "I'll help you make something else, Cherry. It'll only take a few minutes."

"No," said Cherry quickly. "Everybody out of the kitchen. Shoo! Shoo! You too, Lulu! I'll come up with a substitute dish real quick. Y'all have some wine, and I'll be back in a jiff." Lulu was the last to leave the kitchen, and Cherry caught her by the arm real quick. "You need to be doing some investigating, Lulu! Don't worry with the food." Lulu opened her mouth to protest, and Cherry said, "I know it goes against your nature, but seriously . . . leave the food to me. I'll be out in a jiff, and we'll get started with the game."

So Lulu joined the raucous group in Cherry's den. Peggy Sue was just saying, in a loud voice, "Then my mother told the butcher he could call me up *anytime*. And gave him *my* phone number. Can you believe it? She's still trying to set me up on dates, and I've been married to Grayson for thirty years! She's gone plumb senile."

"Was the butcher cute at least?" asked Evelyn.

"Not likely! That's another of Mama's problems— cataracts. So she's trying to set me up with men who are in their dotage half the time. It's not like she's giving my number to some muscle-bound Brad Pitt look-alikes."

"In which case it would be *okay*, Peggy Sue?" asked a scandalized Jeanne.

"Maybe," said Peggy Sue, batting her lashes.

Cherry's husband, Johnny, a grim-looking bald man with a general air of resignation, appeared at the bottom of the stairs, eyed the group balefully, and headed out the front door.

"Guess we're too scary for old Johnny," said Peggy Sue with a shrug. "Another excuse for him to stay out too late with Eric, playing poker. He thinks that's a *real* game. Except they drink too much and pass out with their faces on the poker table."

Cherry pushed through the kitchen door in a rush. "Okay!" she said. "I've got some more cheese dip made up, y'all." Lulu watched in horror as the dip container bobbled, tilted, and smashed on the hardwood floor in front of them all. Really, thought Lulu, it was almost in slow motion.

They all stared at the pile of yellow mush on the floor. "Cherry, honey," said Peggy Sue in a serious voice, "have you been drinking?"

"Not as much as I'm about to," said Cherry, with her hands on her hips, staring at the cheese-dip disaster grimly.

"Here's a novel idea," said Evelyn in a languid voice. "Why don't we have the actual *cook* make the cheese dip?"

Everyone looked hopefully over at Lulu, who was ready to don an apron and get started cooking. "Don't y'all ever go to parties?" asked Cherry irritably. "Guests don't *cook*. The hostess does. I promised cheese dip, and everybody is going to *get* some cheese dip. And leave that mess alone. . . . It'll keep until I get some paper towels out."

The wine flowed and people snacked on the goodies everyone brought. Really, thought Lulu, there was plenty of food. They didn't *have* to have a hot dish. But Cherry had seemed absolutely determined. So Lulu decided to listen in on the conversations and see if any good gossip churned up in the process.

Pepper was asking Marlowe, "You mean to say that it was all a fake? That Tristan didn't really have a lot of money?"

"Well, at one point she sure did. But I guess if a person spends money like it's going out of style and throws elaborate parties and has a huge wardrobe and a designer-shoe collection, then the money tends to disappear pretty fast," said Marlowe dryly.

"That's why Lulu had the fund-raiser," said Steffi. Her shoulders slumped a little. "I had a feeling that people were going to wonder why I needed money—especially since Mother had been so showy."

Pepper said quickly, "No, I bet they don't. People also realize you want to go to college and that you had to bury your mama and funerals aren't cheap. Besides, who cares what people think? They were all happy to go to Aunt Pat's and support you—and have a fantastic buffet."

Lulu said, "I'm sorry that the evening turned out the way it did."

"Lulu, it was a wonderful night—up until the very end," said Marlowe. "You can't help the way that it ended. And you did such a great thing for Steffi . . . and me, too. That money is a great head start for Steffi's college education. Especially since Tristan didn't provide Steffi with any help." Marlowe's face was brooding.

The doorbell rang, and the women looked puzzled. "We've got our whole group here, don't we?" asked Peggy Sue. She walked to the door and opened it.

It was Loren, who quickly approached Pepper. "Thanks for chucking all my clothes out in the yard, Pepper," said Loren in a bitterly sarcastic voice. "Some of those clothes I wear to work, you know. I can't afford to go buy a whole slew of new clothes because you ruined them."

"The weather has been perfectly clear," said Pepper coolly, but Lulu saw the anger in her eyes. "Nothing was going to happen to those clothes."

"And you changed the locks?" Loren sounded peeved. "There's stuff that I still need to get out."

"When I'm *over* there," snapped Pepper. "I didn't want you sneaking over to the house and coming in while I'm at work or something. And taking *my* stuff, instead of your own. Besides, what on earth are you doing over here?"

"I saw all the cars over here and figured you might be here or I'd ask Cherry if she'd seen you." Loren looked smug at his accurate detective work. This, thought Lulu, was starting to be a party to rival her fund-raiser.

But then Cherry, flustered and sweating from her hot kitchen, pushed her way through the kitchen door crossly. She paused to take in the scene in front of her—the cheese dip still on the floor, Loren looking like he was about to pick a fight. . . . Then she looked down at the bowl she was holding with her third attempt to make a relatively easy appetizer. Lulu leaned over to see, and apparently Cherry had run out of Velveeta finally and made something out of shredded cheese . . . which, as watery as the dish looked, seemed to be cheese soup.

Cherry carefully put the watery cheese dip down on a table and put her hands on her hips. "I've had enough tonight. Loren, you picked the wrong time to come in, buddy. This is a *ladies* night, and unless you're willing to clean up the messes I've made or go to the store for more processed cheese, you need to leave. I don't know how your mama could have forgotten to tell you, but you're not supposed to crash a party. Since this is the second party I've seen you do that to, you're uneducated about it. But I promise that's the rule—if you're not invited, you don't go."

Loren looked crestfallen. "Sorry, Cherry," he mumbled. Pepper was already leaving the room for the direction of Cherry's bathroom.

"It's okay," said Cherry. "But don't do it again." And she watched as Loren meekly left.

She rolled her eyes as the door closed. "Okay, now that that's all over with, what the heck am I going to do about my cheese dip?"

It was decided that everyone had filled up on the cold snacks and wine and didn't even have a spot left, everyone assured Cherry, for any cheese dip. Particularly, thought Lulu, cheese dip that sat in a cup of water. It was time to play Bunko. Lulu was glad that even Pepper seemed able to relax and enjoy the game.

When the game was over and Evelyn was declared the winner (although it seemed a little unfair that wealthy Evelyn would take home the fifty-dollar kitty), everyone talked for a few minutes before the party started breaking up.

Cherry, Lulu noticed, had indulged in a few glasses of wine as the evening progressed. Lulu guessed that she was entitled, and she sure wasn't driving anywhere, since she was already at home. Another thing she noticed was that wine seemed to eliminate any filters that Cherry had, as far as what came out of her mouth.

Pepper was getting ready to leave when Cherry suddenly stopped her. "Hey! Can you help Lulu and me clean up?" Pepper looked surprised, and Cherry said in a low voice, "I only ask close friends and neighbors, so really, it's an honor!"

Pepper looked longingly at the door but agreed to stay. She started busily picking up wine and water glasses and bringing them into the kitchen.

The kitchen, thought Lulu, looked a little like a crime scene itself. She wasn't sure why every bowl and spoon Cherry owned had been conscripted into the Great Cheese Dip Disaster, but they all seemed to be out on the counter in varying degrees of mess. Maybe Cherry had planned it that way, since they'd needed a cleanup as an excuse to keep Pepper there. Or maybe not, thought Lulu, looking at how frazzled Cherry appeared and how cheese dip seemed to be on every bowl and spoon that was pulled out.

They'd been doing some washing up for a few minutes when Cherry said, "Pepper, I don't really know how to ask this, and I sure wouldn't invite someone I thought was a *murderer* to my house for Bunko, but where were you exactly on the night of Lulu's fund-raiser? Because there's some debate about that. And thanks for staying to clean up."

Lulu held her breath at Cherry's rambling question. Pepper froze up for a second before jerking around to look at Cherry and Lulu. Her face was pale. "Cherry, I don't know what you're getting at."

Cherry batted at the air with a hand. "Sure you do, Pepper. Where *were* you? Because I'm hearing that folks noticed you weren't around. And there was som 'k that Dee Dee was meeting up with people in the parking deck. So . . . were you away from the fund-raiser? If not, were you just spending a whole bunch of time in the restroom?"

Pepper pressed her hands against her eyes as if she was blocking out some unwelcome images. "Both," she finally said quietly, and Lulu released her pent-up breath. "It was both. Yes, I was away from the party for a little bit. And yes, I was also in the restroom for more than the usual time. That's because I was positively sick to my stomach by what happened that night."

Lulu and Cherry drew closer to Pepper, all ears.

Pepper sank down onto a kitchen stool. "It was that awful Dee Dee. I'm not sorry a whit that she's dead because she was a really horrible person. Nobody is going to be crying any tears at her funeral." She looked over at Lulu. "Except I guess you'll miss shopping at her store, right, Lulu?"

Pepper gave a sigh and leaned her head back, looking at the ceiling. "I was a fool to even come to your fund-raiser, Lulu. I'd read about it in the paper and took it into my head to go. I knew Loren was going to be there, of course, considering his total obsession with anything to do with Tristan. And Steffi had to do with Tristan, but not much." She gave a short laugh.

"I apologize for not coming to your party in the right spirit, Lulu. I wasn't there to raise money to help Steffi, although I guess I did that, since I was sure eating and drinking there. But I wasn't in the giving state of mind—I was actually royally ticked that night."

Cherry drunkenly veered off topic. "What the heck got into Loren tonight, by the way? And what's with that huge dog that you installed in your backyard?"

Pepper sighed. "Brutus? Well, he's there for protection. A single girl's got to look out for herself, and I seem to be becoming a single girl again. Loren was bent out of shape because I'd changed the locks on the doors, and he wanted to sneak in there and get some stuff out. And I guess he wanted to get back at me for messing up his evening at Aunt Pat's."

Lulu tried to navigate the conversation back to the fund-raiser. "Going back to the benefit, honey, I can't blame you for being royally ticked. Of course you were wanting to make the man uncomfortable. Besides, I don't think anybody really even knew what you were doing, anyway. You probably looked real ominous, didn't you, dear?"

Pepper nodded her head. "That's right. I could have really made a scene, but I wasn't looking to totally destroy the evening—I was just thinking I would make Loren nervous until he left. Then maybe I'd pick a fight with him on the way over to the parking deck."

"But while you were there, Dee Dee came over and talked to you," prompted Lulu, trying to shepherd the conversation away from Loren a little.

Pepper now looked purely spiteful. "Yes, she did. Witch. She said that she had something with her that I *might* be interested in seeing. She handed me a note that said to meet her at the second floor of the parking deck at eight o'clock."

Lulu's stomach churned a little with excitement—or maybe with the cheese dip she'd eaten out of pity for Cherry. "So you slipped away from the restaurant around eight o'clock."

"Yes," said Pepper, "but after she spoke to me, I started

really paying attention to everybody else that she talked to. I figured if she was trying this on me, then she's probably trying it on everybody she spent time with that night."

"Who else did Dee Dee talk to?" asked Lulu after she took a deep breath.

"Well, she tried to talk to Sara, for one. But don't worry, Lulu—Sara just shook her head at Dee Dee like she didn't have the time to bother with her."

"Who else?" asked Cherry breathlessly.

"Oh. Well, every one of the people who had been at Tristan's party. I guess I was the very first one. She talked to Steffi, Pansy, Colleen, Loren, and Sara."

"So you went out to meet her at the assigned time," prompted Lulu.

"Yes. And I saw Steffi outside, smoking," said Pepper.

Oh, thought Lulu. So that's probably where Steffi was during that pocket of time where Loren wasn't sure where she was. Lulu hadn't realized that Steffi smoked—she sure didn't see her do it while she was working at Aunt Pat's. Stress did funny things to people, though.

"I'm sure that Steffi probably told the cops that she saw me leave and come back. Because she was *still* smoking when I came back to the restaurant a little later." Pepper sighed heavily. "Maybe all that fund-raising money will end up going to lung-cancer treatments. What a shame that would be."

Lulu said, "What happened during your meeting with Dee Dee?"

"Nothing." Pepper held her hands out in a beseeching way. "Nothing happened. Because when I walked up to Dee Dee's car, I saw her lying on the ground—dead."

Chapter
20

Cherry and Lulu gaped at Pepper now. "So she was dead before you even got to talk to her," repeated Cherry in a breathless voice. "Gee whiz!"

Gee whiz? Cherry must really be tipsy to be pulling those kinds of phrases out. "So you didn't see or hear anything or anyone?" asked Lulu. "No pounding footsteps running from the scene? No suspicious-looking people lurking around?"

"No, although it wouldn't have been a suspicious-looking person who did it, would it? It would be someone we know—and I guess the same person who murdered Tristan. But, you know, any of the people who Dee Dee talked to could have slipped out of the restaurant to kill her. Nobody was keeping track of anyone's going or coming. We were all moving around a lot. I might've kept track of Dee Dee . . . for a while. But then she obviously left to go to her car. Once she left, I really wasn't watching any-

one except for Loren. And keeping half an eye on the time
because I wanted to go out there and ask Dee Dee what she
was playing at, trying to blackmail me." Pepper was looking annoyed again, just thinking about it. "I did notice that
kind of slick-looking guy, Steffi's boyfriend, come back
after I got out of the restroom. At that point, I was sitting
out on the screen porch, so I noticed him coming back into
the restaurant. He'd arrived at the fund-raiser the same
time I did—so I thought it was a little weird that he would
leave and come back. "

Lulu said, "But that would have been after Dee Dee was
already dead, right?"

"Sure. But he must have seen her body if he was out at
his car. He and I parked right next to each other and walked
over to Aunt Pat's at the same time that night. Nobody
could have missed seeing Dee Dee's body spread out on
the ground like that."

"Wonder why he didn't say anything?" asked Lulu.

"Same reason I didn't, I guess! He didn't want to be a
suspect. I'm guessing that he probably hasn't got a spotless
record—he might look like a logical suspect to a cop."

"Do you have any idea what Dee Dee wanted to talk to
you about?" asked Lulu.

"Sure I do. I saw that painting lying next to her on the
floor of the parking deck. She wanted to talk to me about
Tristan's messed-up portrait," said Pepper coolly.

"You're the one who destroyed it?" asked Lulu.

"Yes. The night of Tristan's party. And I'm sorry because I know that Sara spent a long time painting it. I
promise that I didn't have a single thought in my head
about Sara or the time it took, or the picture as art. All I
thought was that I couldn't stand that woman. She told the
Women's League that I wasn't good enough to join—she

blackballed me. But somehow, my husband, who doesn't make enough money for her to consider letting me in her club, is having an affair with her. Tristan comes into the picture and wrecks my marriage; then, on top of it all, she's still insulting Loren and me for not being good enough for anything."

Lulu said quietly, "So when you saw the opportunity at the party to ruin Tristan's portrait, you took it."

"I did. I think I was possessed, Lulu. I'd followed Loren's car over to Tristan's, not knowing that she was having a party. Of *course*, I didn't know she was having a party! She wasn't likely going to invite Loren or me, seeing as how she looked down on us as dirt."

"But seeing the cars there didn't stop Loren. He was desperate to see Tristan, who wasn't returning his calls or answering the door when he rang the bell."

"Yes," said Pepper, rolling her eyes. "Loren was being an idiot."

"Seeing the cars at Tristan's didn't stop you, either. You went inside and talked to Tristan—but she didn't want anything to do with Loren anymore."

"Which almost made things worse," said Pepper thoughtfully. "He was disposable to her. And *I* was disposable. She was done with him. Yes, it made me even more furious than I already was. So when I saw the portrait, it had been put off to the side—sort of near the back of the house."

Lulu nodded. Tristan had grabbed it from the auctioneer and was probably trying to hide it in her bedroom where no one could see it when Sara had come up to talk with her about it.

"So I whipped my lipstick out of my purse and scribbled all over the canvas. Even that wasn't good enough for me.

Like any good southern girl, I carry a pocketknife—my daddy gave it to me when I was a girl. I took it out and slashed that portrait to pieces."

"Dee Dee somehow ended up with the portrait," said Lulu. "She must have seen you mess with it and decided that it would be the perfect thing to hold over you. . . . At the time she probably thought you'd fork over a few bucks to keep her quiet about it."

"Yeah. But then she really hit pay dirt when Tristan was murdered. I guess she thought that the police would love to know that I had vandalized Tristan's portrait. They probably would have jumped to the conclusion that I was also the one who killed her. Dee Dee was planning on blackmailing me, I'm sure." She shrugged. "And now the cops are going to find out it was me who messed up the portrait anyway, I guess. Since I used my lipstick, there's bound to be DNA all over the painting." Lulu raised her eyebrows in surprise, and Pepper shrugged again. "I watch all those crime shows on TV."

"I guess it would have been easy enough for Dee Dee to swipe the portrait," said Lulu. "Everyone was leaving with big canvasses, anyway."

Pepper said, "Or maybe someone *else* took it. Maybe Dee Dee had a picture of the damage. Or, who knows, maybe she even took a picture with her cell phone of me when I'd originally vandalized it."

"And so, maybe the person who murdered Tristan actually took it to plant near the body to point suspicion at you," said Lulu thoughtfully.

"If I'd had any sense, I'd have swiped that portrait and stuck it in my car. But seeing Dee Dee like that with the picture next to her made me sick—literally. I rushed back to the restaurant and straight into the restroom." Pepper looked a little green at the memory.

This made Lulu think. Why would the killer have gone to the parking deck at his or her assigned time to meet with Dee Dee? If Pepper had the first meeting and Dee Dee was already dead for *that* one, then the murderer would have known there was no point in going out there. Maybe they should be looking for the person who *didn't* leave after Pepper returned to Aunt Pat's.

"What a mess I'm in," said Pepper with disgust. "My husband is hounding me. My marriage is in ruins. And now I'm probably the main suspect in a murder investigation. Life just doesn't get any better."

Pepper was in such a state that Lulu and Cherry excused her from any further cleaning up. It was too bad, thought Lulu. Considering the disaster that Cherry had created in the kitchen, they could have used all the help they could get.

The wine was now making Cherry sleepy. "What's the next step in the investigation, Lulu?" she asked, yawning.

Lulu stopped scrubbing dishes for a minute. "I'd like to follow up with Pansy and Steffi on the night of the fundraiser and exactly where they were. Although it sounds like Steffi's cigarette habit probably explains some of her absence that night. And I do want to talk to Steffi's boyfriend again and see if he has any information to give us from that night."

"Sounds good," said Cherry sleepily. She looked around the kitchen. "This is good enough for tonight, Lulu. We've reached a stopping place, right?"

Lulu blinked. The kitchen still had pots and pans lined up on the counters, empty wineglasses, trash to go out . . . "You don't want to tackle the mess tonight?"

"The dishes will keep," said Cherry positively. "Cleanup is quicker the next day, anyway. This stuff will . . . soak."

She reached over and turned out the kitchen light, and Lulu had a feeling Cherry would be in bed two minutes after she left.

An opportunity to talk to Steffi presented itself the very next day when Steffi poked her head around the Aunt Pat's office door. "Lulu? Is it okay that I'm working the early shift today? I traded shifts with Abby. I know I've switched around a lot, but I've got to go to the bank with Marlowe this afternoon."

"Sure, honey, that works out fine," said Lulu, closing up the desk drawer. "Did you have fun at Bunko last night? Even if you didn't win the big pot of money?"

Steffi grinned. "It was great to go out and have *fun*. And it was nice of Cherry to invite me. She was so hilarious last night. I kept wondering why she didn't just leave the cooking to you. . . . You'd have solved her cheese-dip worries in a second."

Lulu rolled her eyes a little. "Yes, well, she can be really stubborn. I think she thought she should be able to at least pull together a cheese dip."

Steffi smiled and pulled an apron off a hook on the office wall. "Oh, and is it okay if I take thirty minutes or so for lunch? My friend is coming over for an early lunch—we made it for ten forty-five so it wouldn't be during the lunch rush."

"Friend?" asked Lulu innocently. "Anybody special?"

Steffi flushed. "David. You met him—taking care of the yard? He came to the fund-raiser, too."

"That's right," said Lulu. "I'm glad that's working out so well for you, Steffi." Lulu couldn't bring herself to say that he seemed like a nice young man. She *wanted* to, but she simply couldn't do it. Steffi obviously couldn't see through him and glimpse the guy he really was underneath the smarmy charm. "By the way, Steffi, someone mentioned to me that they'd seen you smoking recently."

Steffi said quickly, "I'd never smoke in Aunt Pat's, Lulu. I haven't even needed a smoking break—I really don't smoke all that much."

Lulu shook her head. "I wasn't trying to say that, honey. But I thought I'd mention it because Derrick—you know Derrick, don't you?—quit smoking six months ago, and he could probably give you some tips if you want to try to stop."

Steffi looked rueful. "Thanks, Lulu. I guess it's stress that's made me pick it up. If I see Derrick today, I'll ask him about it."

"I just like to look out for my employees' health!" said Lulu. She hesitated, then asked, "Were you out on smoke breaks during the fund-raiser? There were a couple of times when people couldn't track you down."

Steffi gave Lulu a swift look that Lulu couldn't really read. Was Steffi hurt that she'd suspect her? "Smoking. Guilty as charged," said Steffi. She shrugged. "It started out as a way to rebel against my mother, who hated smoking—said it gave people leathery skin and yellow teeth." Steffi gave an unhappy laugh. "That's the thing—it wasn't that she didn't want me to smoke because it might *harm* me. She didn't like it because of how it made people *look*. That's all she ever cared about . . . appearances."

Lulu stood up and gave Steffi a hug. "I'm so sorry I brought up bad memories for you, sweetie. I really meant to say that I *do* care for you, and I hate for you to have a habit that could end up killing you later. That's all. And that I rode Derrick about it the same way, and he managed to stop the habit."

"Thanks, Lulu," said Steffi. "That does mean a lot. And thanks for shifting my hours today and for lunch, too." And she hurried off to start getting the dining room ready.

Steffi's friend David actually arrived at Aunt Pat's around ten thirty, and to look at him, thought Lulu, he came straight from doing yard work. He obviously did a lot of his work first thing in the morning, before it got too hot.

Lulu saw Steffi glimpse him, then hurry over. "David! You got here early. I'm not really ready yet—I've still got to roll the silverware into the napkins and stuff—just get ready for the day."

He shrugged and stood up. "It's not a big deal. I'll go outside and have a quick smoke. Take your time—it's not important."

As he headed out to the front porch, Lulu said, "Steffi, you can finish up with the napkins after your lunch break if you want to. Or I can do it for you."

Steffi smiled. "Lulu, you've done enough. Really, it's fine. I think David is probably happy to take a smoke break anyway. And thank you for not telling him about the dangers of smoking while you had it on the brain."

Lulu said, "Well, I was able to dig up some self-control—for a little while, anyway. If he goes out for another smoke break while he's here, I might not be able to help myself."

Steffi disappeared back into the kitchen to finish with the silverware, and Lulu decided to sit on the porch for a bit before the lunch rush started—and try to catch David on his own before he joined Steffi inside.

Beale Street had plenty of tourists walking around it, despite the early hour. The never-ending parade of people kept the porch entertaining. Visitors came from all over the world, and you never knew what you were going to see or hear as they walked down the street.

Another nice thing about the porch was that you could overhear people talking sometimes. And Lulu was over-hearing a conversation now—David was apparently talk-ing to a friend on his cell phone in between puffs of his cigarette.

"What? No, I'm at the barbeque joint where she works. Yeah. Who knows? I guess she's still working here because she doesn't want to let the old lady who owns the place down—Steffi is that kind of goody-goody. She sure doesn't need the money."

The friend talked for a couple of minutes more. "Yeah, there was that fund-raiser thing, too. I guess they wanted to do something for her—she's planning to go to school, so maybe they were just getting her some extra money for tu-ition or books or something. How should I know? I tell you who needs a fund-raiser—me! I'm the one who can use some money. And I'm not like Steffi—it won't bother me a bit to quit my job. I don't care if I ever cut a blade of grass again in my whole life."

There was another pause on David's end of the conver-sation, and then he said, "Look, I've got to go. She's going to be waiting for me in a minute." A rough laugh. "Are you kidding? I wouldn't date that chick in a million years if she wasn't loaded. Not pretty like her mom was, is she?

"See? That's what I'm saying! Oh, shut up—I'm not al-ways hustling a deal. But I do have something starting up now that looks pretty good." His voice dropped a little, and Lulu strained to hear him. "Yeah. I'm not saying, except that if getting hooked up with Steffi doesn't work out for the long haul, then maybe this will help me have more *reg-ular* income."

There was another pause, and then David said quickly, "Got to go."

Lulu closed her eyes as if she was dozing in the rocker and gave what she hoped was a convincing startle as David pushed through the porch's screen door. "Sorry," he mumbled.

Then he paused and looked sharply at her. "I guess you heard some of that," he said.

Lulu said dryly, "I couldn't really help it."

"I'll make her happy, you know," David said in a defensive voice. "Who cares *why* I'm going out with her as long as I treat her like a queen and make her happy?"

Lulu decided to let that pass. "I'm curious what you meant when you were talking about the thing that would provide you with regular income. Do you have some sort of information from the night Dee Dee was murdered?"

David shrugged. "I guess it doesn't hurt to tell you. I'm pretty sure it was that woman, Pepper, who killed Tristan—and Dee Dee, too. I got bored at the fund-raiser—didn't know anybody there except Steffi, and she was busy talking to everybody. So I went out on the porch to listen to the band and text a couple of friends. I saw Pepper leave the party. She and I had parked on the same level of the parking deck, and I'd followed her into the restaurant that night. When she came back a few minutes later, acting like she was trying not to be noticed? I noticed her. That's the kind of thing I pay attention to."

David really was a hustler, then, thought Lulu. It sounded like he wasn't above blackmail, either. She was starting to think the whole world was into extortion.

"Anyway, I saw her come in, and she was all sweaty and kind of sick looking. She disappeared into the bathroom. I was ready to take off from the party and head home—it was getting pretty boring. So when I got to my car, parked real close to Pepper, I saw this body lying on the floor of the parking deck." He shrugged again. "It doesn't take a genius to put two and two together. And I saw that painting beside the woman on the floor—I figure it has something to do with the fact she's dead."

Lulu said, "So you're planning on getting Pepper to pay you to keep quiet. If she murdered two people, do you really think that's a good idea?"

"I can take care of myself," said David sullenly. He continued walking into the restaurant. When Lulu turned around to look into the dining hall, she saw David greet Steffi with a kiss. She shook her head. She was going to have to figure out a way to break it to Steffi gently that David didn't have her best interests at heart. Steffi didn't deserve to be in another cold relationship after a lifetime of living with her mother.

# Chapter

## 21

Lunch was in full swing when Lulu noticed Pink had come up to the lunch counter. "What'll it be, Pink?" asked Lulu, taking out an order pad. "Or will it be your usual barbeque plate with a side order of coleslaw and a sweet tea?"

"My usual," said Pink with a grin. "Gotta love coming to a restaurant where they know your order before *you* do! And what a great honor having the restaurant owner actually taking my order."

"It's on the house, too," said Lulu with a flourish of her hand. "Got to keep our men in blue happy. Aunt Pat's appreciates her law enforcement officers!" She handed off the order to a passing waitress.

Pink drawled, "And I surely do appreciate the free lunch! But tell me, Lulu, what brought all this on? You're not still messing around in the case, are you?"

Lulu developed a sudden interest in the menus she was

holding. "Oh *no*. Not me. I'm a mild-mannered restaurant owner."

Pink raised his eyebrows at her.

"Well, maybe I'm just interested in getting an update, Pink. Just some general information, you understand." She lowered her voice to a hush. "Like whether or not you found Dee Dee's black notebook."

Pink scooted his stool a little closer to Lulu. "Funny you should bring that up, Lulu. Because we've found neither hide nor hair of that notebook anywhere. Not in Dee Dee's house or car or shop."

Lulu frowned. "Pink, I promise you that I'm not making all this up . . ."

Pink raised a hand to stop her. "Oh, I believe you, Lulu. I think that whoever murdered Dee Dee probably swiped the notebook, too. And whatever evidence was pointing in his or her direction." He paused as the waitress put his barbeque plate in front of him.

He opened up a packet of Aunt Pat's secret sauce and squeezed it onto the pulled pork. "Lulu, think back. Was there anything that you can remember from that book? Anything that might help us figure out who's behind all this?"

Lulu thought, then shook her head sadly. "Nothing that really stands out. Well, there were notes about Tristan having an affair. . . . But I think you already know about that, right?"

"With Loren, yes," said Pink with a quick nod as he took a big bite from his sandwich.

"She *did* have an affair with Loren—but she also had one with Steffi's boyfriend."

"What?" Pink's eyes opened wide. "That scruffy-looking kid that I saw on my way in? That's hard to believe."

"Well, Dee Dee made some notes about it. And I have heard from the boy himself that it was true. Who knows what Tristan was playing at, but the affair did happen."

"And you can't remember anything else?"

Lulu said, "No. And what *really* got her killed is probably whatever she wrote in there that she saw the night Tristan was killed. She likely thought she'd hit pay dirt, but instead, she was messing with something that was bigger than she was. And it's too bad she couldn't tell the difference."


The stress of the last few days finally caught up to Lulu, and she slept like the dead that night. She was shocked to look at the clock and see that it was nine o'clock—Lulu couldn't remember the last time she'd slept so late. It was probably all that worrying about the case; things like that just wore on a body after a while. Lulu decided it was time to do something completely different for a change—housework. She hadn't really done much to her house since Steffi had moved her things out, and it was starting to show.

The nice thing about housework, thought Lulu, is that you get that great feeling of accomplishment—and it's a completely mindless activity. Lulu dusted her tables and her favorite figurines, vacuumed the house, and decluttered. She remembered that she'd planned on getting rid of one of the tables that was in her living room. She didn't need it, and she really would rather have something else there instead. She picked up the phone. "Sara, do you want that table in my living room for anything? No, the one that's by the wall—it has a lamp and pictures on it. I was thinking I'd put a recliner there—seems like I'm falling asleep while watching the news more often than I used to, and I'm thinking about recliners that are good for nap-ping." Lulu turned the volume up on the phone. Maybe she *was* losing her hearing a little. "Sara? Sorry. You said no? Well, how about on the wall that leads into your kitchen? Oh, I don't think it would block the pathway too much."

But Sara definitely wasn't interested in the table. "Lulu, honestly, I really don't have any use for it, and it would re-ally be more clutter for me. How about if you ask Steffi if she needs a table? I know she's with Marlowe now, but she said she's looking at apartments."

"She's got all that furniture from Tristan's house, though," said Lulu.

"Not according to Steffi. They're planning on having an estate sale and using the proceeds from the sale of the fur-niture to pay off some of Tristan's debts."

Lulu clucked. "Poor Steffi! I'll give her a call and see if she wants the table, then. How is she supposed to furnish an apartment?"

"She'll probably check out consignment shops and yard sales, Lulu. Or friends who have extra furniture they don't need."

When Lulu hung up with Sara and called Steffi, she sounded really pleased by Lulu's offer. "That would be fan-tastic, Lulu! I've been looking at some apartments that I can afford so that I can get out of Marlowe's hair. She's been great," said Steffi quickly, "but I know she's used to living on her own. And now that I have a boyfriend and everything . . ." Steffi broke off, embarrassed.

Lulu made a face at the thought of David. She was really going to have to warn Steffi about him at some point. But she wasn't looking forward to it. "I'm sure it would be much better for both of you for you to have your own place,

Steffi. No, you're welcome to the table. Do you want to bring a friend to help you carry it out?"

"David's working, I think. I'll call Pansy because I know she's not doing anything this afternoon. We'll come by in about an hour."

Despite the lack of a qualified piece of furniture for napping, Lulu found that she dozed off for a few minutes on her sofa. There was a light rap on the door, and she shook herself awake. Honestly, she thought with some irritation as she struggled to stand up, she didn't know what was wrong with her. But she knew—it was stress from the murders and worrying about who might be behind it all.

She peeped out the front door and saw Pansy and Steffi there. "Hi, girls," she said brightly. "Come on inside and let me show you the table, Steffi. Now you're not going to hurt my feelings if it's something you're really not interested in—you just need to let me know, okay?"

"Okay," agreed Steffi. "I'm sure it's going to be fine, though. I'm not in a position to be picky!" She followed Lulu over to the table, which Lulu had cleared off before taking her nap. "It's really pretty, Lulu. Are you sure you don't need it?"

"Positive. I think I'm going to get a recliner for that wall, instead. With the way I've been taking naps lately, I think a recliner would come in handier than a table that I never use."

Steffi and Pansy carefully lifted the table and took it out to Marlowe's minivan, which Steffi had borrowed for the occasion. "Won't y'all come in for a few minutes? I have some fresh-squeezed lemonade and some cake, if you'd like a little snack."

Steffi looked like she was ready to leave, but Pansy said,

"Sure! No way am I going to turn down homemade cooking from Lulu."

The girls followed Lulu into her kitchen and sat down at her kitchen table as Lulu bustled around for the drinks and cake. "Pansy," said Lulu, "you must be one of those lucky people who can eat anything and not gain any weight."

Pansy laughed. "I wouldn't go *that* far, but I don't gain a whole lot, no."

Steffi sighed. "Wish that was the case for me. Everything I eat seems like it goes right to my hips. And all I've wanted to do since all this started is to eat."

Lulu said sympathetically, "Oh, honey, believe me, I know! That's the way I am, too. I'll head off to the kitchen anytime I start worrying about things. It's hard not to, isn't it?" She filled the glasses with ice. "You haven't heard anything from the police, have you? About how the investigation is going?"

"No, I sure haven't. I hope they find somebody soon. I just can't stop thinking about Mother. I think it's gotten worse in the last few days. I've even been dreaming about her. In the dream she's been killed, but she's somehow still talking to me—with that awful crown on her head." Steffi shuddered.

Lulu shivered. "What an awful dream to have! Well, try to put it out of your head for right now—have a little slice of cake. This is my famous Lady Baltimore cake. I know a lot of people *think* they won't like a cake with fruit in it, but it's *not* fruitcake. Give it a try."

Steffi took a big bite right away, but Pansy was a little more cautious after the word "fruit" was used. Both of them lit up, though, after they tasted it. "It's delicious," sighed Pansy.

"This is why you should have been cooking on Bunko

night," said Steffi. "I mean, I love Cherry and everything—
she's funny and sweet. But she's an awful cook."

Lulu smiled. "I wouldn't have said she's an *awful* cook,
but she's definitely a distracted one. And she pulls out
every pot, pan, and measuring cup in her kitchen in order
to cook anything. It took forever to clean up, and we weren't
done when I finally left that night."

Pansy snorted. "That night was really a disaster from
start to finish. I think Evelyn should have been disqualified
from winning the kitty, since she's already rich. And then
when *Loren* came in . . ." She shook her head and rolled her
eyes, and Steffi laughed.

"Do the impression you did of him from that night,"
said Steffi, urging Pansy on. "It's *so* funny," she said to
Lulu with a smile. "It really sounds like Loren. Pansy
cracks me up with it."

"Okay," said Pansy, grinning. "Here I go." She wiped
her face clean of all expression, then her face suddenly
transformed until she'd perfectly mimicked Loren's
pinched, concerned look. "Pepper, I'm here at Bunko to
bug you just as much as you bugged me at Steffi's fund-
raiser. Is it working, dear?" Steffi rolled with laughter, and
Lulu blinked. It was unbelievable how well Pansy had
mimicked Loren's voice.

"But that sounded exactly *like* him!" said Lulu, amazed.
"How are you able to do that—and with a man's voice, too?
Oh, wait—that's one of your talents, isn't it? For the pag-
eants?"

Pansy said lazily, "It's my talent for some of the smaller
competitions. I mean, I wouldn't want to do it for Miss
Memphis or something like that. In the big pageants, I'm
singing or dancing, for sure. But it's fun . . . and I'm good
at it." She looked over at Steffi with a smile. "I don't like

doing it to be mean to anybody or make fun of them. But with somebody like Loren . . ." She and Steffi cracked up again.

Then Pansy changed expressions and went with an exasperated look. "Loren. Oh . . . Loren. For heaven's sake, Loren." Lulu recognized it as Pepper's voice, right off the bat. Pansy giggled. "Pepper is just about as bad as Loren for getting on my nerves. And I'm sure she's the one who destroyed Tristan's portrait. Although I think she should get a standing ovation for it. Sorry, Steffi, I know she was your mom, but . . ." Pansy made a face.

Lulu started. "Would y'all . . . would you like some more cake?" She got up, almost in a daze, as Steffi said sadly, "She was awful. I know. I wish things could have been different with us, that's all. Maybe if both of us had tried a little harder."

But Lulu was barely hearing the girls talk. Her mind was whirling as she processed the new information she was getting. The girls must be getting more relaxed as time went on after the murders. . . . Steffi wasn't supposed to know her mother was found with the crown on her head. The police had specifically told Lulu that they did *not* want that information leaked—even to Steffi. And how did Pansy know that the painting was destroyed? That was something else that the police had hushed up, unless Derrick, Pepper, David, or Cherry had been talking about it. She was sure that Pepper wouldn't have said anything about the portrait, since she was embarrassed about destroying it, and neither would David.

But there was something even more chilling, thought Lulu, as she cut two more pieces of cake. Pansy's mimicry.

Pansy, Colleen had told Lulu, could imitate anyone. Lulu had just seen that she could. What if . . . what if Pansy had been in the office area with Steffi and pretended to be Tristan having an argument with Steffi?

What if Pansy and Steffi murdered Tristan right after the auction. They knew that either Sara or Lulu would be looking for Steffi at eight o'clock to give her a ride home. Pansy pretended to be Tristan during the "argument" that Lulu and Dee Dee overheard, giving Steffi the perfect alibi. Lulu would say that she'd heard Tristan's voice, alive and well . . . and that then Steffi and she had left. But Tristan could already have been *dead*.

Lulu thought back to the night of the party as she put cake on their plates. She remembered that Dee Dee had been lurking around. What if she'd stuck her head in the door of the office after Lulu and Steffi had walked away? What if she'd seen that Tristan wasn't even in the office? She probably would have written the whole thing off as a practical joke—until it became known that Tristan was dead. Then all the pieces would have started coming together for her. Dee Dee being Dee Dee, she would have started thinking about blackmail—and that was what ended up signing her death warrant. It was probably Pansy who murdered her, since it would have been harder for Steffi to have gotten away from the fund-raiser, unnoticed.

Lulu took a deep breath. She wouldn't have a chance if she said anything now—not against two girls. Better to just talk to Pink later, when she had an opportunity.

"Lulu?" asked Steffi in a strange voice. "Lulu, I asked you a question."

Lulu gave a shaky laugh. "Well, you know, people keep telling me I've lost my hearing. It's one of those things that you don't *want* to happen so you pretend it's *not* happening. You know? I guess I should be making an appointment to do something about it."

Pansy said, "Funny, though—your hands are shaking, Lulu."

"That *is* funny," said Steffi in a flat voice.

"That's what happens when you have too much caffeine," said Lulu with a shake of her head. "I really need to cut back."

"I didn't really notice anything but lemonade and tea in your fridge, Lulu," said Pansy.

There was silence for a moment. "I think," said Steffi slowly, "that Lulu is being clever. I know you've been poking around in the investigation. Asking questions."

"Only because I like to know what's going on," said Lulu quickly. "I'm just a nosy old lady. Plus, I've been worried about Sara, too—she's had some suspicion thrown on her with all of this."

Steffi had a faraway look in her eye like she was trying to remember something. "Let's see. What were we talking about before Lulu got up to get us refills?"

"I remember!" said Pansy. "We were talking about Loren."

"Not only that, though," said Steffi impatiently. "That's right—you mentioned that the portrait was destroyed. I don't think you were supposed to know that." Her voice had censure in it.

"Shoot," said Pansy. She opened her purse and rummaged around in it, finally bringing out a package of cigarettes. "Well," she said, lighting it up without even looking at Lulu, "you screwed up too, Steffi. Didn't you say something about the tiara? So you can't blame it all on me."

"She definitely knows," said Steffi, looking dispassionately at Lulu. "Look at her. Face white, hands shaking. She knows."

Chapter 22

"So we'll take care of it," said Pansy coolly. And Lulu shivered at the girls' tone, as well as the fact that they were acting like she wasn't even there.

"How?" said Steffi. "I'm getting so tired of this, Pansy. Isn't it ever going to stop—the covering up? The fixing things?" She rubbed her eyes with both hands.

Lulu cleared her throat a little. "Girls, if I can offer any advice? Don't keep running. And don't do anything else to make it worse. Do you really want a third body on your conscience—and your record? Because I know that the police will find out. If *I* was able to put two and two together, they'll definitely be able to do it. And you're talking about a *lot* of jail—a lot of time in prison."

Pansy gave a cold laugh. "Well, of *course* you're going to say something like that, Lulu. It's not like you have our best interests at heart—you're doing it to save your own skin."

"I thought we were friends," said Lulu, her voice getting stronger. "Steffi? I wouldn't have had that fund-raiser if I hadn't been trying to help you. And would I have invited you over here to take this table if we hadn't been friends?"

Steffi seemed to hesitate for a second. Pansy said, "Some friend, trying to get us to turn ourselves in!"

Lulu said quickly, "Think about it, girls. Sara knew you were coming over to take this table. And Pansy, you borrowed the van from your mother, so she knows about it, too. Don't you think that as soon as everyone realizes I'm missing—and they'll realize it in a couple of hours when I don't show up at Aunt Pat's for the supper rush—that they're going to be retracing my steps the very first thing? They're going to find out really fast that you were the last people to see me alive."

"Then I guess," said Steffi slowly, "we'll have to be real careful about covering our tracks this time, Pansy." Pansy smiled at her, and they stood up. Steffi took Lulu's arm, and Pansy put on a kitchen glove and picked up a butcher knife from the wood block that Lulu used. "And I'm thinking we need to take the car out of town a little ways—it'll take longer to discover you that way, too."

Lulu said, trying to stall them, "Don't you see that with every crime you're slipping a little? That you're making more mistakes? Pansy, you even were doing that trick with mimicry that you do so well. That's really what made me think of it. You must have been faking Tristan's voice that night at the party to try to make an alibi for yourself and Steffi."

They weren't going to be stalled, apparently. In fact, Lulu was wondering if they'd even heard her. They were too concerned about figuring out how to kill her and where to dispose of her body. And their coldness shocked Lulu.

"I know this place that's real deserted," said Pansy. "I see it sometimes on the way to out-of-town pageants. Let's head out there. Maybe grab some matches."

Lulu knew that they said a victim should never allow herself to be moved from one location to another. But what was she going to do? They had the knife, not her. She glanced around real quick to see if there was anything she could use as a weapon. The problem was that there were two of them. If she picked up one of the kitchen chairs? But then the other one would just take it away from her. There was no way she could reach her rolling pin or the knives. Could she break away from them for long enough to lock herself in her bedroom and call the police?

Then the doorbell rang, and Steffi and Pansy froze, looking at each other with panic. Lulu yanked her arm away from Steffi and tried to run to the bedroom, but she tripped a little in her hurry, and Pansy was quick to reach out and grab her. "*Don't* do that again," she hissed. "We're all going to answer the door because whoever it is knows we're here because the van's outside. But you better make this natural."

It was Cherry at the door. "Hey, I was just stopping by for a visit," she said, wiggling her eyebrows at Lulu to show that she was really there for one of their meetings about the case. "But then I saw Colleen's van, so I thought I'd check and see if it's a good time. Is it?" She smiled engagingly at the group.

The last thing Lulu wanted was for Cherry to get mixed up in this, too. Steffi and Pansy were clearly starting to get desperate. And in their desperation, they might take Cherry along, too, and make up some excuse.

Pansy gave her one of her pageant smiles. "Actually, we were just going to leave with Lulu—she was going to go

with us to go through some of Tristan's things and see if
she had any ideas about what stuff Steffi needed to try to
keep and what needed to be sold."

Steffi looked at Lulu with a grim expression like she
needed her to say something to support what Pansy had
just said. "Yes," said Lulu. She paused. "Although I don't
know if it's a good day for it. It *looks a lot like rain*."

"I think it'll be fine weather for it, Lulu," said Pansy
cheerfully.

Cherry looked puzzled. "I don't think there's a cloud in
the sky. But these weathermen—who knows?"

Steffi and Pansy seemed to be hoping that Cherry would
take the hint and go ahead and leave. But Cherry wasn't
particularly good at hints or picking them out. "Lulu, I
thought you were on tonight at the restaurant—that's why I
was coming by here, to see you now, because it's hard to
visit when you're working."

"Oh. Well, I think they'll have it under control there
tonight."

"Isn't Steffi working nights now?" Cherry knit her
brows.

"It's my night off tonight," said Steffi smoothly.

"Too bad it's your night off when it *looks like it might
rain*," said Lulu. But this was met by a confused look by
Cherry.

"Okay," she said, standing up. "I guess I'll let y'all go,
then. Lulu, I'll catch up with you sometime later. "

"Where are you headed to?" asked Lulu, feeling panic
rising in her.

"I've got docent duty at Graceland this afternoon," said
Cherry carelessly. She put her helmet back on. "So I guess
I'll head over there a little early."

"Did you know," said Lulu, trying to sound casual, "I

heard something about Priscilla Presley the other day. I heard that she and Elvis actually met each other in Germany!"

Now Cherry was looking sharply at Lulu. "Is that so?" she asked slowly. "What are the chances of that? I'll have to ask the staff about that when I'm over at Graceland today. That's very interesting."

Lulu nodded.

"Okay, well, I'm off. Good luck with the furniture and stuff, y'all," said Cherry. She hurried out. They heard her motorcycle roar off moments later.

"That was smart thinking, keeping your mouth shut while Cherry was here," said Pansy. "No point hurrying things along any faster than they're already going. Besides, then we'd have had to take Cherry along with us, and that might have ended up being ugly."

"Not to mention difficult," said Steffi thoughtfully. "Two against two."

"I think," said Lulu, feeling calmer now that she knew Cherry had been alerted, "that you're probably going to have to find a story to tell the police later. Cherry is sure to mention that she saw y'all with me here at the house. You'd end up being the last people to see me alive." Lulu hoped if she could stall just a couple of minutes longer, then the police would be able to catch up with them quicker.

"Don't worry—we'll come up with something," said Pansy quickly. "Besides, everybody already knew about the table—you probably mentioned it to a couple of people, didn't you? And there shouldn't be any surprise that you'd help Steffi go through her mom's stuff—you've offered to help out a couple of different times. Mother knows why I borrowed the van, so she'll be able to give a good reason for us having been over here. Besides, we had a good alibi for Tristan's murder, didn't we? The police aren't going to be able to pin that on us."

"A good alibi until it unravels," said Lulu. "I'm sure the police will eventually reach the same conclusions that I did. They're bound to."

Steffi moved restlessly. "Let's go ahead and leave, Pansy, before someone else ends up coming over."

The three walked outside and got in Pansy's mother's car. Lulu took a deep breath. Ordinarily, she would fight like crazy to keep from being taken away from her home—but she had faith in Cherry's ability to get help.

Steffi and Pansy sat in the front seat and Lulu in the middle row of the van. Pansy turned the key in the ignition—and there was no sound. "What?" she asked, frowning. She tried the key again, and the motor wouldn't turn over.

"Great timing," said Steffi in a low voice. "What's up with the car?"

"How should I know?" asked Pansy. "I don't know why Mama keeps using this old heap anyway—I keep telling her to get something else." She tried again.

"Well, clearly this car isn't going anywhere," said Steffi. "So let's go in Lulu's instead."

Pansy perked up. "Good idea. So Lulu *can* get her pocketbook and keys. She can act like she's going on a drive—a very dangerous drive."

Lulu said, "Well, let's see. I think my pocketbook is in my bedroom. But I might have left it in the kitchen when I came in from the grocery store."

Pansy gave an exasperated sigh. "Let's go in and look for it, okay?"

Lulu hurried in and found her pocketbook in her bedroom. "Got it!" she said cheerfully.

Pansy looked at her in disbelief. "You shouldn't be nearly this happy, you know. You're about to meet your Maker."

"Well, that's something to be happy about, isn't it?" said Lulu quietly. "At least I can meet him with an easy conscience."

"Just get going," said Pansy between gritted teeth.

They stepped outside and walked to Lulu's car. Lulu said, "Oh! Got to lock the back door."

Steffi rolled her eyes, and Pansy said, "Lock your door? Lulu, have you lost your mind?"

"Won't it look kind of strange if I *don't*?" asked Lulu. "I *always* lock my door and my family knows that. If I left my house wide open, then they'd know I met with some kind of foul play here at the house—and y'all were the last ones seen here with me." Lulu was amazed how calm and reasonable she sounded, considering how hard her heart was beating. But she really did have faith in Cherry. She just hoped it wasn't misguided.

"Lock it," said Steffi in a resigned voice. She waited beside Lulu's car as Pansy hovered behind Lulu as she took her key out of her pocketbook to lock the door.

They climbed into Lulu's car, and Steffi turned the key in the ignition. There was no response. Steffi's eyes narrowed. "Kind of a coincidence, isn't it, Lulu? That your car isn't working either?"

Pansy's voice was starting to sound shrill. "Let's get out of here. This is freaking me out. Come on, Steffi—we'll take Lulu with us."

"And exactly where are we *going*, Pansy? How are we going to get there? On foot? Holding an old lady hostage at knifepoint as we run down the street?" asked Steffi in a panic.

There was the sound of a car speeding down the street, and Pansy turned quickly to look through the car's back window. "The cops! Cops are pulling in!"

Immediately, Pansy jumped out of the car and ran around the back of the house, with Steffi following close behind her.

Lulu was trotting after them as fast as she could go. She turned to look behind her and saw the police cars in her driveway—and she also, with some disgust, noticed that Gordon had driven by, looked out his window with horror, and was now quickly driving away again.

Now she was *mad*. Her close brush with an unnatural death (never mind the fact that her so-called suitor had just fled at the sight of trouble) made her furious. She'd been a friend to both those girls, and they were going to *kill* her in cold blood? Uh-uh.

She heard, at a distance now, the police car doors slamming and them shouting to each other and then to the girls. Out of the corner of her eye, she saw something lying on the ground. It was Cherry's helmet. Then she saw Cherry run up from the side and grab Steffi by the shirt and yank her to the ground. But Pansy was still running. And in a couple of minutes, she'd be able to cut through to the woods and maybe even make an escape. Lulu decided she wasn't willing to let that happen. She was not happy with Pansy and her attitude.

Almost out of impulse, Lulu reached down and grabbed Cherry's Elvis helmet off the ground. In the perfect bowling form vaguely remembered from her early married days, she pulled her hand back and bowled that helmet toward Pansy.

She was off—the helmet never touched the ground. But, in some ways, Lulu thought later, her aim had been perfect—she hit Pansy squarely on the back of her knee, knocking her to the ground.

The police were on top of them at once and put Steffi and Pansy in handcuffs. Lulu and Cherry looked on silently as they fought to catch their breath. "See," said Cherry hoarsely, "I keep telling y'all that my helmet is perfect for emergencies!"

Chapter 23

After the girls were taken away, Lulu and Cherry retired to her kitchen, which was Lulu's favorite place to go when she was stressed. Two police officers took down their stories. Cherry was extremely excited over her role in the rescue and was promoting helmets as a personal safety device ("in so many different ways!") to anyone who would listen to her.

Finally the police left, and Cherry took off to tell the world about Lulu's narrow escape, and it was only family left, and Lulu started to relax. They all sat there quietly for a minute, enjoying the peace.

Ben was the one who spoke first. "I can't believe that Gordon would take off like that," he grumbled. "What kind of a man leaves a lady in distress? Mother, I really don't think you should see him anymore."

"I never wanted to see the man to begin with! It was all your doing, Ben. Besides, he and I really didn't have all that much in common . . . except for food. I don't think you can build a relationship around food. But he sure did take off at a fair clip as soon as he spotted those police cars. I guess he thought I was some kind of lawbreaker or something."

Sara said, "I still can't get over the fact that those girls were cold-blooded killers! Okay, I can believe that Tristan totally warped her daughter. But Pansy? A beauty queen!"

"Only beautiful on the outside," said Lulu with a sniff. "I think Pansy made me the maddest. She was really hateful toward me when she was trying to kidnap me."

Ben, Sara, and Lulu all shuddered at the thought.

There was a light tap at the door, and Derrick stuck his head in. "Granny Lulu? Are you okay? So—the cops came and took Steffi and Pansy away?"

"They sure did, sweetie. Those girls are in some major trouble."

Derrick shook his head like he was trying to clear it. "What I don't understand is why they'd do something like this. Well, I *do* understand why Steffi would want to—sort of. Her mom was awful to her, but she didn't have to *kill* her. She was moving out, anyway."

Lulu sighed. "It's kind of hard to imagine, isn't it? Steffi had really been emotionally abused by her mother her whole life. But it sounds like the final straw was when Tristan stole Steffi's first boyfriend away from her. Marlowe had said that Tristan had done the same thing when she was in high school—like it was a game for her to steal boyfriends. This was Steffi's first serious relationship, though, and she was really upset to find out that her mother had been seeing David."

Ben said, "So she killed her mother out of revenge?"

"Yes, but not just revenge. She also killed her for the

money she *thought* she had. David was completely motivated by money and wasn't going to give Steffi the time of day if she was only a poor student living in an apartment. The money was always the draw. But when Tristan kicked her out of the house and threatened to write her out of the will, Steffi realized it was going to mean the end of her relationship with David. Steffi was as surprised as anyone that there wasn't any money. One time I was talking to David about the fund-raiser in front of Steffi, and her face pleaded with me not to say how *much* she needed a fundraiser. So I made an excuse about Steffi needing the money for college."

Derrick said, "But where does Pansy figure into all of this? I really don't get it."

"Pansy really was there for emotional support early on. Remember, those two girls, despite the age difference, had grown up together on the pageant circuit. Steffi was never in the pageants, but she played backstage with Pansy while her mother was busy coaching or judging. Pansy had really gotten fierce in her defense of Steffi and had upped her ammunition against Tristan in recent days—slamming Tristan on Facebook and showing up at the party to get on her nerves. Although Pansy had sabotaged her own dress and shoes for the Miss Memphis contest, she still did blame Tristan for keeping her from winning more pageants—and getting the scholarships she craved."

Lulu continued. "At some point, one of the girls got the idea for Pansy to imitate Tristan's voice having an argument with Steffi. Pansy was a great impersonator and had mimicked celebrities for some smaller pageants. They decided to kill Tristan first—using a candlestick that Steffi took from the kitchen at the start of the party but that any guest could have had access to. Pansy put the tiara on her head to make fun of Tristan, I think. . . . That was more of the kind of thing that Pansy would think of to do."

Sara twisted a long curl of red hair around a finger thoughtfully. "But how did they get out of Tristan's room without anyone seeing them? And how did they not have any blood on them?"

"It was easy enough," said Lulu. "Tristan's bedroom was on the way to one of the bathrooms. They'd just listen for some of the noise to die down, then slip out, one by one. Then they set up shop in Tristan's office, knowing Sara or I would be looking for Steffi at eight o'clock to head back home. Pansy pretended to be Tristan, giving Steffi an alibi—she was with me the rest of the evening after the argument with her 'mother.' And Pansy wasn't even supposed to have been there, so she wouldn't be considered a suspect."

Derrick still looked puzzled. "So why that old lady? What did they kill *her* for?"

"Dee Dee? Well, Dee Dee was with me when she heard that fake argument. I was so busy trying to help calm Steffi down that I didn't even notice what happened to her—but I bet that she peeked into the office and saw Pansy in there, not Tristan. And Dee Dee being Dee Dee, she would have tried to extort money from the girls to keep their secret. I guess that didn't make them feel very secure—and Steffi didn't have much money anyway. Pansy sure wouldn't. During the party, Steffi visited with others, and Pansy hurried out to the parking deck. No one noticed her go because during the height of the fund-raiser, there were a lot of people coming and going—trying to get food or use the restroom or go out on the porch to hear the band."

Sara said, "What about the portrait, though?"

"Dee Dee had taken the portrait from the party as a way

to get money from Pepper, who'd destroyed the painting. I guess Pansy saw the portrait in the backseat and decided to pull it out beside Dee Dee as sort of a red herring for the police. Because she had nothing to do with the destruction of the painting."

Lulu turned to Derrick. "I do feel real bad about Doug. It looked like he and Pansy were really hitting it off the other day. Poor fella."

Derrick said, "Oh. Well, I actually called him before I headed over here. It's kind of an irresistible story, you know."

"Was he very upset?"

Derrick gave a snort. "Not so you'd notice. He was already calling up girls on his cell phone for a sympathy plea . . . giving them some kind of 'I fell for a felon' line."

Ben rolled his eyes. "Sounds like he'll be all right if he's using the old sympathy ploy to try to get some attention from the girls."

Derrick cleared his throat. "I noticed something else, too. I was leaving Beale Street and passing 201 Poplar and saw Gordon pulling up there with Pansy's mom." Two-o-one Poplar was the well-known address for the Memphis jail.

Ben gave a second eye roll. "Another romantic ploy. He's *comforting* Colleen. Right."

"He did seem awfully interested in the beauty-pageant world. And Colleen has been divorced forever," said Lulu. "Maybe it'll be a good match."

Sara said, "Getting back to the murders, though, I simply can't believe these girls thought they were going to be able to get away with it. That takes a whole lot of confidence."

Lulu nodded. "Steffi didn't have much self-confidence

herself, but she did believe in Pansy. And, remember, for a while, they *were* getting away with it. That made them feel a lot cockier, I think. Well, y'all, I think I'm about ready to put my feet up for a little while and rest. It sure has been a long and scary day."

"Can I get you anything, Mother, before we head back to the restaurant?" asked Ben.

"Oh, honey, if you could maybe get me a sweet tea?"

"Sure I will. Is that all you want?" asked Ben.

Lulu said, "That's it. But be sure and put a little shot of vodka in there, would you?"

# Recipes
## Put Some South in Your Mouth

### Lulu's Chicken Soup

5½-pound hen, boiled, skinned, and cut in bite-sized
   pieces
3 cans creamed corn
2 cups cooked rice
1 small jar sliced mushrooms
2 cans cream of chicken soup
3 cups chicken stock (let cool and skim off fat)
1 chopped onion
1 small jar pimentos
salt and black pepper to taste
2 chicken bouillon cubes
1 tablespoon parsley flakes

Combine all ingredients and heat.

## Lulu's Favorite Boiled Custard

1 pint milk
3 eggs, well beaten
1 cup granulated sugar
½ teaspoon vanilla extract

Use a double boiler to prepare this recipe—and prevent the water from the bottom pan from touching the top pan. While water is rising to a boil in the bottom pan, mix together the milk, eggs, and sugar. When the water boils, pour the mixture into the top pan. Cook until the custard coats the spoon, stirring often. Strain the custard into a bowl, and add one-half teaspoon vanilla extract. Serve cooled. This recipe is best if made the day before.

◇◇◇◇◇◇◇◇◇

## Vegetable Sandwiches

2 tomatoes, cut very fine
1 large bell pepper, cut very fine
1 large cucumber, cut very fine
1 medium onion, grated
2 envelopes plain gelatin
1 pint commercial whipped salad dressing or mayo
thin-sliced white bread, crusts removed

Put small amount of cold water on gelatin to moisten. Add one-half cup boiling water and dissolve gelatin. When gelatin is cool, combine other ingredients and put in fridge to cool. Stir with a spoon before spreading. Spread mixture on bread very thickly and refrigerate. Better if spread hours or a day ahead.

## Tomato Pie

4 sliced tomatoes (squeezed gently to remove seeds and
    juice)
8 chopped fresh basil leaves
½ cup chopped green onion
1 9-inch prebaked deep-dish pie shell (cooked until
    golden brown)
salt and black pepper to taste
chives to taste
¾ cup grated mozzarella or Monterey Jack cheese
1 cup grated cheddar cheese
¼ cup grated Parmesan cheese
¾ cup mayonnaise

Preheat oven to 350. Cook the pie shell according to package instructions. Layer the tomato slices, basil, and onion in the prebaked pie shell. Season with salt and pepper and chives to taste. Combine the cheeses and the mayonnaise, and spread the mixture on top of the tomato layer. Bake at 350 degrees for 30 minutes or until golden brown.

## Corn Pudding

1 can creamed corn
3 tablespoons flour
1 tablespoon granulated sugar
½ teaspoon salt
dash of black pepper
1 cup tepid milk
3 tablespoons melted butter
2 well-beaten eggs

Preheat oven to 350 degrees. Mix together the corn, flour, sugar, salt, and pepper. Add the milk and the butter to the mixture. Add the eggs, and mix the ingredients together well. Pour the mixture into a greased casserole dish. Bake at 350 degrees for 45 minutes or until the pudding is firm.

## Pepper's Bourbon Balls

1 package crushed vanilla wafers
3 tablespoons unsweetened cocoa
1½ cups finely chopped toasted pecans
1½ cups powdered sugar (keep some aside for rolling
    the balls in)
4½ tablespoons light corn syrup
¼ cup bourbon

Mix together the wafers, cocoa, pecans, and powdered sugar. Mix together the corn syrup and bourbon, and then combine it with the wafer mixture. Cover the mixture and refrigerate for several hours or overnight. Form the mixture into small balls; then roll them in powdered sugar. Keep refrigerated.

# Ben's Shrimp and Garlic Cheese Grits

    1 cup heavy cream
    2 cups water
    1½ cups hot chicken stock
    ¼ cup butter
    salt and black pepper to taste
    1 cup stone-ground grits (if you use quick-cooking grits,
        reduce heavy cream to ½ cup, and reduce chicken
        stock to 1 cup)
    1 cup sharp cheddar cheese
    ¼ teaspoon hot sauce
    1 pound large raw shrimp, peeled, deveined, and cut in
        half lengthwise
    3 tablespoons lemon juice
    1 small, finely chopped Vidalia onion
    1 clove minced garlic
    6 slices of chopped, cooked bacon (reserve the bacon
        grease after cooking)

Combine cream, water, and chicken stock in a large sauce-pan over medium-high heat and bring to a low boil. Add the butter, salt, and pepper to the pot. Stir in the grits slowly, and reduce the heat to medium-low. Cook the grits for 20 minutes or until soft. Remove from heat and stir in the cheddar cheese and hot sauce. Cover the pot with a lid to keep the grits warm.

Spray shrimp with lemon juice and sprinkle with salt and pepper; then set the shrimp aside. In a large frying pan over medium-high heat, cook the onion and garlic in the reserved bacon grease for 5–7 minutes or until the onion is soft. Add the shrimp and bacon and sauté for another 5 minutes or until shrimp are cooked (opaque). Remove the mixture from the heat.

Spoon the hot grits onto plates and top with the shrimp and bacon mixture.

**THE FIRST IN THE NATIONAL BESTSELLING
CANDY HOLLIDAY MURDER MYSTERIES**

# TOWN IN A
# Blueberry Jam

## B. B. HAYWOOD

In the seaside village of Cape Willington, Maine, Candy Holliday has an idyllic life tending to the Blueberry Acres farm she runs with her father. But when an aging playboy and the newly crowned Blueberry Queen are killed, Candy investigates to clear the name of a local handyman. And as she sorts through the town's juicy secrets, things start to get sticky indeed . . .

**penguin.com**

M772T0910

THE WHITE HOUSE CHEF MYSTERIES FROM
ANTHONY AND BARRY AWARDS WINNER

# JULIE HYZY

Introducing White House
executive chef Ollie Paras, who is rising—
and sleuthing—to the top...

"Hyzy may well be the Margaret Truman
of the culinary mystery."
—Nancy Fairbanks

"A must-read series to add to the
ranks of culinary mysteries."
—*The Mystery Reader*

# STATE OF THE ONION

# HAIL TO THE CHEF

# EGGSECUTIVE ORDERS

# BUFFALO WEST WING

M546AS0810

# The delicious mysteries of Berkley Prime Crime for gourmet detectives

## Julie Hyzy
WHITE HOUSE CHEF MYSTERIES

## B. B. Haywood
CANDY HOLLIDAY MURDER MYSTERIES

## Jenn McKinlay
CUPCAKE BAKERY MYSTERIES

## Laura Childs
TEA SHOP MYSTERIES

## Claudia Bishop
HEMLOCK FALLS MYSTERIES

## Nancy Fairbanks
CULINARY MYSTERIES

## Cleo Coyle
COFFEEHOUSE MYSTERIES

*Solving crime can be a treat.*

penguin.com

M7G0610

# Searching for the perfect mystery?

Looking for a place to get the latest clues and connect with fellow fans?

**"Like" The Crime Scene on Facebook!**

- Participate in author chats
- Enter book giveaways
- Learn about the latest releases
- Get book recommendations
- Send mystery-themed gifts to friends and more!

**facebook.com/TheCrimeSceneBooks**

Obsidian

M884G0511